THE SHADOWS OF PIKE PLACE

A THOMAS AUSTIN CRIME THRILLER,
BOOK 2

D.D. BLACK

DARKNESS AND LIGHT PUBLISHING

PART 1

THE FAMILY

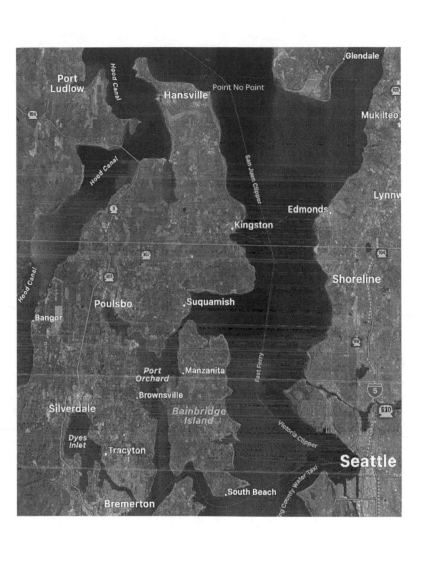

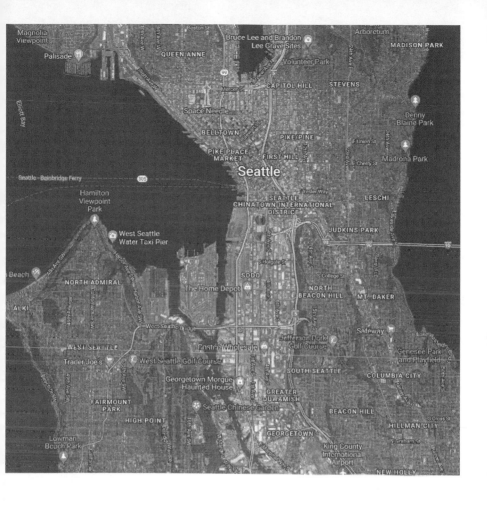

"Do nothing secretly; for Time sees and hears all things, and
discloses all."
–Sophocles

"Nothing makes us so lonely as our secrets."
–Paul Tournier

"Three may keep a secret, if two of them are dead."
–Benjamin Franklin

CHAPTER ONE

Seattle, Washington

ELEANOR JOHNSON LOVED HAVING her whole family together in one place. Well, *loved* might be too strong a word for it.

But it only happened once a year and she never knew how many years she had left. At eighty-two years old, she'd learned to appreciate every day. On her best days, she could even love the difficult moments, like the one she was about to have.

She'd called the family into the grand living room of their Seattle mansion to hear her decisions regarding the allocations of the family charity fund. She'd done this once a year for over forty years and it always left someone upset. But when you spent enough time giving away money, you got good at disappointing people.

Today, she'd be leaving everyone in the room fuming.

"Alright," Eleanor said, smoothing the creases of her dress. She stood in front of the giant, empty fireplace, both savoring and dreading the moment. "I've read the proposals, investigated the charities, and spoken to you individually about why you'd like me to donate to your chosen organizations. Here are my decisions."

The living room was large enough for a gathering of forty people, but only held seven at the moment. Looking on were her two daughters, her only son, her decrepit brother-in-law, and a reporter from the *Seattle Times*. Mack, her chef, had refilled the canapés and taken a seat in front of the large bay windows. Behind him, the setting sun cast a gold-orange light on Lake Washington. For the last ten years, Mack had been allowed to make requests of the family fund and sit in on the meetings.

"This was a good year for the market," she continued, "so we have more money available than usual. The family accountant says twenty-two million, when all is said and done. Karen..." Her eldest daughter sat on the sofa before her, eyes peering out above the rim of her Champagne flute. She was striking in her red Chanel suit, though Eleanor couldn't help but be a little jealous. Karen had grown up in a world where women could run companies and move through society in a way that women of her generation couldn't. "Karen, you requested twelve million for a research grant to Greenville Children's Hospital. I'm allocating one million."

Karen's eyes flashed and she shifted uncomfortably on the sofa, but Eleanor turned quickly to Susan, her second daughter. As always, Susan sat beside Karen but somehow made herself subordinate, slouching and leaning away as though she was on the verge of upsetting the elder sister. She was Karen's second in command at their pharmaceutical company, second in all things. "Susan, you asked for four million for Seattle Parks and Recreation, and four million for homeless shelters. I'm allocating one million. Split it up between the two causes as you see fit."

Susan, always less able to control her emotions than Karen, let out a little gasp. But she knew better than to object out loud.

"John Junior." Her son leaned on the billiard table, sipping golden-brown Cognac out of a thick-bottomed whiskey glass. He'd lost weight in prison, and his light gray suit hung a little looser than it had before his time in the minimum-security Federal Detention Center at Sea-Tac. "You requested ten million for prisoner education programs and halfway houses. I—"

"Yes, mother..." As he said 'mother,' he turned to Brenden, the brilliantly handsome reporter who'd been jotting notes in a Moleskine notebook. Brenden looked like a millennial Paul Newman, and Junior couldn't help but try to impress him. "Having seen the plight of those incarcerated first hand"— Junior's voice had grown lofty, self-important—"I've come to understand the needs of those less fortunate, to *truly* value—"

"No speeches, Johnny. I read the memo." Eleanor had no idea where Junior had learned to love the sound of his own voice. His father had loved to hear himself talk, too, but Junior never met John senior. "I've allocated one million."

Junior set his whiskey glass down hard on the wooden frame of the billiard table. "What? I lived two years in prison and—"

"It was eighteen months," Karen chimed in. "*Minimum* security."

"Still," Junior objected.

"Children, stop. We have *company*." She smiled at Brenden, who leaned against the wall in the back. She'd been inviting the press to their annual gathering for the last ten years because Seattleites loved reading about old-money Seattle, especially when that old money was being given away. Sure it made the family look good, but every once in a while it also led another wealthy family to piggyback on their donations, doubling or even tripling the gifts. Brenden was more than a reporter though, he was a rising star, destined for the *New York Times*, or maybe even TV. He was certainly good looking enough.

He was also ghostwriting her memoir.

Her brother-in-law sat isolated from the rest of the group in a leather armchair to her right. "Andrew, you requested twenty million for an overhaul of the library."

"Let me guess," Andrew said, affably. "One million?"

Unlike her ungrateful children, Andrew knew better than to complain. After all, she'd been funding his lifestyle for years.

"Very perceptive of you, Andrew."

He winked at her, a nasty habit he had before saying something intended to be clever. "You could've just said 'a million each' from the get go."

She smiled sarcastically. "Yes, but that would have deprived us of this *lovely* time together."

"Plus," Karen chimed in, "it's in the bylaws. All family members must be present for a complete reading of requests and allocations."

"These days," Andrew said, "a million will get the library half a bathroom remodel." He sighed, his wrinkled cheeks flapping. "But it will do."

"It will," Eleanor agreed.

She turned to her cook, whose bright white hair matched his chef's coat. "And Mack, you requested five million for World Central Kitchen. To feed disaster victims. A noble cause indeed."

"One million?" Junior called out bitterly, pouring himself another Cognac.

"Indeed," Eleanor said.

Junior walked an angry lap around the billiard table. Karen sipped her Champagne, crossed and uncrossed her legs pointedly. Susan, following Karen, did the same. Andrew chewed at the flesh on the inside of his cheeks. Mack stood slowly, retrieved a tray of appetizers from the end table, and walked around the room, offering them to her children.

Eleanor put on a pleasant smile. "Mack, has Brenden tried one of your Bánh bèo?" She looked at the reporter. "Have you? They're delicious. A traditional Vietnamese street food. Please."

Mack held up the tray.

Brenden tried one, chewing as everyone watched him. Finally, he smiled. "Are those dried shrimp?"

"And pork belly," Mack said, smiling proudly.

Brenden scribbled something in his notebook. "And this bread thingy is..."

"Steamed rice cake."

Brenden surveyed the room. "You don't have any Vietnamese heritage, though, do you?"

"None at all," Eleanor said. "French and Scandinavian, though, as you know, my great-great grandfather practically founded Seattle. We are simply adventurous eaters. I've told Mack, try *anything* on me. I don't want to die before having the entire world served to me on a platter." She said the last sentence with a dramatic wave of her arms, hoping it would end up in the memoir.

They sat in silence as Mack continued around the room, offering the tray to the rest of the crowd.

Finally, Junior spoke, his voice full of disdain. "So what are you doing with the *other* seventeen million?"

She had no idea where he got the nerve. Other than a father, he'd been given everything. The best clothes, the best schools, the best tutors when he flunked out. He'd learned little, but had mastered one skill: turning money into more money. Real estate, stocks, companies. Like her other children, he'd been given a million dollars on his twenty-fifth birthday. By his forty-seventh birthday he'd turned it into ninety million. That was also the day he was arrested for insider trading. The government had clawed back about half of his fortune, but he had little to complain about. He'd now been out of prison for six months and acted as though he'd spent two decades in solitary confinement.

Eleanor cleared her throat. "The remaining seventeen million from this year's disbursement of our charitable fund will be donated to Douglas Senior Living, for the creation of a new senior aquatics program."

From the sofa, Karen let out a little *pffft* sound, something like disgust.

Junior stared daggers at her, mouth half open.

Andrew shuffled to the bar and poured himself a drink.

To Eleanor's surprise, it was Susan who finally spoke. "Selfish."

Eleanor had expected this. It was no secret that she planned to retire to Douglas next year. It was already the third-best retirement community in America, but why not ensure that it had all the amenities she'd need when she arrived? After all, it was *her* money.

And she didn't have to defend her decisions. "If there's nothing else, then?" She looked from child to child, then to Mack and Andrew. "Good, now let's adjourn and go find those grandkids."

The grandkids, nine in all, were gathered in the giant playroom in the northeast wing of the house. The grand Tudor had been built in the 1930s, but the playroom wing was added in the early sixties, just before she and John bought the home. When her kids were little, it had been full of rocking horses, art supplies, and more dolls than any family needed. Now it housed a department store worth of electronics she'd never understand. Her eldest grandson Kyon had assured her it was "a state-of-the-art gaming center." Three widescreen TVs, handheld games, beanbag chairs, something called "VR" headsets, and a fridge for drinks and snacks.

As usual, Kyon sat alone, little white headphones sticking out of his ears. Eleanor was all for counter-culture—after all, she was a child of the sixties—but Kyon just seemed grim. He wore tight jeans and a black hooded sweatshirt and his nose had more piercings than a pincushion. It made her sad, even though she didn't blame him. John Junior had never been much of a father, and his time in jail had done little to help his relationship with Kyon.

Karen sidled up and re-filled Eleanor's wine, a delightfully stony Chablis. "Giving away your money to, well, essentially to yourself, won't look good." She nodded at Brenden, who observed the whole scene from the corner.

Eleanor was glad Karen had gotten over her disappointment so quickly. "He's writing my memoir, and I'm paying him handsomely. He'll write what I tell him to write. A million for your cause isn't bad, and you can always add some of your own."

"Until the sale is final, I don't have a lot of capital."

Karen had been working to sell her company for a year, running into delay after delay. Eleanor could understand her frustration, but having to wait a little longer for her multi-million dollar payout was not exactly a Dickensian tragedy.

Eleanor smiled. "Somehow, I think you'll manage."

Karen sighed and put an arm around her shoulder. "It's nice, isn't it, having everyone together?"

Eleanor nodded. Karen had always been quick to anger, quick to forgive. She loved that about her.

Mack approached and offered a small plate of finger foods. "Fresh rolls, and grilled beef in betel leaf."

"You never cease to amaze me," Eleanor said.

He smiled. "Who would have thought an old army cook would be learning regional Vietnamese dishes at age seventy-five? Praise be to YouTube tutorials."

Karen smiled. "Seventy-five isn't what it used to be. You look sixty."

Mack nodded politely and headed back to the kitchen.

As the teenagers yelled at screens both small and large, Eleanor savored the spicy, tart, savory Vietnamese appetizers and sipped the wine.

Sasha, Karen's eldest at eighteen, pulled off a VR headset and came over. "Chocolate, Nanna?"

Eleanor smiled. "Don't mind if I do."

Sasha was her eldest granddaughter, and nothing like Kyon. Polite, smart, beautiful, and, above all: normal. In the fall she'd be heading to Stanford to study engineering.

Sasha put her arm around Eleanor just as Karen had. "Love you, Nanna."

Eleanor popped the raspberry-creme into her mouth and washed it down with the Chablis. "Love you, too, sweetie."

Life wasn't perfect—it never had been—but it was good enough. For the first time in a long time, all felt right with the world.

∼

The sound of her grandchildren's squeals and playfully angry shouts followed her up to bed. As matriarch of the family, she'd done her best to keep them together, keep the core of their fortune intact, and keep them respected, even revered, in Seattle. Though her children didn't always appreciate her, the happy sounds of her grandchildren were thanks enough.

In the master suite, Eleanor changed into her nightgown, took her evening medications, and slid between her cool cotton sheets. In a life full of responsibilities, her one guilty pleasure was watching an hour or two of TV at night. Until recently, she'd refused to bring a TV into her bedroom, but now that she could watch *Law and Order*, *CSI*, *Monk*, and even old episodes of *Murder She Wrote* from the comfort of her bed, she'd never go back to the media room.

Tonight it was *Cracker*, a British crime drama that was darker than her usual shows. She preferred programs where the good guys had clear and decisive victories, but it was enjoyable nonetheless.

After the first episode, she stood to go to the bathroom, but something was off. She felt unsteady, like she'd had too much to drink. She finally made it to the bathroom, but stumbled on the way back, collapsing onto the bed and almost careening off the edge.

She'd only had two glasses of wine, so it couldn't be that. Was she coming down with something? Had the dried shrimp gone bad? No, Mack was too conscientious for that.

Was it the chocolate? She'd watched a documentary about a child who'd died by eating a bunch of his parent's chocolates, not knowing they were full of THC. Surely the teenagers weren't eating marijuana chocolates in her home?

Her eyes were fuzzy as she studied the clicker to try to start the next episode. Fumbling with the buttons, she accidentally switched off the TV.

Suddenly, she felt violently ill. Her stomach twisted painfully and she barely got her head over the side of the bed in time as she threw up.

She lay back, throat burning, head heavy on the pillow. She tried to yell for help, but her voice drowned in her throat, unable to escape.

What was happening?

Her mind was a cloud of confusion. A darkness closed in, like she was sinking to the bottom of a deep, black sea.

And yet, she could still hear muffled cries of delight twenty feet below. Her children and grandchildren were playing games, munching appetizers, and sipping wine in the game room.

Her thoughts were slipping. She closed her eyes and couldn't open them again.

She tried once more to kick, to move, to flail, but her limbs were frozen.

The darkness was everywhere.

In the moment before she died, Eleanor Johnson gripped a single thought long enough to fill her last breath with bitterness: *which one of those scheming bastards poisoned me?*

CHAPTER TWO

Hansville, Washington

One Week Later

THOMAS AUSTIN WAS no pasta expert, but he was proud of his ravioli. It was his fourth batch in as many days, and he'd finally gotten the dough thin enough to be almost translucent, but sturdy enough to hold the lobster and ricotta filling without breaking in the boiling water.

Outside, his front gate screeched on its hinges and his corgi, Run, bolted for the doggie door. Austin listened. Run didn't bark, which meant she recognized the visitor. Probably the Amazon delivery lady, who came at least twice a week and always brought treats.

Hansville was pretty out of the way—a tiny peninsula jutting out from the larger Kitsap Peninsula, which itself extended from the Olympic Peninsula. The *Triple Peninsula*. People sometimes joked that you couldn't get to Hansville from where you were. No matter *where* you were. He rarely got spontaneous visitors.

"Who's the cutest dog? You are! Yes, *you* are." He recognized the voice. It was Anna Downey, the local crime reporter.

Using a slotted spoon, he fished the ravioli out of the boiling water and tossed them in the pan of sage brown butter.

Run burst back through the doggie door just as Anna knocked.

"I'm at the stove," Austin called. "It's open."

He picked up the pan, flicked his wrist to toss the pasta with the butter, then slid the ravioli onto a plate.

Anna came in as he turned.

She eyed the plate of ravioli. "Looks like you were expecting me." She nodded at the kitchen table. "You mind?"

He grabbed a couple beers from the fridge with his free hand and sat, handing one to Anna. "To what do I owe this surprise visit?"

It had been only two months since they'd met, but in the first few days they'd been to hell and back, so they shared something deep, something unspoken, that few shared. He'd seen her once or twice since—they'd even watched *Titanic*, which Anna had assured him was an essential part of his introduction to the nineties popular culture he'd missed. But she'd been busy writing follow-up stories and doing the rounds on local TV, and Austin had been clear that he wasn't ready to date.

Anna took a long swig of beer and, without asking, snatched a ravioli off his plate and popped it in her mouth.

"Hey," Austin objected, "that's my lunch."

She chewed and washed down the bite with a swig of beer. "I probably just saved you forty calories. You *did* say you're trying to get back into your NYPD shape." She waved at the food. "Plus, those are amazing. Is that lemon?"

"Lemon zest. Want a plate?"

"Nah, I already ate. Just couldn't resist. Are you adding them to your menu?"

Austin nodded. His little apartment was attached to his business, the Hansville Café , General Store, and Bait Shop. He was no trained chef—he'd spent twenty years in the NYPD—but he loved experimenting with recipes. "We're closed this week. Complete kitchen overhaul. Figure now's the time to test new dishes." Late winter and early spring were especially slow in the little beach town, but he wanted to have everything ready for the busy summer season.

Run lay on the floor by Anna's feet and she scratched the corgi behind her ears. She clearly had something on her mind, and he'd never known Anna to be shy about broaching a topic.

Austin swigged his beer. "Out with it. I know something's up."

"Ever heard of Eleanor Denny Johnson?"

Austin shook his head.

"Well, she's dead, and I think she was murdered."

Austin cocked his head. He tasted tart cherries, a ping of excitement he could never contain when an unanswered question hovered before him. "Okay, who was she?"

"Very wealthy Seattle woman. Eighty-two years old. Big family. Old money. Died a week ago."

"How'd she die?"

"At home, alone, in bed."

"So what makes you think she was murdered?"

"Her family is, well, a little *sus*, as my son would say."

Austin shrugged.

"*Sus*, as in suspect, sketchy, shady."

"Okay." Austin popped a ravioli in his mouth, giving her a look over his fork as if to say, *more details, please.*

"Officially, she died of natural causes. She *was* eighty-two, after all. But I'd spent time with her in the two months leading up to her death. First of all, she seemed healthy. Told me she had a clean bill of health from her doctor this winter. Second, her kids are—like I said—kinda sus."

"Wait, back up," Austin said. "She died of *natural* causes?"

"That's what her *doctor* says. Heart failure, peacefully in her sleep."

"Did they do a full tox report?"

Anna shook her head. "Nope. More sketchiness."

"Not really. When an old woman dies in bed, they don't do an autopsy or tox screening unless there's reason to suspect foul play."

Anna stood. "And there is! In this case there *is*."

Austin followed her with his eyes as she walked a lap around the kitchen. Anna wrote a column about crime in Kitsap County and, though it was a part-time gig, she knew the area as well as anyone and had developed great instincts about crime. She also had more guts than half the officers he'd worked with. Even in the face of danger, she was unflappable. So her agitation surprised him. "Tell me how you're involved in this."

Anna sat. "Six weeks ago, I was contacted by Eleanor's daughter, Karen. Her mom was looking for a ghostwriter for her memoir and she'd seen me on TV after everything that went down a couple months ago." She tossed her sandy-blonde hair back playfully. "My *fifteen minutes of fame*. Anyway, she saw me on TV, then read a few of my stories. Liked my writing. Long story short, I went to her mansion on Lake Washington, spent the day with her, and she offered me the job."

"You were going to write a book about her?"

"No, I was going to write *her* book. Ghostwriting. She wanted to tell her story for her family legacy, but she was well-known enough around the city that it would have sold some copies. I was going to spend a day or two a week with her, read through her journals and letters, write the thing, and she'd get all the credit."

"And you'd get?"

"Fifty thousand dollars. More than the standard rate. But she's filthy rich. Family had farms and timber in the late 1800s, helped build sections of Seattle in the 1900s, were part of the group that built out the downtown and started the Pike Place Market."

"Is that the place where they throw the fish?"

Anna's mouth dropped open, then she dramatically raised her chin to close it. "You've lived here over a year and you *haven't* been to Pike Place?"

Austin shrugged. "I left New York to get away from cities. Among other things." After the shooting that had taken his wife and left him in the hospital, Austin had accepted early retirement, happy to live the rest of his life in this sleepy beach town. He'd only visited Seattle once, despite living an hour away. "Wait, you said '*was*' going to write her book. Past tense."

"She fired me two weeks ago. Replaced me with a hotshot from the *Seattle Times*."

"Sorry to hear that."

"Thanks. It kinda sucked. But she paid me five grand for the five days I'd already put into it, so I couldn't be too harsh on her."

Austin finished the ravioli and took the plate to the sink. "I'm still trying to figure what her death has to do with you or—more to the point—with me."

"You're a PI now, right?"

"Sort of." After helping the detectives of the Kitsap Sheriff's office in the case around Christmas, Austin had declined an offer to become a consultant. Instead, he'd started his own private investigation business.

"Any clients yet?" Anna asked.

"I found a missing object for someone."

"Awesome. Your first case?" Anna was impressed. "Jewelry, bearer bonds?"

"One of Run's tennis balls. She'd lost it under the couch."

Anna laughed. "Well, here's your first job offer: come to Seattle with me. Today. I'm meeting with Eleanor's family to return a couple diaries she gave me when I started working with her."

"What do you want me to do?"

"Just, I don't know, *observe*. I can't offer any money, but as payment I'll let you take me out to dinner."

Austin raised an eyebrow.

"Okay fine, I'll take *you* out to dinner."

He said nothing.

She tried again. "I'll *cook* you dinner."

He smirked. "*Definitely* not, then."

Anna laughed. "Hey, I can cook. Swedish meatballs."

Austin sat. "Tell me this: why do you seem so sure she was murdered?"

"First of all, she was rich. Personal money, properties valued at over ninety million, plus a charitable family trust that gave away millions every year. Second, during the week I spent with her, she told me that the family had secrets. She said a hundred articles had been written about her, but none had ever told the full story. She was getting on in years, and was ready to come clean."

Austin considered this. When rich people died, someone always benefited. After all, the money had to go somewhere. But the simplest explanation was usually the right one. When an old woman died in her bed, chances were that she'd simply died. But he couldn't deny that he was intrigued. "You have sources in the Seattle PD, right?"

Anna nodded.

"And?"

"So far, no investigation. No suspicion of anything."

"Alright, I'll come, but not in any official capacity. And you're cooking me dinner sometime."

"Deal. I'll tell the family you're a friend. Leave out the whole PI thing."

Austin nodded. "When's the next ferry?"

CHAPTER THREE

SINCE MOVING TO WASHINGTON, Austin had noticed that dogs were allowed in far more places than they were in New York City. That included the ferries that ran every hour or two from Kitsap County to Seattle.

He, Anna, and Run caught the one o'clock boat and took a seat under an awning on the upper deck. It was nearly spring, but still fifty degrees and gray, a typical day in the area. The wind chilled Austin's face as the ferry eased out of the terminal at Eagle Harbor, leaving a gentle slash through the water. As they moved from shore, Austin took in the estates along Wing Point, a mix of grand modern homes and smaller, older Island getaways.

"Eleanor," Austin said, sipping the black coffee he'd grabbed from a machine in the passenger cabin below. "Tell me more about her. You mentioned her kids, her family. Was she married? Divorced?"

"Her husband was John Johnson, and he was *definitely* going to be part of the book. Second Air Division, injured in the early days of Operation Rolling Thunder. Honorably discharged from the Air Force in 1965. Returned to Seattle and got involved in all sorts of businesses. Met Eleanor, who, like I said, was old-money Seattle. A *very* rich family. They had two kids—Karen and Susan

—who now run a startup pharmaceutical company. Designer cancer drugs. While Eleanor was pregnant with their third— John Junior—rumors started to spread about John's business dealings. He'd grown up poor in eastern Washington, scrapped his way up. Eleanor was born rich. It was a real Han Solo, Princess Leia kind of thing."

"Now *that's* a reference I get."

Anna mocked him mercilessly about his lack of pop culture knowledge, but even *he'd* seen Star Wars.

"John Johnson had his fingers in a lot of businesses around Pike Place," Anna continued. "Some real estate, too. Long story short, police were onto him for all sorts of fraud, corruption, extortion, even murder. I read a few articles from the time, clearly leaks from the police, that said an arrest was coming. He killed himself in 1971, just before John Junior was born."

Austin shook his head. "Whoa. And Eleanor? Was she involved in any of the shady dealings?"

"Not that I know of. Definitely wouldn't be the first time a wife was clueless about her husband's business affairs. Although maybe that's what she meant when she told me about the secrets no one knew. She also said that Vietnam had messed up his head pretty bad even though he was discharged early in the war." She reached over and pet Run behind the ears. "Overall, Eleanor seems to have been a helluva woman. Kept the family together, settled various fraud cases against John after his death, revived the family name, and has done a lot of good for the city. I was thinking we should call the memoir, *The Phoenix of Pike Place* because she rose from the ashes of a horrible situation."

Behind them, a man cleared his throat loudly. Anna turned. "Brenden?" Her face tightened and her lips made a hard line. Austin knew immediately she was not fond of this guy.

"Anna, good to see you." Brenden was tall, with dark hair and a jawline straight out of an action movie. His tone of voice was falsely friendly, as though there might be an awkward past between them. An ex-boyfriend, maybe?

Anna stood. "Austin, this is Brenden McNeery, *Seattle Times* reporter."

Austin stood and shook his hand.

Run tried to get Brenden's attention by gently head butting his shins, but he ignored her and turned back to Anna. "I owe you an apology."

"Oh, why?" Her tone told Austin she knew *exactly* why he owed her an apology.

"The memoir. When she gave it to me, I had no idea she'd been planning to offer it to you."

"She *had* offered it to me." Anna patted her large handbag. "I have two of her diaries in here right now. I'd already begun work."

"Like I said, I'm sorry." Brenden offered a frown that told Austin he was not the least bit sorry. "When she saw me on CNN, she called my agent out of the blue. Or was it when I was on *The View?*" He shook his head. "It all happened so fast."

"Without meeting you?" Anna put her hands on her hips. "She called your agent and just offered you fifty grand?"

Brenden took a step back. "Not exactly."

Anna squinted. "*More* than fifty?"

"*The Seattle Times* isn't exactly Goldman Sachs. I'm looking to move to New York within a year and she said, 'name your price,' so I did."

Anna sat back down. "Don't even tell me."

He moved across from her and leaned on the railing. The breeze blew his dark hair like he was in a commercial for expensive boats. "A hundred grand." Now he was rubbing it in her face. "Not bad for a side gig."

"You still gonna write it?" Anna asked.

"Heading over to Seattle right now to meet with the family. Sounds like they want to buy me out of the contract. My agent got a cancellation clause. Could end up being the easiest fifty grand I ever made. And my dad said I'd never make any money as a reporter!"

Anna took an angry sip of her coffee. She was trying to put her son through college—not an easy job in the best of times and, for part-time reporters, these were certainly not the best of times. It made sense that she'd be fuming over the prospect of this name-dropper making as much for *not* writing the memoir as she was going to make for writing it. "That's more than I made in my last two years of freelance stories."

Brenden frowned as though he was looking into a cage at an animal rescue shelter. "Are you serious?"

Anna nodded.

"If you want I could put in a word for you at the *Times*, although we're not really hiring right now. Maybe when I leave for New York they'll take you on. It could be sooner than a year. I'm meeting with producers from both Fox and MSNBC next week. They're looking for a new straight shooting, down-the-middle voice for their panels."

Anna sighed aggressively. "Anyway, I'll be fine. Good to see you and, well, I guess we'll see you soon. We're heading over to Eleanor's house, too."

"Oh?"

"Returning Eleanor's diaries."

"Next time, have your agent get you a contract."

Anna frowned. "Not all of us *have* agents."

Brenden shrugged, and Austin was about to ask him to leave when he said, "I'd be happy to return them for you. The diaries, I mean. Since I have to go there anyway."

Anna pulled her handbag a little tighter, eyed him suspiciously. "No, thank you."

"Really? It's all the way across town."

"I can afford an Uber," she said, flatly. "Why are you so keen on getting the diaries?"

He stepped back. "I'm not. I just...." He shoved his hands in his pockets. "Anyway, good luck."

Anna followed him with her eyes as he strolled down the deck and around a corner. "Jerk," she whispered.

"Do you think I should pick up the names he dropped and bring them back to him?"

Anna laughed. "I admit, I'm jealous as hell, but he doesn't exactly downplay his success, does he? Let's just hope he's in a different wing of the mansion when we get there."

"And if he *is* around?"

Anna scrunched up her nose at him, then she got his meaning. "Brenden may be a jerk, but he's smart, and a good reporter. If he has any inkling of foul play, he'll be sniffing it out like I am. For now, we just need to play everything casual and see what we can see."

The ferry was approaching the dock in Seattle, and they began walking to the front of the boat. To their left, the giant Ferris wheel welcomed them to the downtown.

"Why was he doing the rounds on TV?" Austin asked.

"Other than the fact that he looks like a Marvel superhero?"

"Is it all based on looks?"

"I mean, it's TV. But, as much as I wish I could say it was all superficial, Brenden is the best-connected reporter in Seattle. They had him on TV because he broke the story about that tech CEO who killed his wife a few weeks ago. Big national news."

Austin pointed at Ivar's, the famous clam chowder shop next to the ferry terminal. "You wanna eat first?"

"Nah, I'm good." She scrunched up her nose and tilted her head like she was about to say something.

"What?"

"You don't think..."

Austin knew where she was going. "Brenden was there the night Eleanor died, and you're thinking..."

"He couldn't, could he? What was your read on him?"

"I think almost anyone can kill another human, under the right circumstances. For most, those circumstances never arise. I don't see any motive for him."

"Fifty-thousand dollars to *not* write a memoir."

Austin shrugged. "Maybe, but if it's true he's about to

become a regular on TV, I'd think there'd be a lot more money in his future."

They followed the crowd off the deck, over the metal plank, and into a long, covered walkway that led into the ferry terminal.

Anna looked at Austin and smiled. "Eh, you're probably right. Does it make me a bad person that I was kinda hoping Brenden turned out to be a murderer?"

CHAPTER FOUR

THE DENNY-BLAINE NEIGHBORHOOD bordered Lake Washington on the east side of Seattle. It was one of the most affluent in the city, and the closest thing to an Old Money neighborhood Austin had seen since moving to Washington State. On the ride from the ferry terminal in downtown Seattle, the streets had grown gradually larger, the houses older and more stately, the lawns wider and greener.

Lake Washington Boulevard itself was the peak of grandeur. A mix of classic waterfront homes from the early to mid twentieth century, and modern homes built or remodeled by the tech millionaires of the last thirty years. Just a few miles east of downtown, it felt like a different world.

The Johnson manor was a sprawling two-story home facing the water, its sharp-peaked roof and arched entryways giving it an almost gothic look. But standing on the sidewalk looking in, Austin was quite sure it had been updated with every modern convenience.

Anna thanked the Uber driver and shut the door, then gestured at the house like a game show hostess presenting a *fabulous new car*. "Not bad, right?"

"What does a house like this go for? Five million?"

Anna chuckled. "Try *thirty*-five million. This is the most expensive location in Seattle, and this is one of the top five houses in the neighborhood."

As they walked up the walkway to the front door, Austin said, "It's kind of like the Upper East Side in New York. Insanely expensive homes, but right on the street. No gated community or anything. Not a lot of security."

Anna rang the doorbell, which clanged with a pleasant, digital tone. "You scoping it out to rob the place?"

"Well, beer and bait aren't flying out of the cooler these days, so I've been considering going into the home-robbery business."

Anna smiled. "As a detective, you must have learned how criminals think, but you would be the world's worst thief."

Austin pretended to be offended. "Why?"

She eyed him. "You're not a deceptive person."

"No?"

"I believe everyone has something unique about them, something underneath their personality, what they do for a living, their likes and dislikes. For you, it's that you're incapable of putting on a facade. Literal minded. You're an open book. No secrets."

Before he could respond, footsteps echoed behind the door and Anna grabbed his hand. "Remember. I'm here to return the diaries. You're not a former detective. *Definitely* not a private investigator."

The door swung open and an older man stood before them, chewing a toothpick. He had a full head of bright white hair and a kitchen towel slung over the shoulder of his crisp white chef's coat. "May I help you?"

Anna smiled. "Are you Mack, Eleanor's chef? She told me a lot about you."

"I am. You must be Hannah, one of the reporters?"

"Anna, and this is my friend Thomas. Joining me to do some sightseeing. Can you believe he's never seen the flying fish at Pike Place?"

Mack smiled and waved them in. "Karen told me you'd be coming." He glanced down and saw Run sitting politely at the end of her leash. "Oh."

"I'm sorry," Austin said. "I meant to ask, is it okay if I bring her in? She's very well behaved."

Mack's expression was pained. "No pets allowed, I'm afraid. I *love* dogs, but I've been with the family for over fifty years, and they've never had a pet. Eleanor wouldn't allow them in the house."

"Allergies?" Anna asked.

"Not that I know of. She simply didn't like animals. But we have a little fenced-in area out back. Happy to take your cute little Corgi out there."

They followed Mack through a series of gardens that ran around the side of the house and into a little grassy area, surrounded by an elaborate wooden fence.

"Look," Austin said, kneeling and offering Run a treat from his pocket, "you have water views." Run gobbled the treat and studied his hand for another. "I've been assured this is one of the most exclusive neighborhoods in Seattle," he told her. "Perhaps you can find a handsome German Shepherd to take you out for a T-Bone while I'm inside." Run ran around the yard looking for something to occupy her, but found only perfectly manicured grass. She stared at Austin with a disappointed look, then did a downward-dog stretch and lay on the grass.

"I have some leftovers I could offer her," Mack said. "Not T-Bone, but skirt steak."

Austin smiled. "Nah, she'll just bored-sleep until we get back, but thank you."

Inside the house, Mack led them through a grand entryway, down a hallway lined with stunning parquet floors that somehow looked both very old and sparklingly new, and into a living room that was roughly the same size as his entire apartment.

"Have a seat," Mack said, waving at a leather couch. "I'll find Karen. In the meantime, would you like a drink? Or coffee?"

"Thanks, but no," Anna said.

"Actually," Austin said, "I'd love a drink. What's your house special?" He glanced at Anna. "Always trust the chef."

Mack gave him a quizzical look, then said, "Actually, lychee mojitos. They were one of Eleanor's favorite cocktails. She was traditional in some ways, but not when it came to food and drink. She had a saying, 'I don't want to die before having the entire world served to me on a platter.'" He looked at Anna. "You sure you don't want one?"

"If it was one of Eleanor's favorites, how can I refuse?"

When Mack was gone, Austin whispered, "Never refuse a drink if you're trying to scope out a situation. The more they serve us, the longer we can stay."

Anna nodded. "This is where they had the meeting the night she died." The room had a grand fireplace, a billiard table, and ornate moldings of a sort Austin had occasionally seen in classic New York homes. The walls were lined with framed photographs of the same man in various settings and outfits. Judging by the fact that he only reached age thirty or so in the pictures, Austin assumed it was John Johnson, Eleanor's deceased husband. In one photo he wore a baseball uniform and held a bat in a hitter's stance, as though posing for a baseball card. One was black and white and showed him in an Air Force uniform when he was in his early twenties. In another he stood on the roof of a building holding a Champagne flute, the Seattle skyline behind him. In another he was older—likely after he'd returned from Vietnam— and wore a sharp black suit and, incongruously, held up a head of cabbage at a vegetable stall in Pike Place Market.

Mack returned with a tray of drinks, followed by two women and a man. Handing Austin a tall, frosty glass, Mack said, "Thomas and Anna, this is Karen and Susan Johnson, and over there is Junior."

"Yes," Anna said, "Karen and I spoke on the phone."

They shook hands quickly, Karen and Susan taking seats on the couch across from them.

Junior hadn't approached, instead grabbing a seat in an armchair to their right. He nodded politely, but, of the three siblings, he was clearly the least interested in pleasantries.

"Well," Karen said. "Two reporters in the house at the same time. Never thought we'd allow *that* to happen."

Anna smiled politely. "So Brenden beat us here? We ran into him on the ferry."

"Oh," Karen said, "so you two know each other?"

Anna nodded.

"He's in the other room." Karen glanced at her watch, a thin, diamond-encrusted thing that looked like it cost more than Austin's truck.

"Don't let me keep you," Anna said.

"Oh no, we were just finishing up anyway. He's on his way out."

Karen noticed Austin noticing the watch and pulled her hand back slightly so it disappeared into the arm of her expensive-looking suit. "I'm sorry about your dog," she said. "Mack told me she's out back. We've just never been big on pets."

"No problem," Austin said. "She's been meaning to check out the Seattle dating scene, anyway."

Anna chuckled, but the Johnson siblings had no reaction.

"So," Anna said, "is the memoir on hold then?"

Karen gave Anna an inquiring look, as though the question was out of line. Before she could answer, the door creaked open behind them and an older man limped into the room. He must have been in his late seventies, but his face had a youth and affability that made him look younger than his stiff walk and thin gray hair indicated.

He gave a little wave. "Hi all. Andrew Johnson." He took a seat in an armchair.

Anna said, "First of all, I'm so sorry about Eleanor." She pulled two leather-bound diaries out of her handbag and handed them to Karen. "Like I said on the phone, she'd given me these when she asked me to start work on the memoir, and I wanted to make sure you got them back."

Karen handed one to Susan, then flipped through the other without stopping long enough to read. "In the sixties and seventies, she wanted to be a writer. Joan Didion or, in her more artsy moments, Sylvia Plath. I always thought she would have been a good reporter, actually, because she liked to chronicle everything."

"She certainly covered a lot in her diaries," Anna agreed.

"So," Junior said, pouring himself a drink from the bar, "you read them?" His tone was a little more accusatory than Austin would have expected, since Eleanor had given Anna the dairies.

"I didn't have time to read them all," Anna said, sipping her mojito, "but I nibbled around the edges, so to speak. I'm sad I won't get to know your mother more. She seemed like an amazing woman."

"She was," Susan said, tears forming in her eyes.

They all sat in awkward silence.

Anna leaned forward toward Susan. "Do you mind if I ask what happened? I know it's impolite, and I promise this is not for a story. It's only that, well, I felt like I was getting to know her, and this came as such a shock."

Susan glanced at Karen. Junior took a loud sip of his drink.

Andrew said, "Heart failure." He double-tapped his chest. "At our age, it happens."

"But what led up to it?" Anna asked. "She seemed so strong, especially for her age."

"People die," Junior said. "Happens every day. And as distraught as we are about it, we'd prefer not to share details with strangers." He stepped toward them and gestured toward the door, trying to end the conversation.

Austin pretended not to notice, sipped his drink, and smacked his lips. "This is excellent, Mack. I heard Eleanor had a love of cuisine."

Karen smiled sadly. "She did. She gave money to charities all over the world—Africa, Southeast Asia, Eastern Europe." She let out a little laugh. "She told me once that all she wanted in return was to sample every food the world had to offer."

Susan said, "I still remember when I was in high school and we had an assignment to interview one of our parents about their favorite things. I asked her what her favorite color was and she said she didn't have one. I asked her what her favorite movie was and she said she didn't have one. I asked her what her favorite food was and she looked at me like I was insane. Said something like, 'In a world as big as ours, why would I *ever* have a favorite?'"

"To her," Karen said, "the *next* thing was always her favorite. The next meal, the next charity she could help, the next thing, the next thing. It was just her personality."

"Not the next *man*, though." Andrew had been sitting so quietly, Austin had forgotten he was there.

"Don't," Junior said.

Andrew held up both hands. "I'm just saying."

Austin looked from Andrew to Junior. There was a tension there, something unspoken, but he couldn't tell what. He wanted to probe more deeply, but he'd promised to keep a low profile, so he stayed quiet.

Anna said, "Is there anything else you'd be willing to share about that night?"

"We really have to be going," Karen said, politely but firmly. She uncrossed her legs and placed both feet on the floor. Ready to stand and see them out, but not yet doing so.

"You're asking a lot of questions," Junior said. "If it's not for a story—and you were fired from the memoir thing she never should have been doing in the first place—why so much interest in our mother?"

Andrew huffed in Junior's general direction, then turned to Anna. "Don't mind him. My little nephew just hates reporters. The press had a party when he went to jail. Headline after headline: 'Silver-Spoon Johnson Boy Busted for Insider Trading.'

Probably kept the papers in business for another six months."
He looked at Anna. "Right?"

"I didn't write any of those stories. I wouldn't." She looked at
Junior. "Really, I'm just curious."

Junior walked over and sat on the arm of the couch next to
Karen. He looked at Austin long and hard, then back to Anna.
"Somehow I don't think that's it. Why are you *really* here?"

CHAPTER FIVE

"THE DIARIES," Anna offered, weakly.

Junior scowled. "You could have dropped them in the mail." He was a slight man, and Austin noticed that his suit was a little too big for him. He had the air of a man who was compensating for a lack he felt inside himself. He had none of Karen's elegance or Susan's emotional vulnerability.

Anna leaned away from him. "I wanted to pay my respects."

"Bullshit," Junior spat, leaning toward them. Austin could smell the Cognac on his breath. "Just like every reporter out there, you're digging for something—anything—that will sell a few papers, get a few clicks."

Austin gave him a hard look. "You're drinking Cognac out of a whiskey glass."

Junior held up the glass. "So?"

He didn't care one way or another how someone chose to get drunk—but he couldn't help but notice little quirks. Sometimes they ended up being meaningless, but sometimes little details like that mattered. "The bar is stocked with gorgeous cognac glasses, and yet you poured a glass of Remy Martin Louis XIII into a heavy-bottomed whiskey tumbler. That's a hundred-dollar shot."

Junior sipped slowly, eyeing Austin over the glass, then he turned to Karen. "Can we see these people *out*." Austin had been trying to get a rise out of him, but the last word was laced with a venom even he hadn't anticipated.

"Sorry," Austin said, holding up his hands apologetically. "Was just curious."

"I'm very sorry if we've offended you," Anna offered in a conciliatory tone. "Really, I'm just curious. No story planned."

Karen put a hand on Junior's knee. "Stop being a jerk, Johnny."

Anna said, "Did Eleanor have any enemies? Was there anyone in her life angling for money from her or..."

She trailed off when she noticed the looks on the faces of the children. This time she'd gone *way* too far.

Susan's face had turned red. "That's, that's..."

"Highly inappropriate," Karen said.

"That's enough," Junior added. "Get out!" He walked to the door and threw it open, spilling his drink in the process.

Andrew, unflappable, smiled at them gregariously as they stood to leave. "Anyone angling for more money? You must not have been around a lot of rich people."

"I haven't," Anna said. "What do you mean?"

"The question should be, can we think of anyone *not* angling for more money? The night she died, she'd denied all of us big donations, and she controlled the money for the whole family."

"Out!" Junior barked at them. "Andrew, stop talking to these people. I *order* you."

"Order me?" Andrew laughed. "Yes sir, captain sir." He was on a roll, happy to piss off his nephew. "When you're as rich as Eleanor, half your time is spent giving away money and *not* giving away money to people who ask for it. Hell, I asked her for ninety grand last month for a vintage 1968 Porsche."

Anna walked to the door. "Did she give you the money?"

Andrew shook his head. "Sadly, no. She dismissed it as my 'three-quarters-life crisis.' No biggie, though. My point is, everyone wanted money from her. Some got it, some didn't. After my wife died, she brought me in and paid my way. If you think someone killed her, you're wrong. And if you're looking for someone close to her motivated by money, it's like looking for blue in a clear summer sky."

"Well," Anna chuckled as the door slammed behind them, "that went well."

Out in front of the mansion, Austin knelt and gave Run a treat from the baggie he carried in the inside pocket of his jacket. "You weren't exactly subtle."

"I tried to be. At first."

Austin smiled and mimicked her voice. "'*Did she have any enemies?*' That's like the first twenty minutes of every detective movie."

"I think I've watched too much *Law and Order*. But seriously, tell me you don't think something is fishy here."

They walked down Lake Washington Boulevard. Across the lake, the tall buildings of Bellevue hung against a gray sky. "The family is certainly a little odd."

"Right? The brother-in-law has lived with them for like fifteen years. No family of his own. The sisters—"

"The sisters seem kinda normal to me actually. And Junior... sure he was rude, kind of a jerk. But his mom just died, he's been in prison. I don't know, money makes people odd. It rarely turns people into killers."

They sat on a bench in Denny-Blaine park, staring out across the water as a pigeon nipped at some soggy popcorn next to a garbage can.

Austin said, "Andrew was right, by the way."

Anna turned to him. "Huh?"

"Money. I had a case in New York in—I don't know—2009 or so. One of my first big cases as a detective. Rich lawyer found dead in his apartment. Head smashed in on his granite counter. No forced entry, so we figured it was someone he knew. I worked like hell the first few days. Looked into family, business associates, neighbors. He had all kinds of business deals, extended family who were getting money in his will. A wife, a mistress, and so on."

"And?"

"Turned out, he slipped and smashed his head on the corner of his kitchen counter. Autopsy showed he'd mixed sleeping pills and alcohol. Later, his therapist told us he'd been struggling with stress and sometimes used that combination to come down after a long day at the office."

Anna raised an eyebrow skeptically. "So it was an accident?"

"Yup. Later we confirmed through the surveillance video that no one had been in or out. Dude took a sleeping pill, drank a little too much, got up for a snack or something, and cracked his own skull."

"Eleanor Johnson was *healthy*, though. She told me herself."

"People lie about their health. Doctors can be wrong. Point is, I spent a couple days certain the case would come down to money. Often, cases *do* come down to money. But sometimes people just die and there's no rhyme or reason to it."

"Okay fine," Anna said, "but what was that between Junior and Andrew? They obviously have beef."

Austin thought back to their exchange in the living room. It had seemed odd at the time, but now something occurred to him. "Two options as far as I can see. Eleanor was a woman who liked to sample everything. And she never remarried, right?"

"Right."

"Any evidence she dated much?"

"None that I've seen."

"The way Andrew said, pointedly, that she didn't go through men the way she went through foods and favorite colors..." He trailed off, sure that there was something there, but unsure exactly what it was.

"What?" Anna asked.

"I don't know. Maybe he had a thing for her and he was jealous because she was still devoted to John even after his death?"

Anna scoffed. "Devoted for fifty years? No. No woman is that dedicated to her husband. Especially not one as badass as her. Remember, she was the one who came from money. John used *her* money to start his businesses. She didn't *need* him the way some women need their husbands. Plus, she barely mentioned John in the parts of the diaries I read."

"Don't tell me you don't believe in true love."

She laughed. "Sometime I'll tell you about my ex and you'll see why."

She pulled her phone out of her handbag, then turned to him suddenly. "Oh, she's probably gay."

Austin raised an eyebrow. "Maybe that's the secret she was going to reveal in her memoir?"

"In the diaries, she talked about her friendships with women all over the place."

Austin pondered this. "Rich Seattle family, mid-sixties. She wouldn't be the first woman who married a man she wasn't attracted to because of societal expectations."

Anna swung her legs around and crossed them on the bench. "And maybe Andrew knew and was pissed on behalf of his brother?"

"Could be, or maybe he was attracted to her and felt rejected? But that's just normal family drama, as far as I'm concerned. Behind the happy family lives people put on the internet, or in their Christmas cards, that sort of drama is not exactly earth-shattering."

They sat in silence, Anna scrolling through her phone as Austin watched a small boat pass on the lake.

Suddenly, he snapped and stood up. "I've got it!"

"What?" Anna asked.

"I know how we can prove the Johnson family is evil and therefore must have killed her."

She looked skeptical. "How?"

"They don't allow *pets* in the house. Any family like that must be full of cold-blooded killers."

Anna kicked him playfully, then tapped her phone again. "Uber is on its way, you jerk. So you really don't think she was murdered?"

Austin considered this. The truth was, he didn't have a gut feeling about it one way or another. "Look, if any evidence emerges, then fine. But for now I've got recipes to test and a kitchen remodel to oversee."

CHAPTER SIX

THE NEXT MORNING, Austin slipped through the back door of the West Sound Community Church, as he did a few times a month, sometimes more. He didn't consider himself a religious person, not anymore. But he came here from time to time during off hours because it's where he felt closest to Fiona. There was something in the smell of the place that triggered his synesthesia. It was the only place he'd ever been that brought the feeling on this strong. It was a feeling that not only was she not gone, but she'd never left.

Usually he had the place to himself, but on occasion, Pastor Johnson would be around, cleaning or doing paperwork. This morning, the old Pastor was in the kitchen, packing brown paper bags with apples and sandwiches. "Morning, New York." The Pastor left the back door unlocked for him, so his arrival was hardly unexpected. "It's been a while."

Austin leaned on the counter. "Been kinda busy."

"Read about the case. That business with those infants." He shook his head. "Horrible."

"It was."

"Thing like that would make anyone come back to church, I'd say."

"That's not why I'm here."

"Alright, alright." Pastor Johnson often brought up the fact that Austin hadn't come to a single Sunday service. But he didn't belabor the point.

"What are the lunches for?" Austin asked.

"Shore cleanup crew we sponsor. Pick up trash that's washed up on the beaches once a month."

"Thanks for doing that," Austin said.

Pastor Johnson nodded. "Got to keep our beaches clean. *'Let the heavens rejoice, let the earth be glad; let the sea resound, and all that is in it.'* Psalms Ninety-Six."

Austin smiled.

"Been meaning to ask you... after all that happened, why haven't you been coming in as much? Or have I just missed you?"

"You're right," Austin said. "I haven't been in as much."

"Is it something about your wife? What was her name?"

"Fiona."

"Right, right." He set a cardboard box on the counter and began adding the paper sacks to it. "Seems to me after seeing what you saw with that killer, you'd need a quiet church more than ever."

Austin smiled. "You sound just like her."

Pastor Johnson leaned on the counter. "I'm listening."

"We had an ongoing disagreement. She was a prosecutor in New York, assistant DA. So she saw the details of some horrible crimes. Some of the worst stuff you can imagine. Things I won't say out loud. Not in here, anyway. In her view, it gave her more reason than ever to go to church, to find meaning and purpose."

Pastor Johnson poured himself a cup of coffee. "You want one?"

Austin shook his head.

Pastor Johnson took a slow sip. "And you didn't agree with her?"

"Did you read the details of what the Holiday Baby Butcher did?"

Pastor Johnson looked in his cup, shaking his head the way people do when coming to terms with the worst humanity has to offer. "I did."

"And you can still have faith after reading that?"

"I can."

"I guess that's where you and I part ways. It's where Fiona and I parted ways."

Pastor Johnson smiled. "Good to hear that you could love each other despite the differences."

Austin nodded, watching Pastor Johnson squint into his mug as though looking for something.

"And yet," the old pastor said tentatively, looking up, "it's still important to you to stop people like that killer. Why?"

"What do you mean?"

"Well, if you have no faith in God, in a higher power, isn't it all just nothingness? Good and evil, truth and lies. Without faith, why does anything matter?"

Austin studied him. "Sounds odd, coming from you."

Pastor Johnson winked. "I minored in philosophy. I've read all the existentialist stuff. Don't agree with *any* of it, but I read it. Just trying to understand how you think."

"I can't explain it," Austin said. "The big stuff, the big picture, the universe, I don't need to have an opinion about any of it to know that snatching a kid out of his crib in the middle of the night is wrong. And doing what she did after that is something worse than evil." He shuddered, thinking back on the little kitchen, the canning pot on the stove. "I don't need anyone or anything to tell me she needed to be stopped."

"What about forgiveness? Would you ever forgive what she did to those babies?"

"It's not my role to forgive. That's up to the families she destroyed, or maybe to pastors like yourself. My job was to stop her."

"And you did."

Austin nodded. "Damn right."

"I wonder, though, what about Fiona? By your logic, it's up to you to forgive the people who took her life. Have you?"

Austin shook his head. "Maybe God can forgive them. I never will."

Pastor Johnson got a fresh cup, filled it with coffee and held it out to Austin. "Black, right? You look like you could use it."

Austin took the cup, inhaling deeply as the steam warmed his face.

"Do you feel like talking about what happened?" Pastor Johnson asked. "With Fiona. You may never forgive, but sometimes it can help to talk. To let go."

"I don't want to let go."

"Then tell me because I'm curious."

Austin sipped the coffee, sucking in air to cool it. "Well, I was hit four times and lived. She was shot once and died. Everyone assumed the shooter's motive had to do with a case she was working on. By the time I got out of the hospital, they'd already looked into her old trials, her pending prosecutions, everything. I tried to get assigned to her case, but they wouldn't let me. Too close. And they were right. I was too angry, too messed up to be a detective on that case. As it turned out, I was too messed up to be a detective at all. I stayed on the job for a few months, then retired early and came out here."

"What do you think happened?"

"I think they were on the right track, but in the detective game, sometimes even the right track leads you to the middle of nowhere. Fiona had dozens of cases—hundreds of people had reason to want to take her out. Drug dealers, murderers, low-level mafia. Or what's left of the mafia, anyway. Could have wanted her out of the way to get them an easier prosecutor. Or simply retribution for a previous prosecution."

The Pastor shoved the cardboard box of lunches into a big silver refrigerator. "You think that's why you're single?"

This caught Austin off guard. "Huh?"

Pastor Johnson chuckled. "Last week I had breakfast over at

your place, heard a group of women at another table. Local gossips, but good-natured. They saw your picture come up on the local news, some follow-up on the case you helped solve. Said you were 'Hansville's most eligible bachelor.' Mostly families and retired folks here, so there aren't many bachelors to begin with."

Austin frowned. He didn't like people knowing about his business, and he liked the thought of them gossiping about him even less.

Pastor Johnson noticed his frown. "C'mon, New York. It's a *compliment*."

"Maybe I'm single because I can't let go, like you said."

"I'm not a psychiatrist, but I like to think I'm not half bad at reading souls..."

Austin cocked his head. Anyone else, he would have been out the door. But he had a soft spot for Pastor Johnson. He was the kind of religious man he wished there were more of. "And what do you see in my soul?"

"At your core, you're a detective. You can't help it. You're never going to be able to let go of Fiona until you figure out who took her from you."

Austin shivered. He'd thought this himself on more than one occasion, but hearing it out loud in the chilly church kitchen hit in a different way. The truth sank in on a deeper level. "The case was never mine to begin with. I know the team who looked into it. They were just as good as me. Plus, now the case is colder than an igloo in a snowstorm."

Pastor Johnson studied him. "Alright then. I'll tell the ladies to take you off the list. For now."

Back at his restaurant, Austin strolled through the kitchen, early-morning sun streaming through the windows. To his surprise, the kitchen renovation was going as planned. The old counters had been ripped out, the plumbing replaced, and new electrical boxes installed. Today would see the installation of a new stove and oven, tomorrow the new sink and countertops.

His phone dinged with a series of texts, as it often did a few minutes after walking into his store. Andy—his former cook and now his manager *and* cook—had gotten wifi for the place. So every time he walked in, all the calls and texts he'd missed while walking and driving through the Hansville dead zones came in at once.

Today, he had three new texts from Anna, the first from about forty-five minutes ago: *You up? Need to talk.*

Then, ten minutes later: *News about Eleanor Johnson. Call me ASAP.*

And finally, five minutes after that: *Hey, Rip Van Winkle. Wake UP! Like I thought, she was murdered!!!*

Austin hurried to the cash register and called Anna from the landline.

She picked up before it had even had a chance to ring. "Oleander."

"Good morning to you, too."

Anna sounded out of breath and Austin imagined her pacing around her apartment like a madwoman. "Eleanor Johnson was poisoned with yellow oleander."

CHAPTER SEVEN

"SLOW DOWN," Austin said. "I thought they weren't doing an advanced tox screening."

"I was wrong. I mean, that's what I'd heard. But apparently one of the kids requested it, and paid for it."

"So they suspected murder all along?"

"It was to make things go smoother with the estate and the life insurance. Can people of that age even *get* life insurance?"

When looking into a suspicious death, Austin's ears always perked up at the phrase *life insurance*. "They can. Sometimes older people will get it to defray costs of unpaid medical bills or funeral costs. It's rarer in wealthy families, though. At least when people are over eighty. Which of the kids asked for the tox report?"

"I... know... Johnson..."

"What? You're breaking up."

"It... nothing... Seattle."

Austin shook the phone, then immediately felt like an idiot. What the hell good would *that* do? "Anna, I can't hear you. Can you come out to Hansville?"

He heard tires kicking up gravel in the parking lot outside his shop. Through the window, he saw Anna's white SUV.

"Start from the beginning," Anna said, sitting across from him at the kitchen table in his apartment.

Austin had pulled up a report on yellow oleander, a substance he knew of but had never seen used as a poison. "There are a few levels of tox screening. The first usually checks for drugs and alcohol. But yellow oleander wouldn't show up on a standard tox report. An advanced screening involves gas chromatography used with either mass spectrometry or infrared spectroscopy."

"Sounds sciency." Anna's phone dinged. She read it, then held it up to Austin.

It was a webpage showing an online fundraising campaign.

"They're offering $25,000 to anyone who can solve Eleanor's murder," Anna said.

"Who is?"

"The campaign was started by Mack, the cook. The kids have kicked in five grand each. So did Andrew."

Austin could see her eyes growing large at the thought of the money.

"I was counting on that memoir money, Thomas. I'm already late on my son's tuition for spring semester. I need this." She looked him in the eye. "Fifty-fifty?"

It was weird to be called "Thomas." Almost everyone called him by his last name. But somehow it didn't sound wrong coming from Anna. He'd planned to spend the rest of the day fishing. Or, rather, casting his line aimlessly into the water while tossing a stick for Run. He didn't have much hope of catching anything at this time of year. There was something about Anna, though. He wanted to help her, and not out of pity. Likely it was because—even though she clearly needed the money—she had the look in her eye that he used to have. That ineffable desire to know what happened. A desire that went well beyond her desire for twenty-five grand.

"I'm in," Austin said. "Who ordered the toxicology report?"

"Karen, the eldest. Do you think that rules her out as a suspect?"

Austin considered this. "You might think so, but no. It's possible one of the others was going to ask for it, or even that the police suspected something and *they* were going to order it."

"In which case, she'd want to order it to get ahead of things?"

"Exactly. Back to the test. I don't know how the science of it works, only that they can detect damn near any compound in the body after death. But they're usually only performed when there's already reason to suspect poison. By the way, where did you hear this?"

"From Karen herself."

Austin was surprised. After they'd been kicked out of the mansion, Austin figured the family would be done with Anna for good. "She called you?"

"Remember when I said I had *two* diaries from Eleanor?"

Austin nodded.

"I had three. I kept one in case I needed an excuse to get back in touch with the family. I called Karen this morning with a whole, 'Whoops, I forgot one of the diaries line. Needed to know where to send it. She came right out and told me that she'd asked for the test four days earlier, suspecting nothing, then done a one-eighty when she got the results. The way she said it, ordering the test had been a routine part of the paperwork for the estate. She sounded truly shocked, fighting back tears." Anna scrolled through her phone, then said, "I need to get my head around this. If this was a case in the NYPD, what would *you* do next?"

"I'd start with what we know. First, everyone agreed that she was at home all evening on the night she died, right?"

Anna nodded. "It was a big family meeting. Like Andrew told us, they were going over allocations for the charitable trust. Did it every year."

"I'm going to assume there's no way she ingested it by accident, which does happen from time to time, but only if you have the plant on site and eat a lot of the seeds. So, someone poisoned her that evening."

"How do we know it was that evening?"

"Oleander takes effect within a couple hours. So unless someone created some special time release form—"

Anna sat up suddenly. "Karen and Susan run a specialty pharmaceutical company."

"That's where my mind went first, too. I was trained to look for a few things: murder weapons, motive, and opportunity. Obviously, we know the murder weapon here. And their company will certainly be something police will look into for the creation of the weapon. A lot of people had the opportunity. Anyone could have slipped her a dose. Jury is still out on motives."

"I have something on motives," Anna said. "Setting aside the grandchildren, we have six suspects. The kids: Karen, Susan, and John Junior. The two older men: Mack the chef and Andrew the brother-in-law. And Brenden. He was there that night, too."

"Motives?"

"I talked to a source inside Karen and Susan's pharmaceutical company. Apparently they've been working to negotiate a sale for quite some time. They're cash-strapped and barely have enough to stay afloat while they try to finalize some big deal. So, money. Maybe they wanted their inheritance a little sooner."

"Or the life insurance. We'll need to find out who the beneficiary is."

"It's the estate itself."

Austin considered this. "Large estates and life insurance policies take a while to settle. If Karen and Susan need the money soon... I don't know. What else?"

"John Junior was arrested twice before his insider trading sentence. Domestic violence, 2010. Hit his wife, apparently. Arrested, but then she declined to press charges and divorced him. And a bar fight in college."

"Okay, not good, but both are a long way from poisoning his

mother. And neither speak to motive. Isn't he the richest of the kids?"

"In terms of liquid cash, yes. Susan and Karen stand to be richer, but only if the sale of their company goes through."

"And if they needed money for their company, why not ask John Junior for a few million for a bridge loan?"

Anna nodded. "Financial motives are trickier when everyone's already rich."

"What about Andrew and Mack?" Austin asked.

"Googling last night, I found an old gossip column, like Seattle's version of Page Six. It ran from 1998 to 2003, but I found a couple articles speculating that Eleanor and Andrew were, well, an item."

"Wait, that she was sleeping with her brother-in-law? Or dating him, or whatever?"

"That they'd been together since John's suicide, but hadn't made it official because of how it would look. I thought she might be gay, but a spurned lover thing could make sense, too."

"It would explain some of Andrew's attitude yesterday." Austin shook his head. "Sex and money. Two most common causes of murder. But was there any substance to the story?"

"No. It was gossip, but I wouldn't rule it out. Mack... I don't know. Got nothing on him."

"And the reporter? Yesterday you seemed keen on—"

"Brenden is a jerk, but I don't think he's a killer." She smiled. "Much as I'd like him to be."

"Let's not rule anyone out yet. How many grandchildren were there? And what ages?"

"I don't know for sure. A lot, and they were all there that night. At least a couple are in their late teens or maybe twenties."

"So they can't be ruled out entirely."

"I guess not, but why kill your grandma?"

Austin shrugged. "Why kill your mother? Or sister in law? Or employer? Or the woman who hired you to write her memoir?"

"Good point. Hold on."

While Anna looked up the grandchildren, Austin brewed another pot of coffee. He'd recently gotten a new coffee maker—one of the ones that ground the beans right before brewing. It made better coffee, to be sure, but sometimes he missed the cheap stuff he used to get at the sidewalk carts in New York, always in those blue and white cups the sidewalk vendors used.

"Sasha and Kyon," Anna said, looking up from her phone. "Ages eighteen and twenty. Sasha is Karen's oldest and Kyon is the only son of John Junior. The other grandkids are all under eleven years old. Can we rule the little ones out?"

Austin handed her a cup of coffee. "For now."

Anna looked at the steaming coffee, frowning as though Austin had served her a cup of sadness. "Sugar? Milk? Not everyone likes their coffee to taste like burnt death."

Austin handed her a quart of milk and a box of sugar, then watched in horror as she dumped half the coffee in the sink, added half a cup of milk, then stirred in tablespoon after tablespoon of sugar.

When she finally looked up, he said, "I could have just grabbed you a candy bar from the store."

She smiled. "Could you? Then I can dunk it in my coffee." She took a sip and smacked her lips aggressively. "What does oleander do to the body?"

"That's where I was going next. Almost everyone who ingests it vomits heavily. When the doctor pronounced her dead, if he'd seen vomit everywhere, I don't think he would have concluded that she died of heart failure in her sleep."

Anna sipped her coffee, then chugged it like a glass of water. "So someone cleaned up?"

"I can't say for sure, but maybe. Or the doctor is covering it up. We'd have to talk to everyone who was there. Did anyone hear vomiting? See any cleaning taking place, or any evidence that cleaning *had* taken place? There are too many unknowns to draw any conclusions about anything."

Anna stood and refilled her cup, then repeated the ritual of adding milk and sugar. "Seems like we have more questions than anything. And I think I know how we can get answers."

Austin raised an eyebrow.

"Tomorrow is the memorial for Eleanor. Your old pals in the Kitsap Sheriff's Department are going, and I think I can wrangle up an invitation. Meet back here at eight?"

Austin nodded.

"Can I use your bathroom?" she asked.

"Through the living room on the right, after the office."

Austin turned back to the description of oleander poisoning, which sounded horrific. The more he read about it, the less he believed Eleanor could have died without leaving evidence of poisoning.

"Whoa!" Anna called from the hallway. "Nice typewriter."

He found her with her head poked into his tiny office. "It was Fiona's."

She stepped through the doorway. "Do you mind?"

Austin waved a hand. He hardly ever came in here, preferring to work on the couch in the living room. But he'd kept Fiona's typewriter exactly as she'd left it, complete with the first paragraphs of the book she'd begun working on not long before she was killed.

"Can I read it?" Anna asked.

Austin nodded. "It's the beginning of a book she was going to write."

He watched as Anna read the lines. He'd read them so many times he knew them by heart.

Michael Lee strolled into the parking lot of his favorite Korean restaurant in Brooklyn at 7 PM on a cold Tuesday in February. He'd never lived in Korea, but he went to Mama Dae's BBQ once a week for their famous galbi and kimchi. The meal made him think of his grandma, who'd raised Michael and passed away when he was ten.

He was at Mama Dae's to meet Megan, a woman he'd connected with in a dating app. He'd worn his lucky outfit—black jeans and an authentic t-shirt from David Bowie's Serious Moonlight Tour.

His lucky restaurant. His lucky outfit.

The unluckiest day of his life.

His "date" turned out to be a stand-in for the Namgung crime family. Megan had come to steal his identity, then lure him to his death.

"Whoa," Anna said, emerging from the office.

Austin didn't say anything.

Sometimes there was nothing to say.

CHAPTER EIGHT

"HOW'D you get us the invite?" Austin asked. "I figured after they kicked us out, we'd be *persona non grata*."

Anna turned her white SUV onto Lake Washington Boulevard. After meeting at Austin's place, they'd driven onto the ferry. "Detectives Calvin, O'Rourke and Jule were coming. I had Ridley get us in."

The street was crowded. Not only was it an unseasonably warm and sunny day, the memorial had attracted at least a couple hundred people. Between the people enjoying the lakeside park and the limousines and Ubers crowding the road, it was stop and go traffic for blocks.

They finally pulled up to the mansion and left the car with a valet in a black suit that was nicer than Austin's own. He wasn't one to wear a suit unless absolutely necessary, but Anna had assured him it was, so he'd pulled his emergency suit out of the back of his closet.

Anna wore a long black dress and heels with a matching black purse.

Austin saw Detective Ridley Calvin from the curb and strode up to him. Detectives Lucy O'Rourke and Jimmy Jule stood next to Ridley, sipping coffee out of paper cups. All three wore formal police uniforms, a sign they were there in an official capacity.

Austin shook Ridley's hand warmly. "Rid, good to see you." Calvin Ridley was the type of detective Austin had always tried to be. Serious, good at his job, and a fair boss to the people who worked under him.

Ridley said, "Good to see you, too. Before I forget, I got a text this morning. Lorraine D'Antonia is being sent to New York to stand trial. When she heard what happened to the Baby Butcher, she went on a hunger strike in prison for three days. Then, well, I guess their bond wasn't strong enough to keep her from eating for more than three days. She's alive, and she'll never see the light of day."

"Good to hear," Austin said. "Jimmy, how's the gut?"

Jimmy Jule was the youngest of the three Kitsap County detectives. He'd taken a kitchen knife to the belly in pursuit of the Holiday Baby Butcher and now stood a little bent forward, as though favoring his stomach. "Healing." He grimaced. "Slowly. Actually I'm here to pay my respects because Ms. Johnson donated a lot of money to Behind the Badge. They're helping with my medical costs."

"It's not all covered?" Anna asked.

"Mostly, but my body is a temple." He put on his cockiest tone. Even in a stiff uniform, his muscles found ways to bulge out visibly. "It has *special* requirements."

Lucy rolled her eyes. "Weird, I didn't think Behind the Badge covered pornography subscriptions?" She had about five years on Jimmy, who self-consciously played the role of meathead to annoy her.

He punched her playfully in the arm. "They're paying for my physical therapy, Lucy O'Loves-Me."

Jimmy and Lucy had been on-again, off-again for a couple years now. This was kind of their thing.

He posed in front of her like a bodybuilder on stage. "I'm gonna come back stronger than ever."

"Get a room, you two," Ridley said. "But in all seriousness, Ms. Johnson gave to a lot of police causes. The Washington State Patrol Memorial Fund was one I worked to help secure. Half a million dollars to the families of fallen officers."

They watched in silence as more and more cars stopped and let out mourners. Austin had been to his share of funerals and memorials—it was why he kept the black suit in his closet—so he was used to moments like this. The awkward silences when there was little more to say about the deceased, but no one felt fully comfortable discussing other subjects. Austin assumed that, like him, the detectives were eager to talk about Eleanor Johnson's murder.

Behind them, the crowd began streaming up the walkway to the house. Men and women of all races, and, judging by the clothes, all income levels. From young men in designer suits to older folks who looked like they hadn't been outside for years. From the look of it, Eleanor Johnson had touched people in every corner of Seattle.

It was Detective Lucy O'Rourke who finally broke the silence. "Alright." She moved a little closer, huddling the group together, and spoke quietly. "Everyone heard about the oleander?"

They all nodded.

"Theories?"

"Before anyone says anything," Ridley said. "This isn't our case. Leave it to the SPD."

"Oh, you're no fun," Anna said. "And it is *our* case." She gestured to Austin. "Family is putting up twenty-five grand to anyone who provides information that leads to an arrest." She looked to Lucy. "If that's you, you can donate it to a charity of your choice if you're not allowed to investigate on your own time."

Lucy smiled. "If I solve this thing on my off days, I'm *keeping* the money."

"Well then," Anna said, "I guess that makes you our competition." She must have seen the disapproving look on Ridley's face because she held up both hands defensively. "You know as well as me that Eleanor Johnson was what people might once have called a 'Battleax.' She was tough and wouldn't want a bunch of sentimentality at her funeral. She'd want a party, and she'd want to know who the hell killed her."

"Speaking of competition." Austin pointed toward the road, where Brenden McNeery stood chatting with a group of women. His head stuck out above the crowd—he was at least six foot three—and he wore the confident smile of someone who'd always been treated like he was special.

Anna frowned. "Is he signing an autograph? At a funeral. And I thought *I* was the inappropriate one."

Brenden seemed to be signing a magazine and handing it back to a younger woman who stared up at him adoringly.

"Who *is* he?" Lucy asked. "I mean, I'd take his autograph just to stand next to him."

"Hey!" Jimmy said. "I'm standing right here."

Lucy looked him up and down. "You're adequate."

Anna leaned in conspiratorially. "So are you two an item, then?" she asked Lucy.

"It's complicated. But if *he's* single—" she waved toward the reporter, who was making his way over to their group—"I'm definitely single, too."

"*Do not* like that man," Anna said. "That is a *bad* man."

"I could bench press two of that guy stacked one on top of the other," Jimmy said.

Anna shushed Jimmy and Lucy and smiled politely as the reporter reached their group. "Brenden, good to see you again. These are detectives Calvin, O'Rourke, and Jule. Kitsap Sheriff's Office. And you remember my friend Austin from the ferry. Everyone, this is Brenden McNeery from the *Seattle Times*."

They shook hands and stood awkwardly, hands in pockets, scanning the crowd.

"So," Brenden finally said. "How did you all know Eleanor?"

"She was a generous donor to police causes," Ridley said.

"Ahh yes," Brenden said. "She came from a previous era where one could support the police *and* homeless people. When one could care about fallen officers *and* social injustice. Better days." Even though Austin agreed with the sentiment, Brenden had a grating way of speaking. It was performative, the rises and falls in his deep voice sounded like he was practicing for a TV appearance, which, Austin realized, he probably was.

"You're not wrong," Ridley said. "She came from a time before all the current BS. Wish we had more like her, though I still think most of the BS is from keyboard warriors."

Jimmy nodded. "In real life, people are less crazy than they appear on the internet."

"Eleanor was a hell of a woman," Anna said. "Wish I'd gotten to know her better."

"Maybe you will," Brenden said. "I assume you're digging now, what with the reward and all."

Anna nodded. "And you?"

Brenden shook his head. "I don't write stories for the money."

Anna put her hands on her hips. "So you're not gonna try to figure out who killed her?"

"Oh, I'll be breaking this story." His tone was confident, but also playful enough to show that he didn't take himself too seriously. Or at least that he wanted people to *think* he didn't take himself too seriously. "But not for the money."

Anna rolled her eyes. "Lemme guess. You're in it for the truth?"

Brenden bowed dramatically. "What else?"

The crowd on the lawn began filtering into the house. The memorial was about to begin and Ridley led the way up the stone path toward the entry.

"I'm surrounded by detectives," Brenden explained, "and I know you all know the feeling. There's something about finding out what really happened that's uniquely addictive. The twenty-five grand is, well, whatever. I just *have* to know what happened. Being the first one to find out—beating you and the SPD—is a happy bonus."

"Challenge accepted," Anna said, pulling Austin toward the door.

She glared back at Brenden. "And we already have a prime suspect."

CHAPTER NINE

"DO we have a prime suspect you're not telling me about?" Austin leaned on the wall, one eyebrow raised as high as it would go.

"Of course not," Anna said. "I only said that to get in Brenden's head. And before you say anything, no, I don't really hate him. But I damn sure want to beat him. And not just because I need the money, which I *really* do."

For the first half hour of the memorial, Austin had hung back, following beside Anna as she worked the room. She was quick to introduce herself to new people, asked a lot of questions, and passed out as many business cards as she could without being rude.

Austin was surprised to learn that the memorial was largely an informal gathering. Hundreds of people drank coffee and ate hors d'oeuvres from little plates. Many drank Veuve Clicquot Rosé, which Austin learned was Eleanor's favorite Champagne.

They'd overheard Mack tell a small crowd that she'd once said she wanted a hundred bottles to be consumed at her memorial. Not just provided, but *consumed*. Her life had been a great adventure, and she wanted her memorial to be a party fueled by excellent Champagne.

Small groups gathered around the photographs of Eleanor displayed on stands in hallways and on the walls of the home. Some signed a guestbook and shared memories of the woman. But there didn't seem to be any formal program or any religious aspect to the ceremony. This, he realized, was a good thing when it came to their reason for being there. The informality allowed them time to pull people aside one-by-one, which was almost always the best way to gather information.

So by the time he'd eaten his share of Swedish meatballs and gravlax on rye toast points, and by the time Anna was on her second glass of Champagne and Austin on his second cup of coffee, he pulled her to the corner of the massive living room. "Let's see if we can get the six adults who were present that night one-on-one. This seems like it's going to go on for a while, and tipsy witnesses and suspects are the best kind."

"I was thinking the same thing." Anna subtly tilted her head to the right, where Karen and Susan were shaking hands, smiling sadly, and speaking with a small group of older women. "Let's hover," Anna continued. "Wait for our moment."

Their moment came when a short woman who must have been in her eighties broke into a coughing fit and excused herself. Moments later, her companions followed her toward the restrooms, leaving Karen and Susan alone.

Anna led the way, sidling up beside Karen, who smiled more warmly than Austin had expected. "Thank you for coming. Both of you." She shook their hands formally, but not coldly. "I was glad when Detective Calvin asked if you could be invited. In my shock, I forgot to invite you."

Austin knew nothing about fashion, but even he could tell that Karen's pantsuit was stunning, likely some kind of designer piece. It was the blackest black he'd seen, sheen and angular, with three gold buttons down the front of the jacket. A simple but elegant pearl necklace was her only ornamentation.

"We wouldn't have missed it," Anna said.

Susan reached out and squeezed Anna's hands as though they were old friends. "Yes. Thank you."

Younger than Karen by two years, Susan seemed to live two feet behind her older sister. She spoke second, stood a step behind her, and glanced at Karen first whenever anyone asked a question. Even the way she dressed indicated this. Like Karen, she wore a black pantsuit, but it was faded and linty, as though it had been worn many times, whereas Karen looked like she was ready to appear on the cover of a fashion magazine about *Fabulous Women Over Fifty*. Austin didn't care much one way or another about how people dressed—it just wasn't his thing—but the contrast was striking.

Karen sipped her Champagne. "I want to apologize to you, Anna. Truly. We were all in shock when you visited, and you were not treated properly. When we learned that mother had been..." she swallowed hard and continued in a whisper... "killed. Well, our shock is..."

Susan glanced around the room. "To think, one of these people, or a member of our own..."

Austin did his best to appear casually interested, understanding their pain but not deeply invested. In truth, he was studying every word and gesture of the sisters. Both seemed genuinely upset, but he'd been fooled before.

He'd once worked a murder case in which police had arrived at the scene two minutes after a shooting. Bodycam footage showed the victim's girlfriend, frantic and sobbing, and telling a fully-believable story about how the husband had been shot in the driveway while taking out the trash. Turned out, the wife had killed him. Austin never forgot the pain and horror on her face from those body cams. The shock, the tears. They were more convincing than any actor in any movie he'd ever seen. And yet, one-hundred percent fake.

"May I ask," Anna offered. "And I'm sorry to do this here. I wouldn't, but I know you are desperate for answers. What do *you* think happened?"

"I truly have no idea," Karen said as Susan nodded along. "We both gave statements to the police this morning, after we told them about the results of the toxicology report. Mother had *no* enemies. And, let me say this: Anna, you were the first to raise the idea that there may have been foul play, and I'll help you however I can, just like I told the police. I know mother pulled the rug out from under you on the memoir job. There's no one I'd rather see get the money than you." She appeared to be fighting back tears. "We just want answers."

Anna reached out and squeezed her free hand. "Thank you. I didn't tell you this before, but Thomas Austin here isn't only a friend. He's a former NYPD detective. One of the best there is. He's going to help."

Susan stepped back.

Karen squinted at him. "Oh?"

"I'm a private investigator now," Austin said. "And again, I'm sorry for your loss. By all accounts, Eleanor was an amazing woman." He paused, cleared his throat. It was always tricky to make the transition he was about to make, especially at a memorial. "It would help if you told us anything you can remember about that night. Or the weeks leading up to it. Any odd interactions, any changes in her routine. Unusual phone calls or visitors, that kind of thing."

Susan said, "There's simply no way anyone who was at our home that night did this. No way. It was only family, plus Brenden and Mack."

"Did she argue with anyone recently?" Anna asked.

Karen shook her head slowly. "I don't think so."

"No," Susan said.

Austin made his expression as warm and innocent as he could. "Your pharmaceutical company. I hear you're in the process of selling it?"

"That's right," Karen said.

"Any chance that could be related?" Austin asked.

Susan glanced at Karen. "I can't see how. Mother had no involvement."

Anna saw where he was aiming and went there on her own. "There are rumors that your company is short on cash, needed money to hang on until the deal goes through."

"That's right," Karen said, shifting from foot to foot. She was clearly uncomfortable with the line of inquiry. "Not uncommon in business deals of this size. We spend millions on R and D, all our capital is tied up."

Austin had planned to ease into the next question, but Anna plowed forward. "Do you think someone in your company could have believed that your mother's death might benefit the deal? Get the two of you the money you need to—"

Susan gasped. "No!"

Karen sipped Champagne. "I should be upset that you'd even raise that question, but I'm not. I know you have to ask." She finished her glass and swapped it out for a full one as a waiter walked by with a tray. "But no. No way."

Anna had been trying to upset them. In his line of work—and hers too—half the questions were designed to get information, the other half to elicit a response that might reveal something beyond words.

Karen sighed tiredly. "I've read *All the President's Men*, too, Ms. Downey. I understand that 'follow the money' are words to live by in your profession. But, no. We'll be signing for a six million dollar bridge loan by the end of next week. It was negotiated *before* mother's death. And I'd expect you know, Ms. Downey and Mr. Austin, large estates like my mother's take months, even years to settle. We won't be receiving anything until well after the deal goes through. By which point—" she lowered her voice to a whisper—"we will be so rich the money from the estate will be irrelevant." She cleared her throat. "As I told the police, I'll happily provide paperwork confirming all this. The sooner we and other family members can be ruled out, the better."

Anna smiled. "I had to ask. So you're quite sure no one in your family could have done this?"

Karen frowned, glanced around the room. "I can't see it."

"Me neither," Susan said.

A small group of women had gathered nearby, waiting to speak with the sisters. Austin said, "We don't want to take too much of your time. I hope we can follow up when the dust settles. Just one last thing. The people who were present that evening, the night your mother passed away: you two, Mack, Andrew, John Junior, Brenden, and the grandchildren. Sasha and Kyon are the only two of adult age. Correct?"

Karen nodded.

Susan frowned. "Tell me you don't suspect..."

Karen put a hand gently on her wrist to silence her. "Let the man finish, Susan. He knows what he's doing."

"Just following every possibility," Austin said. "And who found your mother? Who was the first to know?"

"Myra," Karen explained. "One of Mack's kitchen staff. She wasn't there that night, but found her at six in the morning on the dot. As she did every morning, Myra knocked on mother's door with coffee. I heard her knock because I was staying in one of the guest rooms. I heard the tray of coffee drop to the floor and Myra banged on my door only seconds later. She came and got me right away."

"Why were you staying in one of the guest rooms?" Austin asked.

"I'd had a bit of wine the night before. Didn't want to drive home. And I had things to discuss with my mother the next morning."

Susan looked confused. "You did?"

Karen waved her off. "Nothing important. Minor issue with her ongoing donations."

Austin waited until she looked at him, then cocked his head slightly.

She was smart enough to know what he was thinking. "I

assure you, Mr. Austin, it was nothing. I'd rather not say more now—impolite to talk about money at a memorial—but nothing changed because mother and I never got to discuss it, and it couldn't possibly be related to her death."

Austin filed this away, then said, "So you were the second person in her bedroom that morning. When you went in, was anything out of order, any messes, anything unusual?"

"Other than the tray and coffee and cream on the floor, no. Everything looked normal."

"No sign of a struggle, or illness?" Anna asked.

Karen shook her head. "I called our family doctor immediately. Mother kept him on salary." She pointed to a man of at least eighty years, leaning on a cane near the window. "He was here half an hour later."

Earlier, Anna had managed to corner the doctor for five minutes. He hadn't said much due to doctor/patient confidentiality, but he seemed genuinely devastated by Eleanor's death, though perhaps a decade or two out of the loop when it came to medical science. Still, Austin was left with no reason to suspect he could be involved in a cover up.

"Last thing," Austin said. The crowd of women had begun inching closer, growing impatient. "If she *had* argued with anyone who was there that night, maybe an argument you didn't see, who would you suspect it *could* have been?"

Susan perked up suddenly. "Kyon. John Junior's son. Last week I heard them arguing out in the garden."

Karen scowled at her. "You didn't tell me that."

"Didn't seem like a big deal. You know how Kyon was. That kid would argue with a mannequin."

Anna finished her glass of Champagne and, as Karen had done, deftly swapped it for a full one. "What were they arguing about?"

Susan frowned. "I didn't hear specifics. Only raised voices."

Karen said, "He's a sweet kid deep down. But brooding.

Typical angsty young man. Look at the way he dresses, how he spends his time. And it didn't help that his father was in jail."

"If I may..." One of the women had poked her head between Karen and Susan.

"Absolutely," Anna said. "Thanks for your time, ladies. We'll be in touch."

CHAPTER TEN

THEY FOUND ELEANOR'S BROTHER-IN-LAW, Andrew, smoking a cigar in the backyard, leaning on the fence that surrounded the grassy patch Run had been playing in the previous day.

"Mr. Johnson," Anna said, "do you have a minute?"

Around the side of the house, a little girl of nine or ten played basketball with a young man Austin assumed to be Kyon, the eldest grandson, judging by his piercings, purple hair and the fact that he was wearing a hooded sweatshirt at a memorial. At least the sweatshirt was black, Austin thought.

"I have all the time there is," Andrew said. "I presume you're here to ask about Eleanor?"

Anna smiled. "You'd know I was lying if I said any different." She cleared her throat. "You met Austin yesterday, but I didn't tell you he was a former NYPD detective."

Austin shook his hand.

Andrew said, "Thought you were asking a lot of questions, and I don't mind them. Seen enough *Law and Order* to know you'll probably want to know if I was upset about Eleanor denying me the money for my charity, for the car." He paused, taking a deep puff on the cigar, then blowing it out after turning his head so as not to hit their faces with the smoke. "Sure I was upset. Doesn't feel good for a man my age to be dependent on his brother's widow. Know what feels worse?" He laughed. "Working for a living."

Anna pulled out a notebook. "But you had a career, previously, didn't you?"

"Sure. 1970s all the way to 2003. Small farm equipment company."

"And your wife had passed away around that time, right?"

"Suzanne Margaret Johnson." Andrew ashed his cigar over the fence. "Breast cancer. 2002. Probably part of the reason the company went under. We were already struggling, and I lost the will to continue after Suz passed away. Eleanor said I could move in here, and I never left."

Austin considered this. The rumors that he and Eleanor had been an item had begun in 1998, four years before his wife passed away. "What made you decide to move in here, rather than dating, maybe remarrying?"

Andrew winked at Austin, a kind of sly, rascally wink, bordering on pervy. "Wives are always after your money. Didn't need another. And I had my share of... female callers."

"You're a very handsome man," Anna said.

"Well, thank you, young lady." He ran his free hand over his mostly bald head. "Shoulda seen me when I had my hair."

"But really," Austin pressed. "Why move in here?"

Andrew studied him. "Oh, I get it." He studied the cigar for a long time, then said, "you're wondering about the rumors. Me and Eleanor?"

"I'd be a fool *not* to wonder," Austin said.

"I'll tell you the same thing I told the papers every time they needed to fill column inches in their gossip sections." He studied the tip of his cigar, which had gone out. From the inside pocket of his jacket, he pulled a plastic baggie and a cigar cutter, then clipped off the burnt end, letting it fall to the ground. He stored the remaining half of the cigar in the baggie. "Cutting corners,"

Andrew said, chuckling. "And this is how you can rule me out as a suspect. Eleanor told me she'd cover my living expenses until one of us died. Now I have to rely on her kids. If Junior has anything to say about it, I'll be out on my ass."

"So," Austin said, "she didn't leave you a stipend or anything in her will?"

"Pre-paid the twelve grand a month for a retirement home. So I'll be moving there unless one of the kids steps up." He held up both hands as though anticipating an objection. "I get it, a nice retirement home isn't too bad. But compared to the way I've been living... anyway, I'm the last one on earth who benefits from Eleanor's death."

Austin studied his face as he spoke. He sounded sincere, but also strangely flippant, like he was talking about someone else.

"You and Junior seem to have some animosity," Anna said.

Andrew slipped the cigar baggie in his pocket. "He's a spoiled little shit. But we're family. Families fight."

"What do you two fight about?" Austin asked.

"Mostly his kids. He's a crappy father. Just look how Kyon turned out." He gestured over to the young man, who was now passing the ball back and forth with the little girl. "John's oldest male grandson." He shook his head. "I don't have kids. Suz never conceived. So *that* is the man who must carry on the Johnson name when I'm gone."

"What's so bad about him?" Austin asked.

"Talk to him for yourself. Maybe it's kids these days, but that guy scares me. Keep in mind, I blame Junior, but I wouldn't want to be left alone with Kyon."

"So he looks a little different," Austin said, "but what specifically bothers you?"

"I think about what John would say if he were here. He was a traditional guy in most ways. Served in Vietnam in the early days. Silver Star. He was no conservative, but damn..." he waved a hand toward Kyon, as though it was self-explanatory.

Austin shrugged. "Please, say more."

"That kid was given everything. Now he won't go to college, won't get into business. Wants to be a DJ, which I guess is electronica music or something. John would roll over in his grave."

Anna held up a hand. "We got off track. What about you and Eleanor? The rumors."

"Imagine my wife hearing that crap when she was sick with cancer." He shook his head. "She read the gossip like everyone else, and I'll tell you what I told her: we never had an affair, never would have had an affair. Never *could have* had an affair."

His emphasis on the words 'could have' were supposed to convey something, but what? Then it struck Austin. "You mean..."

"I know there are parades now and everything," Andrew said, "but in the sixties, there weren't. Sure, I had a thing for Eleanor. But she was a big fan of Sappho."

Austin assumed that was another movie reference he should get.

Andrew frowned. "You don't read much Greek poetry, huh?"

"Can't say that I do."

"Sappho was a famous poet," Anna said. "He's saying Eleanor was gay."

Andrew shrugged. "Not a hundred percent. I mean, I don't know, she's got three kids. But yeah. After John died, it was women only for her. That I'm sure of. And I knew it for decades. Does it make any sense that I'd stew for forty years, then kill her?"

There was a loud clattering from the kitchen and all three looked up. The smell wafting through the screen door was intoxicating—garlic and butter and dill.

"Thanks for your time," Anna said.

"Like I told ya," Andrew said, pulling the cigar baggie out of his pocket, "I got all the time there is."

They took the back door and stood in a corner, out of the way of the busy kitchen crew. Mack wore his chef's whites and directed a team of five cooks and six waiters.

The kitchen was brightly lit and equipped with appliances better and larger than most home kitchens, but not quite the size and durability of a restaurant kitchen. The stove, Austin noted, was a $25,000 La Cornue in matte black and gold. He'd drooled over that stove online. Not that he would have spent that much, but it was a gorgeous piece of equipment.

On the walls were family photos: Karen, Susan, and Junior at various ages, as well as other children, some of whom Austin recognized as Eleanor's grandchildren. In one photo, Eleanor sipped Champagne at a banquet. In another, Mack cooked for a barbecue at a park. In another, a teenager leaned on a palm tree in front of a giant library.

Mack finished a platter of food by sprinkling it with sea salt, sent it out in the arms of a young waiter, then looked up across the giant granite kitchen island. "Looking for me?" he called.

Before they could answer, Mack walked up, wiping his hands with a rag. "Only got a couple minutes, but I can talk. I assume you're here looking into Eleanor's death?"

"And to pay our respects," Anna said.

"Sure. Right. Reporters are famous for showing up at memorials to 'pay their respects.' How can I help you?"

"It's nice that such a great kitchen is still informal." Austin pointed at the photos lining the wall. "Who's the girl in front of the palm tree?"

"My granddaughter," Mack said, smiling fondly. "She's in college. Evie, short for Evelyn. Her dad, my son-in-law, wanted her to have a classic name with a modern nickname."

"She's beautiful," Anna said. She was always trying to butter people up before launching the tough questions. She was used to working alone, so she had to be the good cop and the bad cop at the same time.

"She's my heart," Mack said, staring fondly at the photograph. Then, looking back at them, "How can I help you?"

Anna said, "We're looking for more information about the night Eleanor passed away."

Mack shook his head. "I still can't believe it."

"The food," Austin asked. "Do you always have complete control over the menu? Over what leaves the kitchen?"

"Always. Eleanor had suggestions, requests, but then left it to me."

"How many helpers did you have in the kitchen the night she died?"

Mack considered this. "Mike and Priya. They left by five or so."

"What did you serve?" Austin asked.

"Bánh bèo and other Vietnamese finger foods. We've been doing a tour of Southeast Asia. Thai food, Malaysian..."

As he went on, describing all their recent adventures in cuisine, Austin did the math in his head. Oleander acted in two to three hours at most, so there was no way the other cooks could have poisoned Eleanor's food unless they'd poisoned the entire batch, in which case others would have gotten sick as well.

"Eleanor always said," Mack concluded, "she didn't want to die before having the entire world served to her on a platter." He looked at the floor. "I'd like to think she didn't."

Anna patted his arm. "We truly are sorry. We know you were with her for a long time."

"And with John, before he died. He was actually the one who hired me."

"Over fifty years is a long time to work for one family," Austin said. "You don't see that much anymore."

"They always treated me well," Mack said. "Never gave me a reason to leave." He turned and shouted at a waiter. "Thumbs off the platters. Use a napkin!" The frightened waiter got a napkin, then scurried out of the kitchen. "Could have been grinding away, sixteen-hour days in a restaurant all this time. That's no way to live."

"We know you're busy," Anna said, "so I'll come right out with it. What do you think happened?"

Mack scrunched up his face like he was thinking. "Well, I'm glad you asked. Obviously, it looks bad for me because I control the food, and she was poisoned, apparently, though I'd like the family to order another test to be sure. Anyway, after our family meeting, after we all ate, she hung around with her grandchildren for a while. I was in and out." He leaned in. "But I saw her eating chocolates and drinking wine. If I had to guess, that's where it came from."

"So," Anna said, "someone could have slipped the oleander into her drink?"

He scratched his chin. "Or somehow gotten it into a chocolate, yeah."

"Was she on any medications?" Austin asked.

Mack shouted at a young cook. "Baker, check the meatballs. Don't let them dry out." He turned back to Austin. "What were you saying?"

"Medications," Austin repeated. "And, by the way, those meatballs were delicious."

"Oh, um, thanks. Medications... probably. I mean, what person of our age isn't? But she didn't share her medical stuff with me."

"What about Kyon? Heard he has a bad attitude. And he was one of the grandkids she was with that evening, right?"

"Him? No. I mean, yeah, he was here. But I think that kid gets a bad rap. This is Seattle. Just because you have piercings and tattoos doesn't make you a bad kid."

"But Andrew and Junior seem to argue about him a lot."

Mack sighed. "I gotta get back to my pots and pans, but you should really talk to Kyon about it. I was close to family, but I'm *not* family. Whatever is between them is family business."

CHAPTER ELEVEN

AS THEY LEFT THE KITCHEN, Austin heard the gentle *ting ting ting* of metal clinking on crystal. "Everyone, please gather in the living room." It was Susan's voice from the hallway. "We're going to offer loving reflections of mother, of Eleanor."

In the living room, Austin and Anna stopped next to Lucy, who had cornered Brenden McNeery. She was not flirting, as she'd indicated she might. Instead, she was deep into a playful interrogation. Austin listened as the crowd filtered into the living room from around the mansion.

"Did you actually *see* her take food off the tray?" Lucy asked.

Brenden smiled his practiced, chiseled-jaw smile. "I can't claim I had my eyes on her every second, but I saw her take food off a platter more than once. Could someone have laced a bite with oleander? It's possible. And, of course, it's one of the angles I'm considering."

"What about Champagne?" Lucy asked. "Were glasses passed like today, or refilled individually?"

"The latter," Brenden said. "And I've already ruled that out. I was next to her the entire night and always got refills at the same time."

Austin cleared his throat. "Were you with her when she went to see her grandkids?"

Brenden turned, eyes wide as though he was surprised to see him there. "Well, no. I went home after the formal meeting."

"So you weren't there the *entire* night," Lucy said.

"Yes," Brenden said, "that's true."

"What time did you leave?" Lucy asked.

"Around 9:30. And the time of death was around one in the morning, so you can take me off your list."

Lucy frowned. "Just asking questions."

"How do you know the time of death was around one?" Anna asked.

Brenden smirked.

Anna was pissed. "You already have the report?"

"John Junior emailed it to me this morning. I don't think he likes you two very much."

"Care to share it?" Anna asked.

Brenden laughed. "Do your own reporting." Then, trying to sound more friendly. "You understand, I'm sure. I mean, they'll let you have it, but why would I give you the head start I worked for?"

As they went back and forth, Austin thought through the timeline. If the meeting had broken up around 9:30, and assuming Brenden was right about the time of death, that meant she'd been poisoned between 10 PM and midnight. Mack had told them she was eating chocolates and drinking wine around the time.

There was also the question of medications. If she took medications in the evening, it was possible someone had contaminated one of her pills, or perhaps her beverage of choice. For that matter, once she was alone in her room, someone could have snuck up and forced her to inject the powder, then tied her to her bed until she died.

Susan clinked her glass again, then stepped aside as Karen walked to the front of the room. "Welcome, all of you. Though I wish we were gathered here under better circumstances, my mother would be happy to know we are here, all of us, eating her food and—much more importantly—drinking her Champagne." Laughter filled the room as Karen raised a glass. "So, let us toast. The first family member to share his reflections will be John Junior."

As Eleanor's son made his way to the front of the room, Austin noticed a definite sway to his step. Junior's oversized suit was wrinkled and his white dress shirt had a small Cognac-brown stain on the front. He'd been drinking even more heavily than usual.

"Welcome, all," he said, his voice loose. "Today we gather to mourn Eleanor Johnson, my mother..." he waved toward Susan and Karen who stood nearby, looking concerned "*Our* mother." He looked at the floor a long time before continuing. "I never met my dad. He died before I was born, but I can't help but wonder..." he trailed off, then let his head fall back as though he was staring at an especially fascinating section of the ceiling. He stared so long that some of the attendees looked up as well. "Sorry..." he offered an awkward smile. "I'm a bit drunk. What was I saying? Oh right, my father. John. Before he died he was on the path to being a great man in Seattle... a great man. I was brought up to believe that I would be a great man. But, well... And now here we are. Together."

Austin noticed concerned glances passing between Susan and Karen. It probably wasn't the first time John Junior had embarrassed them at a public gathering, though their mother's memorial was certainly a most somber occasion on which to do so.

"A great man I was supposed to be," Junior continued. "And now... well... I think we all know that Eleanor was the only great man—the great person—in our family. And now she's gone. I wish I'd known my father. I wish he'd had the chance to... then maybe I would have..." He let out a long, dejected sigh. He did not look close to tears. He looked like a broken man, a man with little feeling left. He was worth fifty or so million dollars, but

Austin thought that if he looked up "sad sack" in the dictionary, he'd see a picture of John Junior.

"Drink the Champagne!" Junior said, his voice inappropriately loud. "It's what mother would want, and we all know that she got *everything* she wanted in life."

With that, Susan made her way to Junior's side, patted him on the shoulder, and ushered him away.

As Karen lightened the mood with a funny story about the time Eleanor's hat blew into the water while riding the ferry, Austin scanned the room.

There were about sixty people packed in, but not the one he'd hoped to speak with next.

CHAPTER TWELVE

AUSTIN EXCUSED himself and quietly left the living room, wandering down the hallway and loitering by the bathrooms long enough to be sure no one was inside. He peered into the kitchen, where two dishwashers were scrubbing pots and pans over twin sinks. Mack and the cooks had gathered in the living room to keep the Champagne glasses full.

At the end of the hallway, a door opened into an office, which was empty. Outside, a ball bounced rhythmically on cement. *Thwap-thwap-thwap.* Following the sound, Austin cut through the kitchen and walked along the side of the house.

Kyon was no longer there. But the little girl was still playing basketball. She was good, too, cutting and weaving and making more than half the shots she took.

"Mind if I play?" Austin asked. "My name's Austin."

She shrugged.

"How come you're not inside with everyone?"

"My mom said I could stay outside and play."

Austin held out his hands for a pass. "You like basketball?"

She tossed him the ball. "Duh!"

Austin laughed as he caught the pass. She was right. It had

been a stupid question. He didn't have a lot of experience with kids. "Who's your mom?"

"Susan."

He passed the ball back. So this little girl was one of the grandchildren who was there the night Eleanor died. "Where's your cousin who you were playing with before?"

"Kyon left."

She passed him the ball, a single bounce right into his hands. "Good pass." He threw it gently back. "Do you know where he went?"

"That was a basic bounce pass." She began dribbling, between her legs, around her back. Suddenly she stopped and held the ball close to her chest. "I don't think he liked Nanna very much."

"Nanna, is that what you called your grandma Eleanor?"

She nodded.

"And why do you say he didn't like her?"

"They got in a fight."

"Oh, when?"

"Christmas. He makes loud music and she didn't like it. She liked the Beatles. He said the Beatles were trash."

"That's what they were arguing about?"

She nodded.

He held out his hands and she rifled him a chest pass. "I am a friend of the family. Do you mind telling me what you heard?"

"Are you trying to find out what happened to Nanna?"

"What do you mean?" Austin had assumed that no one told the children she was murdered.

"I heard my uncle talking on the phone. He said she was poisoned. Is that true?"

Austin passed her the ball. "I'm sorry."

She looked at the ground for a long time. "I like Kyon. He's my favorite cousin. Mom says he shouldn't dress like he does, he's embarrassing the family. But I don't care."

"I don't care either," Austin said.

"When he fought with Nanna, he said rock and roll was dead. She said his music was bad. He said EDM was forever. That's when he said the Beatles were trash."

Austin suppressed a laugh. It was as clichè a fight as there was. Most likely, Eleanor had had the same fight with her parents in the sixties, except she'd been saying jazz standards were dead and that rock and roll was forever.

"Were they really mad?" Austin asked.

She nodded, then looked up and passed him the ball. "But they must have made up."

"Why do you say that?"

"Because. The night Nanna died we were playing video games, and they were sitting next to each other on the couch, sharing a box of chocolates."

By the time Austin made it back to the living room, the toasts had ended and everyone had broken up into small groups, chatting and sipping Champagne. Classical music played gently through hidden speakers. The mood of the room, though still somber, had lightened.

He found Anna lingering by one of the large bay windows and told her about the conversation on the basketball court. "So far, I'm not loving any of our suspects. Kyon and Sasha are the only adults present that night who we haven't spoken with."

Anna was already on her phone. "Hold on."

"What are you doing?"

"I overheard Junior saying something about a DJ thing Kyon was doing today. He was badmouthing his own kid at his mother's memorial." She leaned in, whispering. "Junior may not be a killer, but he's an absolute jerk."

"So what are you looking up?"

"Hold on... yeah, got it. Let's go."

"Where?" Austin asked, following her across the room. "Without saying goodbye?"

"Yeah, *this party's dead anyway*." She didn't even wait for him to ask about the reference. "*Swingers*. Another nineties movie you should have been watching instead of poring over police procedure manuals as a teenager."

"Okay, but where are we going?"

"Kyon is DJ'ing a twenty-four-hour party in a warehouse downtown." She smiled. "The nineties are back, baby."

She led them through the front door and out onto the lawn. The gentle sound of the string quartet followed them, and Austin noticed tiny speakers mounted on the side of the house.

"As you know, I kinda missed the nineties," Austin said. "What do you mean?"

"Raves, all that stuff. They're back, just with different music. Different clothes. And it's not even that different."

"I'm sure it will surprise exactly no one that I didn't get invited to any raves."

"Neither did I. I was more of a grunge girl. But at least I knew they existed."

She tapped her phone to call an Uber. "So how 'bout it? Want to go to your first rave?"

"Why not?"

"Only, don't call it that. I don't think they call them that anymore."

"Noted."

PART 2

THE CHASE

CHAPTER THIRTEEN

THE UBER DROPPED them in front of a Starbucks, which, Anna pointed out, was the "first" Starbucks. Built in 1971, it seemed to be a major attraction. The line extended down the block and a handful of people posed for selfies out front.

Across the street was Pike Place Market, a sprawling farmers market and crafts fair that stretched many blocks to the north. The first thing Austin noticed was the smell. Fishy, but in a good way. They crossed into the market, where a young woman was grabbing fish from a bed of ice, then launching them at a young man behind the counter. He deftly caught each one in newspaper, then packed it up for the customer.

"This is the famous flying fish deal?" Austin asked.

Anna nodded.

"Betcha five bucks they drop one," Austin said.

"They never drop one."

They watched for five or ten minutes, but they didn't drop one.

"I'll add it to your bill," Anna said.

They strolled north through the market, passing stands of fruits and vegetables, local honey, handmade gift cards, salmon jerky, even paintings and other arts and crafts.

"How often do you come here?" Austin asked.

"Rarely," Anna said. "My son is a sophomore at the University of Washington, so I come to Seattle fairly often, but I usually go through Edmonds and not downtown."

"What's he studying?"

"He's nineteen, so he has no idea. I mean, for now, it's anthropology, but who knows?"

Austin laughed. "I get it. I always knew I wanted to go into law-enforcement, but not everyone skips their teenage years to read police manuals."

"No, not everyone does that. Speaking of our teenage years, did you see *Fargo?*"

Austin clapped his hands together. "Yes! Finally. Something I've seen. Loved that movie. Though I only saw it way later, maybe ten years ago. Fiona made me watch it."

"Does John Junior remind you of the William H. Macy character?"

In the film, Macy had played a down-on-his-luck car salesman who'd hatched a plot to have his wife kidnapped in order to extort ransom money from his rich father-in-law. The plan had failed miserably, devolving into a series of failures and death. Austin had found the film bleak, deeply human, and more representative of reality than many films depicting police work. "Yeah, he definitely has that sad-sack thing going. Doesn't strike me as a killer, but I could see him being involved in some plan gone horribly awry out of sheer incompetence."

"Me, too," Anna said. "But how do you *accidentally* kill someone with yellow oleander?"

Austin agreed. "He's not high on my suspect list."

They stopped for coffee and walked on, leaving the market behind and passing into a more industrial neighborhood. "I've been wondering," Anna said, breaking a long silence. "Did your wife always want to be a lawyer, a prosecutor?"

Austin passed his coffee cup from hand to hand. "No, she wasn't much like me in that regard. Until she was about nineteen she wanted to be a dancer. Ballet. Had a scholarship and danced in college, then got into creative writing, law, even designed websites for a while. She was the opposite of me. Lots of interests, lots of options, lots of directions."

"Creative writing? I thought about trying that, but decided on something 'practical.' Journalism. Got out of school in the early 2000s, right as the whole industry went into upheaval because of the internet and social media."

"I guess a lot has changed. But yeah, she said she always wanted to get back into creative writing. Hence the paragraphs of the novel you saw earlier. She was planning to take a little time off and try to write it."

Anna stopped. "Novel? You didn't say it was a novel before."

"What did I say?"

"You said 'book.'"

Austin stopped. "Isn't a book a novel?"

Anna stopped as well. "Yeah, it didn't really read like a novel, though."

"What do you mean?"

"I'd have to look at it again, but the piece I read—"

"The piece you read is all there is."

"It read like the beginning of a magazine article, or the prologue of a non-fiction book."

As they continued on, Austin considered this, allowing the paragraphs to flow through his mind as he had a dozen times before. Fiona had never mentioned writing non-fiction, at least not that he could remember. Her dreams had always been about writing crime novels. In the paragraphs, the name of the victim was Michael Lee. Austin had assumed this was one of her characters. If he was a real person, that could mean any number of things.

"Austin? Hello?" Anna put a hand on his forearm. "Hello?"

Austin blinked. "Sorry, what?"

"Where'd you go? You stopped in the middle of the sidewalk."

"Sorry." He began walking again. "It's just…"

"What?"

"Nothing."

"Austin, c'mon. You're the worst liar I've ever met."

"Really. Nevermind." Austin's mind was dancing in ten directions at once. Over the last year he'd thought through everything he knew about Fiona, every interaction he could remember. If she'd been working on a piece of non-fiction—maybe a book, maybe a magazine article—why had she not mentioned this? And was there a chance it could tell him something new about her murder?

He didn't want to share all this with Anna. At least not yet. He shook out his head like he was erasing an etch-a-sketch. "Sorry," he said. "I always thought it was the beginning of a novel. Puts me in a weird place to think about it."

They crossed over the train tracks heading east, climbed a few steep hills, then finally came to a street lined with old warehouses. At the end of the block, a two-story brick building rose out of the hill like a toothless brick monster, crooked and missing windows. Thumping bass notes drifted down toward them from what Austin assumed was an unnecessarily loud sound system.

He eyed the old warehouse skeptically. A small line of people —some of whom were already dancing—waited to get in. "How are they getting away with having a party here in the middle of the day?"

"From the website, it looked like it was an official, permitted event."

"I guess that makes sense. As long as the fire department signs off on it and the place is up to code…"

At the door, two bouncers who didn't look like bouncers stood, arms folded, scanning people's phones as they came in.

Austin stopped. "We don't have tickets, do we?"

Anna pulled her phone out of her handbag, swiped a few

times, and held up a barcode. "I bought them online while we were at the memorial."

The bouncers looked at them with concern. Austin and Anna were about twenty years older than most of the people coming through, and their clothes stood out. The twenty-somethings who'd gone in before them wore all sorts of different outfits— everything from skimpy shorts and tank tops to elaborate half-animal princess costumes, probably from shows or comic books Austin had never seen. None of them had been wearing formal black funeral attire.

As Anna held up her phone to be scanned, Austin smiled at the larger of the two bouncers, who was giving him an especially skeptical look. "We are very sad to be here." He gestured at Anna's black dress. "We are in mourning."

The bouncer didn't smile, didn't even offer a courtesy laugh. But he did let them in.

The floor began to shake beneath them the moment they entered. It looked as though the second floor of the warehouse had been torn out, leaving a giant open space of around six-thousand square feet. White and green lights flashed across the walls and ceilings. Occasionally, colorful animals, skeletons, and other creatures were displayed on the ceilings from some unseen light source, and, on the east wall, above a raised DJ booth, various phrases and website addresses flashed a running promotion for the DJ. The current track was called "Ending the Empire" by DJ Khell-yon.

Anna noticed it at the same time. "That's Kyon's DJ name, Khell-yon, like *hellion*."

"I get it. Clever," Austin said flatly, though he didn't think Anna could hear him over the music.

Austin was pretty sure he'd never been so out of place in his life. Young people were everywhere, dancing in groups and by themselves, sipping drinks, in some cases popping pills, making out. He averted his eyes from a couple in the corner who seemed to be even closer than that.

He didn't actually mind the music. It was a rhythmic thumping that shook the walls and floors, layered with dozens of different sounds that ranged from laser gun bleeps to thunderous, tectonic bass drums. Every once in a while, the pitch of the music rose and rose and rose until the crowd hit a frenzy and then, finally, the bass beat would come back in.

"The kids call that the *beat drop*," Anna said, almost screaming to be heard over the noise. "I'll be right back. Gonna find a bathroom."

"Try not to ingest any illicit drugs while you're there," Austin yelled back. "I'll wait along that wall." He pointed to an area beside the DJ booth.

Pushing through the crowd, Austin leaned up against the wall. He could see the top of Kyon's head—purple hair bobbing in and out of a bright spotlight. Every once in a while, the dance floor would part enough for Austin to see Kyon waving his hands, smiling, and jumping. He seemed to be in his element.

The song ended and flowed into a new one, which opened with slow electronic strings and a minor-key guitar melody Austin thought he recognized. After a moment, he was sure: it was a sped-up version of the guitar line of the Beatles' *While My Guitar Gently Weeps*. Then, growing louder every few bars, a slow rising sharpness that sounded like police sirens.

A new track name flashed on the wall behind Kyon. His new song was called "Death to Grandmas."

CHAPTER FOURTEEN

IT WAS TOO RIDICULOUS, too on-the-nose to be true, but that's what it said. Austin waited, eyes darting from Kyon bobbing up and down in the DJ booth to the wall behind him. As it flashed again, he snapped a picture on his phone.

Death to Grandmas

-DJ Khell-yon

After the beat kicked in, every ten or twenty seconds Kyon's voice burst through the cacophony of sound with a "Yeah" or "Jump! Jump!" Even an occasional "Let's get it!"

The song reached a crescendo, then quieted down. The sounds now were like gentle whooshes and bleeps, an outer-space kind of feel. "Everybody chill!" Kyon called, his voice too loud now over the gentler music. "Five minute intermezzo."

Kyon disappeared to the back of the riser and Austin wandered over. It took him a moment to realize that the music had actually been coming from a laptop on the table. Kyon hadn't actually been mixing any records.

He spotted Kyon standing behind the stage, talking to two men, both dressed in jeans and t-shirts. He couldn't hear them, but their body language told Austin they were having a disagreement. Kyon's face went from hard to scared, then back to hard.

In a lull in the music, he heard one of the two men shout at Kyon, "Today!"

At that point, Kyon led them away from the riser, toward a little hallway that led to a sitting area. Austin followed.

They stopped in the hallway, where the music was quieter. Facing away from them, Austin listened. It appeared to be an argument over money. "The money. Today!" one demanded.

"I don't have it," Kyon said.

Then Austin heard a groan. A muffled shout. When he turned back, Kyon was on the ground, one of the men kicking him.

Austin looked around quickly. The security guard near the stage hadn't noticed.

Austin bolted into the hallway, shoulder lowered. At a full sprint, he rammed into the chest of the man kicking Kyon. The man smashed against the wall and fell, but the other guy was on Austin immediately, grabbing around his neck and trying to get him into a headlock. The guy was bigger than Austin, but clearly had no idea what he was doing in a fight.

Austin bent into the headlock and the guy turned, exposing his midsection. Austin brought up a knee, swift and violent, connecting with his stomach. The guy fell to the ground just as the first guy made it back to his feet, squaring up on Austin. He was around Austin's height, with muscles squeezing through his tight black t-shirt. Muscles were nice to have, but in a fight they only mattered when all else was equal.

This guy had fear in his eyes, and that told Austin all he needed to know.

Austin stepped forward, fists raised. The guy stepped back, making his face hard. But his eyes were darting to the side, looking for a way out.

"I can tell you don't want to do this," Austin said.

The man's eyes dropped, but his fists remained raised.

The one who'd just become acquainted with Austin's knee leapt up, then limped away down the hall.

"How about we don't bother with this," Austin said. "I only have this one suit, and I'd rather not get your blood on it."

The security guard appeared behind them, having made his way over from the stage. The guy who'd squared up on Austin shot him a nasty look, then hurried away down the hall.

"What's going on?" the security guard asked.

"Nothing," Kyon said quickly, rising from the floor. "Just a disagreement." He wiped sweat from his forehead. "They were drunk and they're leaving." He turned to Austin. "Thanks, though. Appreciate you stepping in."

The security guard seemed happy not to have to do anything. "Good to hear." He slapped Kyon on the back. "Wicked set, by the way," he said as he returned to the stage.

"Why were they attacking you?" Austin asked.

"It's nothing."

"You owe them money?"

"Bro, thanks for helping but it's really none of your business."

"If you want to press charges, I could help. I saw it go down."

Kyon laughed. "You think cops are gonna care?"

"How much money do you owe them?"

Kyon turned to leave, then stopped, turned back, and studied Austin's face. He looked at his suit. "You were there earlier. At my grandma's house."

"I was. I'm Thomas Austin, private investigator. And I couldn't help but notice that one of your songs was called 'Death to Grandmas.'"

Kyon either didn't understand what Austin was implying, or was good at faking it. He tugged at one of his big hoop nose rings. "I've also got a track called 'Everyone Over Forty Must Die' and another called 'Gen-X Wrecked the World.' That last one is about my dad. What's your point?"

"My point is, your laptop looks expensive. Two or three thousand?"

He laughed. "Try, six thousand, bro. It's a quad-core."

Austin nodded. "Nice. Congratulations. My point is, you're

not broke. You must owe those guys *a lot* of money. Two things I can think of that can get a rich kid like you in that kind of debt. Drugs or blackmail."

Kyon stepped away, eyes scanning Austin's face, questioning.

Austin stepped toward him, eyes hard. "Ever heard of yellow oleander?"

A slow smile spread across Kyon's face, then suddenly his look turned angry and he kicked Austin in the shin.

Austin's leg gave out and he fell to one knee. When he looked up, Kyon was halfway down the hall. A moment later, he burst through an exit and disappeared into the bright day.

CHAPTER FIFTEEN

ANNA'S HAND touched his shoulder as he stood. "I've been looking all over for you."

"He kicked me! That little bastard kicked me after I saved his ass."

At the end of the hallway, the door Kyon had run through slammed shut. The hallway was dark. "I'm going after him. His laptop is on the riser. See if you can get, well, anything."

Without waiting for a reply, Austin sprinted down the hallway, tearing off his jacket and tossing it aside as he burst through the door, which opened into a narrow alley. He blinked rapidly, his eyes adjusting to the bright sun.

There was no sign of Kyon. To his left, the alley ran west, down a hill toward the water. To his right it ran east, a longer stretch that came out near the entrance he and Anna had come through.

He ran west, down the hill, figuring Kyon would take the shorter, easier path. At the end of the alley Austin looked both ways and saw Kyon busting through a small crowd of teenagers. His purple hair was easy to pick out in the crowd.

～

Anna watched the door slam shut. She'd almost followed Austin out, but the unattended laptop of a potential suspect was too good to pass up.

A few people had gathered around the little stage that held the DJ booth. A security guard seemed to be explaining Kyon's disappearance to an event organizer and another young man who looked to be Middle Eastern. Anna assumed he was a DJ because he carried a laptop under his arm and wore a bright pink mohawk. On the riser, Kyon's laptop still played the low-key intermezzo on a loop. From what she could gather by eavesdropping, Kyon was supposed to come back for another hour of music. The producers and DJs were trying to make a new plan on the fly.

Anna decided to take advantage of the confusion and the fact that their backs were turned. Phone in hand, she took the three metal steps onto the stage. A few people in the crowd cheered, probably too high to realize that she wasn't the returning DJ.

Opening her camera app, she walked quickly to the laptop. In a few quick motions, she minimized the window that was playing the tracks and snapped a picture of the desktop. Then she opened his Chrome browser, found Kyon's search history, and snapped another picture. As she did, a hand emerged from around her and slammed the laptop. The music stopped abruptly.

She turned to see the young Middle-Eastern man with the pink mohawk. "Umm, Kyon asked me to, um, get this for him," she stammered, unconvincingly.

"No," the guy said. "He didn't." He ran a hand gently over his pink mohawk, which sprang perfectly back into place, likely due to massive amounts of hair product. His eyes were wide and searching, a *who-the-hell-are-you?* look. "Why were you looking at Ky-Ky's laptop?"

She recognized him from the website where she'd purchased the tickets. He was the headline act. "Are you DJ Normal Hair?"

"Get off the stage, old lady." He gestured to the security guard, who reached for Anna's arm.

She shook it loose. "I'll leave. Just one more thing." She turned back to DJ Normal Hair. "Do you know why Kyon ran out of here? I'm worried he could be in trouble."

"None of your business," the DJ said, now using both hands to make sure his mohawk didn't have a single stray hair. "Why were you taking pictures? You with the cops or something?"

"No. Why would you think the cops are after him?"

"I wouldn't."

"Where does he live?"

He folded his arms.

Anna knew she wasn't going to get anywhere with this guy, but she had to try. "I don't suppose you'd give me his cell number?"

The security guard cleared his throat loudly. "Don't make me drag you out, lady. C'mon."

She knew when she was beat. She made her way off the stage, stopping on the steps just long enough to stare back at DJ Normal Hair. "Love the mohawk, by the way."

Kyon stumbled, crashed face-first onto the sidewalk, and lay motionless just long enough for Austin to think he was seriously injured.

Austin leapt around a man taking selfies, jutted into the road to avoid a woman pushing a stroller, and picked up the pace on a long open stretch of sidewalk. Kyon was still on the ground half a block away.

Just as Austin thought he was going to reach him, Kyon sprang up and crossed the street, pulling away as he accelerated across the railroad tracks. Austin had been trying to get back into shape, but Kyon was twenty years younger and surprisingly fast.

His purple hair disappeared into the north end of Pike Place Market, tracing in reverse the path Anna and Austin had walked earlier.

Forced to slow down by the crowd, Kyon shot a look over his shoulder. He crashed into someone, careened off a flower stand, then darted down a staircase to the right.

Austin followed, noticing the curvature of the thick wooden stairs, worn down in the center from decades of foot traffic. Leaping down two steps at a time, he entered an area under the main market, where bookshops, small restaurants, and gift shops followed a series of maze-like underground hallways with low ceilings.

He heard rapid footsteps and turned. Kyon had circled back behind the staircase, reached a dead end, then come back toward Austin at the bottom of the stairs.

"I just want to talk," Austin shouted.

Kyon froze, breathing hard, and met Austin's eyes.

For a moment Austin thought he might actually speak with him. Panting, he held up both hands, trying to look unthreatening. "I can help. You're not in any trouble."

Suddenly, Kyon darted to the left down another staircase, taking three at a time and smashing into the wall each time he reached a landing.

Kyon burst through an exit door to his left.

Austin followed, his legs now screaming in pain.

By the time Austin made it through the door, Kyon was sitting on a little motor scooter. Casting one more glance back, the kid took off, weaving across two lanes and disappearing into traffic. But not before Austin had memorized the license plate number.

CHAPTER SIXTEEN

TWENTY MINUTES LATER, Anna joined him at a corner booth in a small diner just south of Pike Place Market. A steaming mug of coffee sat next to her place setting. Austin was already nearing the bottom of his second cup.

"For me?" Anna asked, setting her phone on the table.

Austin nodded. "And I already asked for milk."

"Sugar?"

"I told the waiter just to bring the whole bag."

Her lips curled in a half-smile. "Where'd he lose you? Kyon, I mean."

"A few blocks away. He had a scooter. I don't think he stole it. Must've parked it here earlier." He shook his head. "Second time in a few months I've been outrun by a suspect."

Anna laughed and the waiter set down milk and sugar. She handed Austin her full cup. "Can you drink half of this?"

Austin gave her a look, then carefully poured some of her coffee into his own cup, leaving hers only half full. She proceeded to add milk and sugar to it until the cup nearly overflowed. "I got photos of his desktop and browser history."

"Not bad. I got a license plate number."

Anna considered this. "Ridley might still be in town. Want to see if we can get an address for Kyon? Maybe he could have a friend in the SPD run it."

He was already dialing. When Ridley answered, Austin said, "Hey there, it's Austin, I—"

"I *have* caller-ID."

"Oh, right. Okay so I went to talk to Eleanor's grandson, Kyon. When I mentioned the oleander he kicked me and ran."

"Interesting," Ridley said, but he didn't sound interested. "What made you want to speak with him in the first place?"

"A few people at the memorial brought up his name. Apparently he had an argument with Eleanor recently. I don't love him for this, but there's definitely something odd going on with that kid."

"Okay," Ridley said. "You know this isn't my case, and I'm not after the reward money." He paused and Austin could picture the veins in his temples throbbing. Ridley had little time for beating around the bush. "From the tone of your voice, I can tell you want something."

"Did I ever tell you what a *fine* detective you are?"

"What do you want, Austin?"

"After he kicked me, Kyon ran. I got a plate number."

Ridley sighed. "I'm about to have dinner with the chief of the Seattle police. Send it over and I'll see what I can do."

"Kyon has the means to flee," Austin said. He glanced at Anna, who wasn't going to like what he was about to say. "Maybe the SPD is already looking into him, maybe not, but I doubt he will stick around more than a day if he's involved in this. Any chance we could join you and the chief for dinner? Maybe tell her what we have?"

As expected, Anna frowned. Austin turned away.

"We?" Ridley asked. "Though you said *you* went to speak with Kyon."

"Anna. I'm helping her out on this."

"Ahh, I see."

"So, can we join you with the chief?"

"Word from Jimmy," Ridley said, "who heard it from Lucy, Anna has a thing for you." The abrupt change of subject was probably a way for Ridley to buy time while thinking about Ausin's request.

Austin decided to play along. "It's definitely a possibility," he said flatly, glancing over at Anna, whose face was scrunched up dramatically, indicating how upset she was at the prospect of sharing their work with the Seattle police.

"So?" Ridley said.

"What?"

"You could do a lot worse. She's smart, a good mom. And even though I'm contractually obligated to hate reporters— except when I can use them—she's one of the good ones."

Austin held his phone to his ear with his shoulder and sipped his coffee, eyeing her over the cup. "Tell me more."

Anna whispered, "What's he talking about?"

Austin waved her off as though it was nothing.

"Well, you know about her husband, right? Ex-husband, I mean."

"I've heard he wasn't a great guy."

"He, well... know what, it's not my story to tell. All I'll say is that she's earned my respect. Plus, she's not hard on the eyes. And, most importantly, she likes you. I'm sure that's exceedingly rare."

Austin set down his coffee cup. "Very rare."

"What's rare?" Anna asked. "Oleander poisoning? A grandson murdering his grandma? What's he saying?"

Austin waved her off. There was a long pause, then Ridley said, "Sushi Mori, Pioneer Square. Half an hour."

Austin hung up.

"What was that about?" Anna asked.

"I want you to get the money, but, at the same time, Kyon is in the wind. If he *did* have anything to do with this, he'll be long gone before we know it."

"And?"

"Sushi with the chief of police, half an hour."

She scrunched up her face like she was about to offer a rebuttal, then cocked her head. "So, what were you talking about at the end?"

"You."

"Oh?"

"Ridley said he respected you." He thought about asking about her ex-husband, but the truth was, he didn't want to know. Not yet, anyway. Pursuing a case together was one thing. It was safe territory. It felt weird that Anna had read Fiona's writing, and knowing the details of Anna's divorce would only make things weirder. "He just said that you're a helluva woman."

"Always said Ridley had great taste." She smiled, then gulped down half of her cup of sweet, milky coffee in one long swig. She passed the cup back and forth from hand to hand. "So we're going to share our scoop with the police?" She seemed to be weighing the pros and cons.

Austin figured that the allure of a sit-down dinner with the chief of police might outweigh the disappointment of sharing her scoop.

"You cool with this?" Austin asked, putting on his jacket, which Anna had grabbed from the hallway at the warehouse party. "You seem... concerned."

She waved down the waiter. "Fine with it. Just trying to figure out whether I should order rolls or teriyaki."

CHAPTER SEVENTEEN

SUSHI MORI WAS AN UPSCALE, modern place decorated with black lacquer tables. The back wall was a fountain of sorts—a massive sheet of gray stone with water cascading down its face into a little koi pond that offered a pleasant gurgling to fill the spaces between the thumping, electronic beat emanating from hidden speakers. The music reminded Austin of the stuff Kyon had been playing at the warehouse party.

"I've eaten here before," Anna said as they walked in. "Fusion. They've got all the traditional stuff, but they also incorporate many non-traditional foods into their sushi."

Austin spotted Ridley at a large round table in the back, away from the crowd. As they wound through the bustling restaurant, Austin asked, "What sort of non-traditional foods?"

"They'll do stuff like smoked Texas brisket rolls, topped with raw shrimp and avocado. One time I had a traditional spicy salmon roll, but they battered it with tempura and served it with Japanese ranch dressing."

"And? How was it?" Austin made eye contact with Ridley, who sat alone at a table designed for five or six people.

"Kinda embarrassed to say," Anna said as they reached the table, "because of the whole clichè about Americans dipping everything in ranch dressing, but it might have been the best thing I've ever eaten." She flashed a smile at Ridley and took a seat. Austin did the same.

Ridley asked, "What was?"

"The fried roll they have here, with Japanese ranch."

"I'm ordering that," Ridley said. "Rachel might divorce me for coming here without her—she's wanted to come here for a year—but I'm going all out. We call it restaurant infidelity."

Austin laughed.

"She started it," Ridley continued. "Went to Bartollo's with a friend from college without me. Two-star Michelin Italian food. So she started the cheating."

Austin looked around. "Where's the chief?"

As he said it, a woman wearing formal police blues and a bitter frown came around the corner from the restrooms. Ignoring Austin and Anna, she said to Ridley, "Some idiot just chased one of our suspects through Pike Place Market."

Austin swallowed hard.

Then, turning to them as though noticing them for the first time, she cleared her throat. "Oh, right. I forgot Rid invited the circus."

Anna stood and held out her hand. "Anna Downey. Senior lion tamer." The chief shook her hand quickly, without warmth, and didn't smile. "And this is Thomas Austin."

"But we call him Austin," Ridley said, "because, well, something about wrestling I think."

Austin stood and offered his hand, but she was already sitting. "Sandra Jackson. Nice to meet you both. I'm sorry I'm upset. Just got a note from an officer who fielded multiple reports of a man chasing someone through Pike Place Market. Turns out, the guy he was chasing is a potential suspect."

Austin caught Anna's glance, but decided not to say anything just yet. Chief Jackson was known to be a hard ass, one of the reasons she'd risen so quickly and was known to be good at her job.

"Do you mean a suspect in the Eleanor Johnson thing?" Ridley asked.

Chief Jackson smacked her lips. "Yup! Not sure if it's something they're adding to the water these days, or maybe cellphone cameras, but everyone thinks they're a detective. I mean, when did *that* happen?" She shook her head. "It's like half the people hate the cops and the other half want to whip out their phones, record something and help us enforce the laws." She sighed.

"What did the guy look like?" Ridley asked, glancing at Austin.

"White guy, early forties. Brown hair. Black pants, white dress shirt."

As she spoke, a wide grin broke out across Ridley's face. He nodded toward Austin. "Anything like this guy?"

Austin held out his hand across the table. "Sorry about that."

She shook it warily. "That was you?"

"Apologies. We went to speak with him. He kicked me and ran. So I ran after him. Don't think I broke any laws."

"No, but... who are you again? Rid said..."

"Thomas Austin. Private investigator."

"He was NYPD for twenty years," Ridley offered. "Helped us wrap the Baby Butcher case a few months back." He held up both hands, anticipating her objection. "I know you don't want anyone sniffing around a case this important. But they might have something."

Some of the tension relaxed from Jackson's face. "Ahh, the Baby Butcher thing was *you*. Okay, now it's coming together. Ridley had mentioned you." She paused, thinking for a moment. "I know Rid vouches for you, which I appreciate. But a word of advice. In my city, leave it to the actual officers to apprehend suspects, okay?"

Austin didn't respond.

Anna said, "Maybe if you'd figured out this was murder a week ago, amateurs like us wouldn't have to chase suspects through your city."

Chief Jackson opened her mouth, looking like she was about to release a torrent of fire in Anna's direction. Then she let out a long, slow breath as though she'd thought better of it. Public figures like Jackson—the face of the thousand-plus officers in the SPD—had to be wary of cellphone cameras at all times. A little video clip, even taken out of context, could end her career.

"Look," Ridley said, trying to sound conciliatory. "Everyone is on the same team here."

Austin could tell Anna was about to object, but before she could, he said, as diplomatically as possible, "Look, Chief Jackson, we wanted to meet up to give you a plate number on Kyon Johnson's scooter." He scribbled the number on a napkin and slid it across the table.

"We were already on him," Jackson said, ignoring the napkin. "What led you to Kyon in the first place?"

"Couple things people said at the memorial. He'd had an argument with his grandma. Typical stuff. Musical tastes. Sounded like a generational thing. I was following every lead until he kicked me."

"Why did he kick you?"

"Mentioned the oleander."

This seemed to get Jackson's attention, but before she could reply a waiter arrived to take their orders. Austin hadn't looked at a menu, but he always ordered the same thing when he went to sushi, the chef's selection of nigiri. He ordered it along with a Kirin Ichiban, his favorite Japanese beer. Everyone else made more elaborate orders, including Ridley, who ordered the fried roll Anna had mentioned, plus a surf-and-turf roll that included spicy lobster salad and seared filet mignon.

"Interesting about Kyon," Chief Jackson said. "Still don't condone you two playing amateur sleuth in my city, but that's interesting."

"We were hoping you'd pull up his address for us," Austin said.

Jackson scoffed. "But you knew I wouldn't."

Austin smiled. "I choose to believe anything is possible. Had a fortune cookie tell me that once."

Jackson chuckled at this and she seemed to be relaxing a little. "Even if I would give you his address—which I never would—you wouldn't find him. Already checked. He's not at home."

"I wonder," Anna said, "does Kyon stand to benefit financially from Eleanor's death? Maybe a spoiled rich kid who wanted to be richer?"

"Will hasn't been released yet," Chief Jackson said, "but we're looking into the financial angles."

Anna smiled. "C'mon. You already know what's in the will."

"And I don't want it showing up in the paper tomorrow," Jackson shot back.

"Hundred percent off the record," Anna said.

Jackson glanced at Ridley, who said, "You can trust her."

"Tell you what. You send me anything else you find out about this case, and promise not to play Jack Reacher in my city, then I'll tell you about the will."

Austin and Anna nodded in unison.

"Word is," Jackson said, "there's nothing unusual in the will. Bunch of donations to charities she was already supporting, a few million each to her three kids, trusts of a quarter million each for her grandchildren for education expenses, but their parents have total control of those and they expire when they are twenty-five."

"Expire," Anna said, "as in, they go away?"

"If the grandkids don't spend the money on educational expenses by age twenty-five, the money gets donated to charity."

"Any recent *changes* to the will?" Austin asked.

"Doesn't look like it."

The waiter set down Austin's beer and he took a long swig. "The eldest daughter, Karen, mentioned that she wanted to speak with her mother about a financial issue. Said it was minor."

Jackson said, "Rich people are always fiddling with their finances. Look, I don't know all the details, but I'm sure my people are looking into the money angles. Just don't go chasing anyone else through the city. Play by the rules."

Ridley smirked and put on an exaggerated, movie-trailer voice. "*When lives are on the line, he makes the rules.*"

Austin tasted a bitter-sweetness with a soft mouthfeel, like marshmallows made of grapefruit rind. Embarrassment.

"What?" Jackson asked.

Ridley laughed. "Something Austin here said to my boss."

Jackson asked, "How is Sheriff 'Three-Sheets-To-The-Wind' Daniels anyway?"

"He's fine. Drinking less." Ridley leaned in. "Get this. Few months ago, me and Austin are in Daniels' office and he's giving us hell. Ripping us apart for some screw-up or another. This is when we were in the thick of it with the Baby Butcher case. Everyone was stressed as hell. Sheriff Daniels tells him to cut the cowboy stuff. Austin stands up like he's auditioning for *Die Hard 6* or something. Says, '*When lives are on the line, I make the rules.*'" Ridley cackled with laughter.

Anna slapped him on the shoulder. "That's definitely going in one of my stories."

Chief Jackson was less entertained. "Maybe that shit flies in New York. Here, citizens have rights. Police have responsibilities and... I don't even know why I'm talking to you. You two aren't officers and—"

Her phone rang and she excused herself to take the call.

Anna leaned over and whispered in Austin's ear. "Please don't tell her about the screenshots."

"I know you want the money, but—"

"It's not just that." She shot a look at Ridley. "Running a department like you do. You ever make tradeoffs?"

Ridley nodded. "Sure."

"Like sometimes it's not in the overall interest of the department to solve every case?"

"Whoa whoa whoa," Ridley said. "I wouldn't say that. Yeah, it's not a cop show, it's the real world. But I want to solve every case. Sometimes limitations get in the way. Limitations in manpower, resources and, I hate to say it, competence. We're all just people here. Doing our best with limited resources."

"That's my point," Anna said. "If we share everything with Jackson, maybe it gets used to catch Kyon and maybe he's the killer. But maybe one of a hundred competing interests takes over and something else happens."

Austin was conflicted. On the one hand, he wanted to give the chief every chance to catch Kyon, and that included sharing all their information with her. On the other hand, he wanted Anna to win the money. Plus, she was right about conflicting interests. He'd known officers to trade information on one case to make a break in another case. In fact, he'd done this himself. He'd seen corrupt officers tip off suspects so they could flee. And he'd seen perfectly well-intentioned officers blow cases by sending emails to the wrong address or accidentally alerting a suspect about an upcoming raid. He'd seen it all.

Then something struck him. "We *can't* share the screenshots with her. I mean we can, but you obtained them kinda illegally. Gray area because his laptop was in a public place. It's the kind of thing that could get a prosecution thrown out if they have to admit where they got the evidence."

Anna nodded along, relieved.

Turned out, he didn't need to decide. When Chief Jackson returned to the table, she seemed flustered. "I gotta go. Rid, you can eat my sushi. Next time it's on me."

Without another word, she hurried out of the restaurant.

CHAPTER EIGHTEEN

THEY ATE dinner without returning to the topic of Kyon. It was clear that Ridley wanted to stay in his lane, and his lane was across the water in Kitsap County. He'd come to Seattle to pay his respects, but solving Eleanor Johnson's murder wasn't his job.

Austin was on his second beer by the time Ridley and Anna finished their own food and turned their attention to the elaborate rolls Chief Jackson had ordered.

Ridley held up a piece with his chopsticks. "You want some, New York?"

Austin declined. He'd finished his sushi, which was excellent, and was eager to get to the photos of Kyon's laptop.

Ridley finished the last bite, then turned to Anna. "I was telling Austin earlier, he should go out with you."

Anna's face grew red, but she tried to play it cool. "We're already out."

"You know what I mean," Ridley said. "Seriously, you two would be a good match. Over twenty years of marriage I've learned to spot personalities that go together. Austin, you and I are a lot alike. And Anna's like Rachel."

"How so?" Anna asked.

"You haven't met her?" Ridley shrugged. "Guess not. She's

more thoughtful than me. More cerebral." He paused for a moment, as though considering whether to go on. "Not ashamed to admit, we've been in couples counseling for, I don't know, a year now. Nothing wrong exactly, but we're looking to grow, to level up. The way our therapist puts it, I'm a *doing* type, she's a *thinking* type. I'm a *body* type, she's a *head* type. The way he put it..." Ridley laughed softly... "and this was spot on. He said I'd rush into a burning house to save a kid, but it's quite possible I'd be the one who'd accidentally set the fire and left the kid in there. Rachel, she'd just remember to turn off the toaster."

Austin laughed. Anna smiled, sipping her wine.

"But we share commonalities, too," Ridley continued. "We both value independence, both are outgoing by nature."

"What does she do?" Austin asked.

"Runs a small business. Niche fashion blog. Monetizes it through ads, Youtube videos, affiliate links, newsletter subscriptions. Started it from nothing and now she makes more than me." Ridley looked at the table, shaking his head. Austin bit his lip because he saw in Ridley the way he'd felt about Fiona. Ridley not only loved his wife, he admired her.

"What else did he tell you?" Anna asked, turning to Austin.

"He said you were a catch, which I never denied." He'd already told Anna he wasn't ready to date, and that it had nothing to do with her. His chat with Pastor Johnson had driven this home. Truth was, since Fiona died, he hadn't given another woman so much as a chance. "He said you were strong, tenacious."

"True facts," Anna said. "Bet he didn't tell you I'm broke, though. That's a strike against me."

"No, but *you* told me that," Austin said.

"Money ain't shit," Ridley said. "Older I get, the more I realize nothing is better than having someone to spend time with, someone you love and like, family, people you want to be better for, someone you want to grow old with."

Anna studied Ridley's face. "What's brought on this philosophical side?" she asked. "You get a cancer diagnosis or something?"

Ridley smiled and pushed his chair back. He pulled out his wallet. "I gotta get going."

Austin was curious as well. Something seemed different about Ridley. It wasn't that he'd seemed incapable of being this reflective before, but the time they'd spent together had been in a different context: the joint effort to solve the most important case of Ridley's career. "Rid, what is it?" Austin asked. "You seem different."

"It's my day off." His face broke out in a huge smile. "And Rachel and I are having another baby."

He didn't wait for congratulations. He placed a few twenties on the table and strolled out like a man without a care in the world.

When Ridley was gone, Anna took the liberty of ordering after-dinner cocktails called Amakazes. Made from espresso, sake, maple syrup and fresh ginger, they were like nothing Austin had ever tasted. Bitter and sweet, spicy and cold, it made him feel like he was being drugged with sleeping pills and splashed with ice cold water at the same time.

As they drank, they studied the photographs Anna had taken of Kyon's home screen and search history. His desktop was, as Anna put it, "a nightmare." Hundreds of files and images in no discernible order, some stacked on top of others so the file names were unreadable. Music tracks and clips of sound, a few essays from his brief time in college, file folders that appeared to be pornography, and random other images. And all of it on top of a desktop image of Elon Musk riding a bicycle in space.

"What a mess," Austin said.

"This is well beyond *mess*," Anna replied. "I find desktops like this maddening in a way I can't articulate fully. And I write words for a living."

"What about the search history?"

Anna swiped and the photo appeared. Austin read through the list from top to bottom. It felt odd reading through Kyon's search history. Intrusive, yet also necessary.

Directions to LazerHaus Warehouse
Pizza delivery near me
How to get booked as a DJ in Las Vegas
Free audio clips
Directions to Little Huế restaurant
Skrillex tour dates 2022
Seattle Mariners 2022 roster
Assisted suicide laws—WA State

He held up a finger to the last one.

"Yeah," Anna said. "That's where my eyes landed as well."

"What if Eleanor asked him to help her die?" Austin asked. "Maybe she knew she was sick. Something serious. Something terminal."

"Maybe, but she seemed healthy." Anna sipped her cocktail. "And *told me* she was healthy. Plus, why would she ask her *grandson*? Isn't that something you'd talk to your doctor about?"

"Good point."

"Washington passed a 'Death with Dignity' Act in 2009. All she'd need to do is talk to her doctor. If she had a verifiable terminal illness... but she didn't." She sighed. "I don't think it adds up, but it *is* weird. Why would a twenty-year-old kid search that?"

The waiter left the bill on the table and Anna glanced at her phone. "If we leave now, we might catch the eight o'clock ferry. Any later and we'll be boarding with all the members of the sea level high club."

"Sea-level high club?" Austin asked.

"The night boats are full of teenagers and twenty-somethings coming back from concerts and dates in the city. All the excitement combined with the sea air... sometimes people get lucky on the ride back to the Island."

"I get it. Mile-high club, sea-level high club."

"It's a Kitsap County thing. *You know nothing Thomas Austin.*"

That was a reference he understood. Even though he'd never seen *Game of Thrones*, Fiona had been obsessed with it. She'd started saying that exact phrase to him sometime in the mid-2010s. It had taken her fifteen minutes to explain why it was actually a phrase of endearment. It was odd hearing it from Anna, but not in a bad way.

Austin smiled and nodded. "You ready to get going?" He pulled out his wallet. "Couple more things I want to look into, but I can do that on the boat."

"Sounds good. I could use a coffee to wash down that cocktail. Plus, remember when I said I'd given back Eleanor's diaries and it turned out I had another?"

Austin could tell she was up to something by the mischievous look on her face. "Now what? You have *another* diary?"

Anna held up her phone. "I kinda still have all of them."

They were halfway to the ferry when Austin noticed they were being followed. The sake-laced cocktail had left him slightly loopy, and he'd been feeling the urge to go to sleep. Cheek against the headrest of Anna's SUV, he let his eyes drift to the rearview mirror.

As it often did, his brain started looking for patterns. The timing of the traffic lights, the movement of vehicles. He'd read once that the super-power of the human race—dating back a couple hundred thousand years—was making order out of a fundamentally chaotic and unpredictable world. Humans excelled at finding patterns and using them to predict things. Of course, this also led people to create patterns where there was only chaos, to find conspiracies where there was only human fallibility, complexity, and randomness.

But when a black Chevy Suburban makes four turns and six lane changes that match your own, that's not random. And when Anna took a wrong turn on the way to the ferry, then had to loop back around the block, the Suburban did as well. That's when Austin was sure.

"Someone's tracking us," he said as casually as possible when they'd stopped at a traffic light. "Black Suburban two cars behind you."

Anna glanced in the rearview mirror. "I... what? Are you sure?"

"Not a hundred percent, but yeah. Pull over when you can. Keep the car on."

Anna's grip on the steering wheel caused it to release a little pop, the sound of tight leather being twisted. When the light changed, she pulled into the parking lot of a gas station on the corner.

Austin watched as the Suburban disappeared from view, continuing past the station.

"See," Anna said, "You're being paranoid."

"Wait."

The Suburban took a right turn and entered the station from the other side. Now headed straight toward them, it stopped, idling near the entrance to the pumps about twenty yards away.

"They're not even trying to conceal the fact that they're following us," Austin said. "That's the good news." He could see two figures through the windshield, but it was too dark to make out any specifics.

Anna glanced over. "Why the hell is that good news?"

"It means they're not trying to kill us. Head back to the ferry."

Anna pulled out and turned onto Alaskan Way. They were

only a few blocks from the entrance to the ferry. "Why does that mean they're not trying to kill us?"

"Most murders are crimes of passion—domestic disputes, neighborhood violence, gang violence. When people are following you in a black Suburban, they either want to know what you're up to, or they want to kill you."

"Are they still there?"

"Yup. Just drive normal. If they want to kill you, they usually want to conceal the fact that they're following you. It's not like in the movies where people give a cool speech before killing you. These guys wanted us to know they were following us. Or, at the very least, weren't willing to make any effort to hide the fact."

"To intimidate us?"

"That's what I'm thinking." Austin watched the side mirror. The Suburban didn't make any dramatic moves, but there it was, two to three cars behind them with every lane change, every turn.

Anna turned into the lot and stopped at the toll booth. When they'd made it through, she stopped in the line of cars waiting to ride onto the ferry. "I still don't see why."

Austin glanced at the mirror. No Suburban. "Someone doesn't want us looking into this murder."

"But who?" Anna asked. "Someone connected to the killing?" She shook her head. "I don't want to say it, but..."

"What?"

"We just left Chief Jackson, who was pissed you were chasing a suspect through *her* city."

Austin shrugged. "Not likely, but I wouldn't rule it out." He opened the door.

"Where are you going?"

"Stay here. I'm gonna go ask them who they are."

"You're... *what?*"

Austin got out, looking back toward the toll booth. The Suburban wasn't there. He glanced around the lot. Nothing. He stood on the bumper of Anna's car, scanning back toward the road. Then he saw it. Idling near the lane that led to the toll booth.

He couldn't see into the vehicle, but he tried to imagine who might be sitting there. Private investigators hired by the Johnson family? Off-duty cops Chief Jackson had asked to track them until they left Seattle? Friends of Kyon? Or perhaps someone else entirely.

A moment later, the Suburban eased away, past the ferry toll booth and into the night.

CHAPTER NINETEEN

AFTER PARKING HER CAR, Anna sent Austin to the ferry's café, found a booth in a dimly lit corner, and pulled out her phone. She felt guilty for scanning Eleanor's diaries into a PDF before returning them to Karen. It had been a breach of trust, no doubt. But she hadn't had time to read them all and she told herself it was in service of finding Eleanor's killer. It's what Eleanor would have wanted her to do. She wasn't actually sure of this last part, but it alleviated the guilt long enough to begin reading.

As Austin waited in the line for drinks, she returned to a section she'd already read, one that had been triggered during the reflections on Eleanor's life at the memorial, reflections that had barely mentioned her husband John at all.

November 18, 1971

Today was unseasonably warm. Low sixties, when all I want is a nip in the air to accompany the falling leaves. Carrying a baby makes me hot.

I found out last week that John and I are to have a boy. John wanted to name him after himself, John Jr. I told John I wanted to name him after one of the Beatles—Paul or George. We had a laugh and settled on 'John' so we could both get our way.

It will be lovely, having a boy. Despite John's many flaws, he is a man's man. Not afraid to get his hands dirty. I only worry that this time he's gotten them too dirty.

I knew right when I met John that he is the opposite of my father in every way, save one. Though John is rough where my father is soft, stern where he is meek, ignorant where my father is educated, both will do anything to make a buck.

As shameful as it is to admit it, perhaps this is what attracted me to John in the first place. At the time, I felt as though I needed my own money, that it was shameful to live only on the wealth of the past.

Now I fear that John's business is the most shameful thing of all.

November 19, 1971

More bad news from John today. More bad news every day.

In the few hours he's around, it seems all he does is share bad news. He does not tell me everything—I know he has his secrets, just as I have mine—but there are legal troubles coming. The businesses at Pike Place are doing well, at least I thought so, but John has word that he's being investigated regarding kickbacks. Bribes. He says it's just how business is done. That he will take care of it.

Mother always said I should marry someone from my own station, but the men from my station were all so monstrously dull.

At least we have music. Last month we saw The Moody Blues at the Coliseum and next month we have tickets to The Who. Perhaps I should have run off with a musician and toured the world. In retrospect, that may have been more responsible than marrying John.

But I wonder whether there is one man among my mother's banker and lawyer friends who would take his pregnant wife to see The Who?

Despite John's many flaws, he will do that.

November 22, 1971

Only 23 days until The Who come to Seattle. I wonder whether I am getting too old for things like this. I very much doubt there will be another millionaire there who's six months pregnant.

Yesterday Mack brought in a chef from the new Japanese restaurant downtown. I had heard of sushi before, but boy oh boy was it something.

Chef Nakamura says that with all the fresh fish available in our waters, he can make sushi here as good as he did in Japan. I expect that within twenty years, sushi will become the new hamburger as America forgives the Japanese people and our collective memory of the war fades.

November 26, 1971

Yesterday John came home late and we had it out. He reeked of vegetables and liquor. I know he spent all day at "The Farm."

I accused him of not caring about John Jr., not spending any time with the girls. He said Karen and Susan were too young to remember if he was around or not. What a louse!

He told me I knew the arrangement when I married him. I admitted that he was right. He accepted me and I promised to accept him. We've had this same fight a hundred times.

This time something new happened. When we'd both shouted our last shouts, we lay on the bed facing the ceiling and his voice was different. I'd stopped blaming him and he'd stopped resenting me. His voice wasn't kind —it's NEVER kind—but it was soft, like a little boy who needed help.

He said, "El, I think I'm in trouble. Real trouble this time that there may not be a way out of."

He rarely calls me "El" anymore.

I wanted to shout at him, tell him he'd promised it was all handled, that he was just doing business how business was done, but something in his tone had me worried. I asked him whether this was about the bribes, the kickbacks, the business at the Market. What he's really selling at Pike Place.

He said, "No. It's about a murder."

Then he fell asleep without another word.

CHAPTER TWENTY

AUSTIN SET down a cup of coffee, but she didn't look up from her phone. "Anna?" She seemed fully engrossed in whatever she was reading. "Hellooo? Anna?"

No response.

"Brenden McNeery won a Pulitzer Prize and got a million-dollar deal from CNN."

She finally looked up. "Huh?"

Austin smiled. "Reading Eleanor's diary?"

Anna nodded, setting her phone on the table. "I don't know. I'm not buying the Kyon thing. Not fully, anyway. The diary mentions secrets, hers and his. I thought it was weird how almost no one mentioned John at the memorial. I get that he's been dead a long time, but those kids are his, and the grandkids."

"You said he was suspected of various crimes. Maybe they don't want to call attention to the past."

"In the bit I was just reading, Anna hints that he was selling something other than fruits and vegetables at Pike Place."

"Drugs?" Austin asked.

"She doesn't come right out and say it, but I assume so. Also says he was being looked into for murder. She never mentions it again, at least in the diaries I have, and I never found a record of it, though I don't have access to fifty year old police files. I don't know. I just..."

As she trailed off, Austin let his gaze drift out to the Puget Sound. The sun had set, but the sky still held a faint light, making the water an almost-black shade of blue. In the distance, the houses on the shore of Bainbridge Island were dark forms against a dark landscape.

Austin rubbed his eyes. He was a little tipsy and all he wanted was to crawl into bed after tossing a ball for Run a few times. "Lemme see those screenshots again."

"Which one?" Anna asked.

"The desktop from hell."

Anna handed him her phone, open to the photo of Kyon's chaotic desktop. One by one, Austin read the name on every single folder and file. He'd already scanned it, but sometimes the second look brought on the breakthrough. He was hoping to find something about assisted suicide, maybe a PDF about oleander. Something about travel plans. There were dozens of little blue file icons, some for music files, but others with enticing names like "Travel" and "Projects" and "Family."

It was almost painful seeing the files and not being able to click them.

Then it struck him. "Kids and their technology."

Anna raised an eyebrow. "Huh?"

"I was sprinting through Pike Place Market when you took these photos. I doubt Kyon would have gone back to the ware-house after he bolted. If he *does* have anything to do with this, he might have assumed we were with the cops. Or maybe not. But either way, I don't think he would have gone back there, and there's no way he'd just forget about his laptop."

Anna sat up like she'd been hit by an electric shock. "DJ NormalHair."

"What?"

She sipped her wine excitedly. "When I took the photos, another DJ was there." Anna grabbed her phone, tapped, swiped, and tapped again. She held it up to Austin. The photo was of a young man who looked to be in his early twenties, Middle Eastern, with a bright pink mohawk.

"He's the guy who organized the party," Anna said. "He's a DJ and promoter. My guess is, he's the guy who booked Kyon. He's the dude who shut the laptop when he caught me taking pictures."

"And if he did that, maybe he returned the laptop to his pal."

"And if the SPD already checked Kyon's house and he's not there..." Anna was growing more and more excited. "Hold on."

Again she tapped and swiped, studied the screen, then scrolled. "Here. Nassar Ali. His parents are from Kuwait. He goes to UW, junior music major." She swiped again, tapped, and swiped. "Lives in off-campus housing. Apartment only a couple blocks from my son."

"How did you learn all that?" Austin asked, impressed.

"Little thing I like to call, 'The Internet.'"

"I *know*, but—"

"His DJ stage name led me to his Instagram. In the comments on his posts people used his real name a couple times. Concealing one's real name online almost never works. Once I had his real name, a search led to a page for the UW music department. He's a TA for first-year students. From there I searched his name with 'UW Music' and found his personal Instagram, which he keeps separate from his DJ one. Photos of him moving into his apartment last fall. Pictures of him moving in with the address of the building right next to him. I'd say kids are dumb about online security, but I bet people could find just as much about me if they tried."

Austin wasn't sure whether to be more impressed or more concerned. She was a hell of an online sleuth, to be sure. In fact, he was reminded of Samantha, the intern who worked in Ridley's office. Samantha had been critical to solving the case of the Holiday Baby Butcher and seemed to be able to find almost anything about anyone online.

It was the look on Anna's face that had him concerned. She was antsy, like she might jump overboard and swim back to shore, then catch a taxi to Nassar Ali's apartment in case Kyon was there.

"Here's the deal," Austin said. "We're in the middle of the Puget Sound. We have information that may be crucial to an investigation. We have two options." Anna's face broke out in a scowl, like she knew where Austin was headed. "One: we land on Bainbridge Island and immediately catch the next ferry back to Seattle, then drive over to Nassar Ali's apartment and—"

"Exactly," Anna said.

"And then what?" Austin stared at her.

Anna said nothing.

"The way this usually works is, police have enough to bring someone in, then they work like hell to get a confession. It's not always pretty, but they'll lie, cheat and steal to get a confession when they don't actually have enough evidence to hold someone. And unless the SPD has a lot more than us—which they might—then they don't have enough to hold Kyon long. We've got even less. The one thing the SPD has that you don't have is the ability to get Kyon or Nassar to come in for questioning."

Anna looked at the table. "I'm guessing your second option involves calling the SPD?"

"Ding ding ding." He paused, watching Anna's face darken. "But hear me out. We call Chief Jackson, tell her about Nassar and the laptop. They're looking for Kyon. If he's with Nassar, maybe they're able to bring him in for questioning. If they do, she owes you. Big time."

"But..." Her objection faded before it could fully form. "I'm not calling that woman. Giving my scoop to her goes against everything I... wait, what if I don't just *give* it to her?"

The ferry was slowing as it reached Bainbridge Island. "We need to get back down to your car," Austin said.

Anna stood and led the way through the passenger deck to the stairwell that led down to the bottom floor of the ship, the parking garage. "You call her," she said. "She liked you more anyway. See if you can get her to promise me an exclusive if anything comes of the Nassar tip."

"Okay," Austin said, "but I thought you said you weren't going to publish on this."

"I wasn't, but that was when I thought I was gonna get the twenty-five grand. If I'm handing my chance at the money over to the SPD, at least I can make five hundred bucks from a solid freelance scoop. Hell, maybe I can sell it to the *Seattle Times* and take Brenden's job when he moves to New York."

CHAPTER TWENTY-ONE

AUSTIN TOSSED the rubber ball into the darkness. The only light on the beach came from a dim half moon, which illuminated the foam of small waves washing up on the shore in front of his shop. Other than Austin, Run, and the waves, the beach was deserted.

He wasn't the paranoid type. The amount of violence and evil Austin had seen working in the NYPD had the counterintuitive effect of making him *less* paranoid. When you know that monsters are real, when you spend your life figuring out how they think and act, there's less reason to worry about them hiding under your bed.

Still, the nip in the air, the blackness of the water, and the way Run's panting breaths cut through the silence, left him a little on edge. As sure as he was that the Suburban hadn't followed them onto the ferry, and that no one had followed him home, the unknown of who'd been following them in the first place left him wary.

Austin had made the call to Chief Jackson and she'd accepted the offer. She admitted that she didn't yet have anything on Nassar Ali. If the tip led to Kyon, and he turned out to be involved, Anna would get an exclusive sit-down interview with

Seattle's police chief. Not nearly as good as twenty-five grand, but a good get for any crime reporter.

Run dropped the ball at his feet, ready for another sprint. Austin picked up the ball and launched it as far as he could. Run took off. When he was away, Austin gave Andy an extra thirty bucks a day to let Run out three or four times, but this was her first chance all day at real exercise.

As she disappeared into the night, Austin breathed in the cool air. He was finishing his second winter in Hansville and he could almost taste the first hints of spring.

Spring in New York was different because the winters were much harsher. Back east, spring felt like a desperately needed transition, a physical and emotional thawing, a celebration shared by ten million New Yorkers who'd made it through another winter in the big city.

In Hansville, winters were milder. Day after day of the same. Forty-eight degrees and cloudy. Fifty-one degrees and drizzly. Forty-seven degrees and gray. It rarely snowed, and the occasional dustings never lasted more than a day or two.

He'd had a good laugh at the local response to the half-inch of snow the county received last February. Closed schools, people stocking up on food, slippery roads. The area just wasn't prepared for it because it was such a rare occurrence.

He tried not to think about New York because, when he did, it made him think of Fiona. And not the good times, but her death. For him, New York would always be associated with gunshots in front of a midtown steakhouse.

Austin's weary mind kept returning to what Anna had said, that the opening paragraphs of Fiona's novel didn't sound like a novel. At first it had struck him as impossible. For over a year he'd lived with the certainty that the few paragraphs he kept in her typewriter had been the novel she'd always wanted to write. But it was certainly possible they were something else.

Maybe she'd agreed to write a magazine article or an op-ed. Maybe she'd decided to try a non-fiction book. They were a happy couple, but both working professionals with demanding jobs and not the type who texted back and forth all day with every detail of their lives. It was certainly possible that Fiona had started a project and just not gotten around to mentioning it.

And this was especially true if the project had something to do with a case, a case she might not be allowed to talk about yet.

Austin crouched and repeated the process of tossing the ball down the beach. This time it landed in the water, a couple feet from the sand. Austin had learned that Run had no fear of water, and though it was too cold to swim, she'd happily wade in and fetch it.

Austin ran through the lines in his head.

Michael Lee strolled into the parking lot of his favorite Korean restaurant in Brooklyn at 7 PM on a cold Tuesday in February. He'd never lived in Korea, but he went to Mama Dae's BBQ once a week for their famous galbi and kimchi. The meal made him think of his grandma, who'd raised Michael and passed away when he was ten.

He was at Mama Dae's to meet Megan, a woman he'd connected with in a dating app. He'd worn his lucky outfit—black jeans and an authentic t-shirt from David Bowie's Serious Moonlight Tour.

His lucky restaurant. His lucky outfit.

The unluckiest day of his life.

His "date" turned out to be a stand-in for the Namgung crime family. Megan had come to steal his identity, then lure him to his death.

The more he thought about it, the more he thought Anna was right. It definitely wasn't just notes on a case. It sounded like the opening of a true crime book or...

It struck Austin just as Run dropped the wet tennis ball on his shoe. It sounded a little like an opening statement she might perform at a trial.

Fiona had usually written her opening statements on yellow

legal pads, refining them late into the night on their kitchen counter. She liked to say that the key to winning over a jury was telling a story about the victim, including key details that would make the person real to the men and women whose job it was to deliver justice. Details like the lucky shirt he was wearing and the exact meal he'd ordered.

The more he thought about it, the more sure he felt. The words would have made an excellent beginning to an opening statement. Most likely, they would have been followed by a neat, linear presentation of the facts, followed by a return to the "character" in the story and another emotional connection for the jury.

If he was right, Michael Lee wasn't a character in her planned novel. He was a murder victim, and Fiona had been preparing to prosecute his killers.

He'd gone through a list of all her pending cases, as had the official investigators, and it didn't ring a bell. But maybe something had been missed.

He picked up the ball, led Run back to the apartment, and fell onto the couch, exhausted.

Opening his laptop, he typed out an email to his closest friend in the NYPD. His name was David Min-Jun, and though Austin had been a year ahead of him in the academy, they'd bonded over their shared experience as Navy brats.

DMJ,

Sorry I haven't been in touch for a while. I think you know it's hard for me to put myself in the New York frame of mind these days.

You probably saw on the news, the Baby Butcher re-emerged. Wouldn't you know it, I came three thousand miles to escape that kind of thing, and it found me anyway.

But that's not why I'm writing.

Fiona may have been working on a case involving a murder victim named "Michael Lee." Would you see what your system pulls up?

Open invitation to come out here to fish if you can ever find a week off.

Austin

Technically, David wasn't supposed to share this kind of information, but "DMJ," as he liked to be called, was a little less by-the-book than Austin. At times, his tactics bordered on recklessness.

And that's exactly what Austin was counting on.

CHAPTER TWENTY-TWO

THE INTERROGATION ROOMS at the downtown branch of the Seattle PD were about the same size as the ones Austin had used back in New York. The ones depicted on TV usually showed two stiff plastic chairs lit by a single lightbulb dangling menacingly over an old metal table. But in reality, most interrogation rooms were much less dramatic.

Kyon Johnson sat in what looked to be a decently padded chair of maroon cloth, the type you'd see in a mediocre hotel conference room. Across from him sat two detectives Austin had never met, one leaning toward Kyon, the other leaning back and looking through papers.

Austin and Anna watched through a double-sided mirror in an adjoining room. Chief Jackson stood next to them. Anna had no notebook or recorder because Jackson agreed to let them observe the interrogation only if it was one-hundred percent off the record.

When Chief Jackson had called Austin at seven that morning to invite him to Seattle, she'd explained that Kyon hadn't been at Nassar Ali's place, but their tip had led directly to his apprehension. Nassar Ali had been dying his hair an even brighter shade of pink when two officers banged on his door a little after ten.

Luckily for the officers who questioned him, Nassar had been dumb enough to open the door with a mirror sitting on his kitchen table, a mirror speckled with white powder. That had been enough to bring him in for further questioning. Now Nassar sat across the hall, where he was being questioned by two other detectives. Nassar had spent the first five minutes denying that he knew Kyon, the second five minutes denying that he'd seen him that day, the next five denying giving him his laptop, and the final ten minutes telling them everything.

After ditching his set and fleeing on his scooter, Kyon had messaged Nassar through a secure app called Signal. They'd met up for dinner, where Nassar had given Kyon his laptop. According to Nassar, Kyon had admitted to being in some kind of trouble, though he hadn't said more than that. He'd told Nassar he was going to stay at the White House, their name for a little motel in South Seattle where they'd partied a few times.

The detective closest to Kyon was a bear of a man. Around Austin's height, but at least sixty pounds heavier. Barrel-shaped and hard like he'd put on more muscle than his frame could handle. Austin hadn't gotten his name, but he'd already started calling him Cueball in his mind because of the way his bald head gleamed in the fluorescent light. He was taking the lead, and his interrogation style was like a bull in a china shop. "So. Mr. Johnson. Why'd you kill your grandmother?" His voice was like a series of gunshots, his words loud, hard, and clipped.

After a long silence, Kyon looked up, tears in his bloodshot eyes. "I didn't kill her."

Cueball scoffed. The other detective seemed lost in his papers, shuffling and shuffling as though sorting through the mountain of evidence they had on Kyon. It was all an act, Austin knew. But Kyon probably didn't know that.

"Let's go back a little way, alright?" Cueball tapped the floor with his dress shoe. "Yesterday. Two guys jumped you. At a warehouse party. Vincent Mignolo and Darius Fishburn. Why'd they do that, Kyon?" Cueball was good. He had a way of cutting his sentences short, speaking in fragments. It was both threatening and disconcerting. A good combination when trying to squeeze a confession out of a scared twenty-something who might also be a killer.

Kyon shrugged, then fidgeted with his nose ring. His clothes and piercings made him look like a kid who wanted to come across as angry and defiant, but to Austin he looked beaten, dejected. Everything about his mannerisms said he had little fight in him.

"They're drug dealers," Cueball said. "Vinny and Darius are drug dealers. We already know. You've bought special K from them. On more than one occasion. Your buddy Nassar—DJ NormalHair. He's in the next room. Telling us everything."

Kyon's eyes darted to the door, as though he might be able to see his friend confessing to a whole list of crimes. Just as quickly, they fell back to the floor.

"Try this story on for size," Cueball said, standing and looming over Kyon. His voice had gone up a few notes, lighter and friendlier, but Cueball's presence was as intimidating as any Austin had seen. "A few weeks ago. Your friends Vinny and Darius sell you a couple pills. Molly. You mention wanting to get your hands on some yellow oleander. As stupid as it is, young idiots like yourself take it as a downer on occasion. When you can't find enough regular drugs to kill yourself with." He walked a little circle around Kyon's chair. "Being the intrepid young entrepreneurs that they are, Vinny and Darius tell you, 'No problem.' After all. You're one of their cash cows. A sad little rich kid who overpays for drugs."

"You saying they ripped me off?" They were Kyon's first words and they brought a smile to Cueball's lips. His teeth were yellow and stained. Too much coffee, not enough flossing. The little things Austin couldn't help but notice.

Cueball had been trying to get a response out of the kid, and it had worked. "They didn't rip me off."

"I'm sure they charge you the same as the skanks walking the corners downtown." Cueball chuckled. "But setting aside *price* for a moment. Actually. Wait. How much did they charge you for the oleander?"

Kyon looked at the floor. "I didn't do anything."

Cueball turned to the other detective, still shuffling through papers. "Hear that, Mike? Kid says he didn't do anything. Should we let him go? What do the papers say?"

Mike took off his glasses. He was the opposite of Cueball. An older Black guy who could have passed for a college professor, he was thin, soft-faced and relaxed, even studious looking with a neat gray beard. "It doesn't look good," he said, shaking his head sadly. "Not good at all."

"What's in those papers?" Kyon demanded.

Mike frowned like a disappointed English teacher who'd recently graded Kyon's D- paper on *The Grapes of Wrath*. "Not good at all."

Cueball sat again and crossed his thick right leg over his left. "Allow me to finish my story." He cleared his throat. "Roughly ten days ago. Possibly as much as two weeks. Vinny and Darius deliver the yellow oleander. You use it to murder your dear grandmother. A woman who personally thanked me for my service at a police fundraiser last year." He stabbed a meaty finger in Kyon's face. "You killed her. Then went on about your business."

Kyon shook his head, but said nothing.

Austin studied his eyes, which seemed to grow hollower, more dead by the second. Next to him, Anna and Chief Jackson watched in silence.

"Everything looks good," Cueball continued, "until the second toxicology report comes out. Somehow your good pals Vinny and Darius see a report. A rich widow has died from yellow oleander. They notice she has the same last name as a certain spoiled rich kid. Same one they'd sold the oleander to." He uncrossed his legs, then crossed them again. "Now, a smart pair of drug dealers would have fled, knowing they were accessories to murder." He smiled and turned to Mike. "Anything in those files about whether Vinny and Darius are smart?"

Mike held up a paper, smiling. "Says right here they are dumb as a sack of hammers."

"And that," Cueball said, "is a big problem for you, little buddy. Instead of fleeing, they came to the warehouse party to blackmail you. Knew you'd killed your grandma. They demanded money to stay quiet. You declined. They beat you up." He laced his hands behind his head and leaned back, like a fat uncle after a Thanksgiving meal. "My hunch? You were coming up with a plan to pay them off when we found you in that dump downtown."

Cueball leaned in close now, waiting for Kyon to meet his eyes. The young man finally looked up. His cheeks were wet with tears, his face the color of wet ash. Cueball was a bully, to be sure, but in this instance, that was his job. And it worked. He'd broken Kyon in minutes.

And yet, despite the guilt painted across his face, Kyon admitted nothing. "I didn't kill her."

Cueball shook his head. "Hey Mike." He leaned in, spitting words in Kyon's damp face. "Anything in those papers about whether Mr. Johnson here is a spoiled little lying bastard rich kid?"

Mike flipped through the papers, as though studying them carefully. "Nothing says that specifically," he said softly. "But we do have an ATM withdrawal on the day Vinny and Darius sold you the yellow oleander. Happens to be for the exact amount they claimed you paid them."

"Doesn't sound great," Cueball said.

"There's more," Mike continued, his voice as dry as if he'd been reading the phonebook. "You see, Nassar showed us a private message from two weeks ago where you asked him about oleander. He told you that shit will kill you and he'd never touch the stuff, despite being a drug addict himself."

"So," Cueball turned to Mike, "and please correct me if I'm wrong. The papers in your hands seem to indicate that our spoiled little deviant friend here is completely screwed. That about right?"

Mike set the papers down on the desk. "I'd say that's an accurate assessment."

They sat in silence a long time, Kyon's eyes straight ahead and unmoving, like he was staring into a long future behind bars. "Lawyer," he said softly. "I want my dad's lawyer."

CHAPTER TWENTY-THREE

AUSTIN AND ANNA walked out into a heavy rain. The sky was a gray so thick it seemed to block out any possibility that the sun would ever return. The sidewalks were deserted except for a lone crow taking shelter under a tree, nibbling at an unidentifiable food smear on a wet napkin. Even the occasional passing car gave Austin an empty, forlorn feeling.

Anna ducked under the awning of a bank. "Where are we going?"

"I don't know." Austin tasted bland, unseasoned meat. Like he'd taken a bite of boneless skinless chicken breast, cooked in the microwave with no seasoning. Textureless, meaningless. "Let's find somewhere to talk."

"Lunch?"

Austin nodded. His synesthesia had never come on in this way. The flavors he experienced were usually strong, striking. Tart cherries and lemon zest. Even the bad ones, usually associated with negative emotions like disgust or sorrow, were usually accompanied by similarly negative flavors. This was something else. He couldn't understand what he was feeling, but he knew it had to do with Kyon.

Anna pointed to a diner across the street. Austin stepped out from under the awning, then Anna grabbed his arm. "Wait," she said. "We're only a few minutes away from somewhere I want to check out."

"Where?" Austin asked.

"Just follow me."

She opened a large umbrella and led Austin through the rain into the International District. Lots of little restaurants and shops lined the wide streets, though people were still few and far between. They passed the famous Uwajimaya Market—said to be one of the best Asian grocery stores in America—but even that couldn't grab Austin's interest.

As they walked, rain came in from the sides, bypassing the umbrella as easily as a kid hopping a turnstile in a New York subway. Austin studied each car, each face, each storefront. They weren't being followed—he was quite sure of that—which made him think that the people in the Suburban hadn't been Seattle PD. That meant it had been someone associated with the murder, or perhaps someone associated with the Johnson family. Either way, he didn't think that the sad, angry, and broken kid he'd seen in the interrogation room had anything to do with it. Even if Kyon had wanted to, his life was too much of a mess to hire professionals to follow them.

As they walked, Austin also thought about the last thing Chief Jackson had said to him before they left the station. "Don't call us, we'll call you."

After Kyon had demanded a lawyer, Cueball and Mike had come out, received praise for their performance, and huddled with Jackson. Austin had asked whether they could stick around in case there was another interrogation, or a deal struck with the lawyer, but Jackson had declined. The SPD had their guy, and the last thing they wanted was a meddling reporter and a know-it-all private investigator hanging around their case. So, after Anna had gotten assurances that she'd get her sit down with Jackson, they'd headed out.

Sopping wet despite the umbrella, after ten minutes they reached a nondescript white building. The kind of building you'd walk right past without noticing. Two stories, it was marked with a tiny sign, green lettering painted on peeling white paint: *Little Huê.*

It was the restaurant that had appeared in Kyon's search history.

They stood before the windows, which were covered in dusty white lace curtains. "Great minds think alike," Austin said. "I was wondering about this as well."

"Kyon searched for this restaurant only a week before Eleanor died. One of my old editors used to say that, at their core, people aren't extraordinary. Sometimes the key to breaking a story is following the most mundane lead you have. Most people—even killers—spend most of their time doing everyday, mundane things."

It was 11 AM and the restaurant appeared to be closed. Not that there was any sign to indicate this. It didn't have posted hours, and the dining room was dark. There was no evidence anyone was inside preparing for a grand lunch opening.

Austin leaned on the side of the building, thinking. "In the interview with Kyon, I started getting a weird feeling."

"Your synesthesia? Must be cool having a weird superpower."

Austin chuckled. "I'd hardly call it a superpower. Usually it's more annoying than anything. And it's not like it gives me magical crime-solving abilities."

"Oh I'm aware. You developed those by skipping childhood. Watching interrogation videos instead of Saturday morning cartoons and reading crime scene manuals instead of comic books."

"I'm being serious. If this were a CBS show, I'd taste peppermint when a suspect was lying, or garlic when I was in the presence of a killer. But this is real life. My thing has to do with what *I'm* feeling. And like a lot of guys, knowing what I'm feeling is like knowing where the fish are biting. In fact, one thing I read about it said it might be a mechanism to compensate for lack of emotional intelligence."

Anna walked a little circle under the awning of the restaurant. She stopped, smirking in his general direction. "I'd buy that."

"Point is, during Kyon's interview, I got an odd feeling. I've never seen someone act so guilty. Someone so obviously guilty."

"But..."

"You agree there's a 'but'?"

Anna paced, arms folded. A few cars splashed by, spraying oily water in their direction, but not far enough to hit them.

Finally, she said, "I think we need to be looking for an accomplice. But tell me, what was the feeling you had?"

"It started with a taste. Like bland boiled chicken. Almost like tap water. Like nothing at all." Austin thought back to the interview room. "Murky, like we're missing it, missing something, missing everything." He sighed. "I mean, he bought oleander. Obviously that's not a coincidence." He sighed. "I don't know *what* I'm saying."

Anna seemed to have stopped listening anyway. She was on her phone. Austin was about to object—one of his pet peeves was when people started scrolling in the middle of a conversation. "Here." She held it up to Austin.

"What?"

"This joint has a website. They open at noon."

Austin took the phone and searched the homepage. It looked like the site had been built in 2006. Weird pale green lettering was barely readable over a yellow background. There were no colorful photographs of enticing Vietnamese food. The only image was pixelated clip art of a steaming bowl of noodles.

Squinting, Austin scrolled down to read the menu. The font made it difficult to read, but—despite the lack of images, the menu *did* sound enticing. The area was flush with Vietnamese restaurants—mostly specializing in phở, which was as much a staple around Seattle as pizza was in New York. This place was different. No phở on the menu. Instead, it offered regional Vietnamese cuisine like *bahn da cua, bánh it ram, bánh bèo,* and *bun cha.*

Austin stopped. "Bánh bèo."

Anna leaned in to read the screen next to him.

"That's what they had the night Eleanor died." He knew something had been bugging him. And that was it. "Kinda odd that Kyon would google this restaurant, which is across the city from his apartment, only a week before he kills his grandmother. And that same night, they are served a specialty Vietnamese food they also serve here."

"What is bánh bèo?"

"They're amazing." Talking about food instantly lightened Austin's mood. "Usually an appetizer or street food, it's a thin rice paper crêpe topped with dried shrimp or pork, served with an amazing fish sauce and scallions. Sometimes fresh herbs."

"Could be a coincidence, though, right?"

"Definitely *could* be."

"But you're thinking of Mack?"

Austin nodded. "He told me Eleanor often threw out ideas for food, but he had final control of the menu."

Anna began pacing again, still sheltering under the restaurant's small awning. "So we know that Kyon had something to do with this. He bought the oleander. He was obviously guilty."

"I guess I'm wondering whether that bland taste in my mouth—which I've never experienced before—is the flavor of solving the case without solving the case. We know Kyon did it —did *something* anyway—but there's no motive I can see. I'm not buying the whole clash over musical tastes thing. And no one makes a song called *Death to Grandmas* and then goes and kills their grandma."

"So maybe he bought the oleander and gave it to Mack, who poisoned her food?"

"Maybe. Or it could be something else."

"Like what?"

"I don't know, but I think the answer might be in this restaurant." He thought for a moment. "I have an idea, but it involves coming back here tonight."

"Okay... what?"

"Are you up for a double date?"

CHAPTER TWENTY-FOUR

JIMMY AND LUCY were already sipping drinks at a table near the window when Anna and Austin arrived. They were ten minutes early, but their detective friends had arrived even earlier.

"You beat us here," Anna said as she sat.

Lucy said, "It was either twenty minutes early or thirty minutes late. Ferry schedule."

Jimmy sipped from a green bottle labeled *333 Premium Beer*. "Before we go any further, I'd like to announce that this is in no way a 'double date.' Lucy has made it abundantly clear to me that —though I have the body of a Greek God—I am too dumb for her."

Lucy slapped his shoulder. "That is *not* what I said."

Jimmy raised an eyebrow.

Lucy poked at her cocktail with a little white straw. "I said you're *waaaay* too dumb for me."

Jimmy leaned back, clutching at his heart like he'd been struck by an arrow. "That hurt more than getting stabbed in the belly with a kitchen knife."

Anna laughed. "When are you two gonna quit the Sam and Diane thing, get married, and pop out a precinct or two worth of crime-fighting babies?"

"March 74th," Lucy said, "in the year two-thousand-and-never."

A surly waiter set down menus, frowning at them as though their presence was an imposition. He left without saying a word.

Anna chuckled nervously. "Service with a smile, huh?"

Lucy leaned in. "Seems like they're not that interested in selling us food. We had to beg them to take a drink order."

Austin glanced around the restaurant. It was a Saturday night, prime dining hours, and the only other customers were a pair of old men in the corner, sipping bottles of *333* and playing a game involving dice and a little mat. They spoke loudly in Vietnamese and appeared to be gambling large sums of money, judging by the pile of crumpled bills they were passing back and forth between rolls of the dice.

The whole place was dimly lit, but not in a carefully crafted, moody way. As Austin was in the process of renovating both the kitchen and dining room of his own little café, he was more aware than usual of how a guest would experience the space. He was no interior designer, but even he knew you needed enough indirect light so your patrons could see the food and the faces of their companions. Here, the little window sills were dusty, the only decorations a lone plastic flower sticking out of a small plastic vase on each table. No candles. No lighting.

It was the least inviting restaurant he'd ever been in.

Austin could tell that Jimmy, too, was scoping the place out. When he'd called to ask Jimmy to bring Lucy to dinner, he'd explained that he had a hunch the restaurant was somehow involved in Eleanor Johnson's death. It was simply too much of a coincidence that Kyon had searched for the place and, a week later, their house specialty showed up on his grandma's dinner menu the night she died. Austin wasn't sure what was going on, but he felt better knowing that, if anything went down, he had two armed officers next to him. Not that he couldn't handle himself, but he no longer had a badge.

Anna and Lucy excused themselves to find the restroom and

Jimmy made eye contact with Austin, then pulled out his phone and typed a text at lighting speed. The waiter was now standing by the door, close enough to hear their conversation.

Austin's phone vibrated with Jimmy's text.

When I worked patrol, my partner and I would drive around the county and bet on which run-down restaurants and stores would turn out to be criminal fronts. A pizzeria in Bremerton, a dog-grooming place on Bainbridge Island that never had any customers but reported $11 million in income. That sort of thing. Second I walked into this joint, my radar went off.

Austin finished reading the text and gave Jimmy a nod. It was the same in New York City. The vast majority of businesses were legit, but there were some that screamed *Criminal Front* from a city block away. They were easy to spot because they were the ones that didn't make any effort to please customers. Businesses like that either failed, or they had illicit sources of income.

The ladies returned from the restroom and the waiter finally appeared to take their orders. Jimmy, it turned out, spoke just enough Vietnamese to order for them, and everyone deferred to him to order a selection for the table to share. When the waiter was gone, he turned to Lucy. "Could a dumb jock be that multi-lingual?"

She scoffed. "So you spent three months in Southeast Asia with your bros and learned enough Vietnamese to pick up chicks. Big whoop."

The waiter had disappeared to the kitchen and the two gamblers had staggered out, so they now had the place to themselves.

Austin put his hands flat on the table. "Lucy, did Jimmy explain what we're doing here?"

She nodded.

"I'd be interested in your impressions."

Lucy cocked her head slightly, making sure no one was within earshot. "The restroom was nice. Passed by the kitchen on the way. Smelled fantastic. This place definitely screams Drug Front, but sometimes the worst-looking restaurants have the best food. Maybe they focus on takeout?"

Jimmy waved a hand at the empty restaurant. "You seen any Doordash or UberEats delivery folks coming through here? It's Saturday night. Should be bustling."

"Maybe they specialize in catering," Lucy offered weakly. "All I'm saying is, don't judge a book by its cover. What I *do* think we should talk about is a certain gray-haired chef. Mack."

"We know Kyon procured the murder weapon," Anna said. "And we know he looked this place up. And we also know that not long after, Mack served this place's specialty the night Eleanor died."

Jimmy flexed his bicep, which almost popped out of his black v-neck sweater. It was a habit he had while thinking. "So maybe Mack and Kyon met here—a restaurant one of them knew would be empty, where no one would recognize them—and Kyon passed along the powder, which Mack then added to the food?"

"Definitely an option," Austin said. "But let's step back for a second. To potential motives. I keep coming back to Eleanor's husband. John. It was odd—right?—how his name barely came up at the memorial? Made me want to look into his death a little more closely. Maybe something about one of his shady deals, or something about his suicide, or maybe it wasn't a suicide... I'm just throwing stuff out here."

"He's got the Vietnam connection, too," Anna said. "But there's very little information about his death. Obviously, the newspapers covered it, but it was nothing like today. I've got one article on it."

"Show us," Austin said.

Anna pulled up the article on her phone and handed it to Lucy, who read it quickly and handed it to Jimmy.

"Damn," Jimmy said, "warn a guy before showing him a crime scene. It's my night off." When he'd finished reading, Jimmy handed the phone to Austin, who saw what he meant.

The article was a scan of a yellowing newspaper clip from

1971 and included a photo of John Johnson, face down on the floor, one side of his face visible, including a single lifeless eye. A pistol lay beside him and a small pool of blood had dried around his right temple.

The headline read: *Local Businessman and Vietnam Vet Takes Own Life*

Austin scanned the article, which was short on detail. In fact, it contained no real information other than the fact that Eleanor Johnson had reported her husband missing around ten in the morning. Police had found the body around six the following evening in the office of a farm store attached to an orchard about twenty miles outside of Seattle. Apparently John owned a stake in the orchard and hired people to sell the fruit it produced at Pike Place Market. Like the restaurant they were sitting in, Austin thought the little orchard business may have been a front for something else.

Anna said, "In her diaries, Eleanor is always talking about 'The Farm.' Apparently John spent a lot of time there. Definitely shady as hell. I mean, he's a sketchy entrepreneur making a lot of money, and his only legal business is a twenty-acre apple orchard? Not likely."

Jimmy said. "It's got a very *Satriale's Pork Store* vibe."

Lucy and Anna laughed.

Austin didn't get it. "Pork store?"

"*The Sopranos,*" Jimmy said. "Greatest TV show ever?"

Austin shrugged.

"You'll have to explain it," Anna said. "His TV only plays interrogation videos and reruns of *Leave it to Beaver.*"

"I mean, I've *heard* of that show," Austin said, a little more defensively than he intended.

"Jersey mob," Jimmy said. "They spend half their time hanging out at a pork store, butcher shop."

"Got it." Austin nodded and stared down at the article. Something bugged him about the photo, but he wasn't sure what. Johnson wore a slim-cut, black suit with brown shoes and white socks. The white socks were a no-no with the outfit. Even Austin knew that and he was definitely not big on style. There was something else, though. The blazer rode up his back slightly, revealing a white dress shirt and a belt holster a little back from the right hip. Not a normal carrying position.

He held it up to Jimmy and Lucy. "Anything look weird there?"

Lucy studied it. "Holster is too far back."

"Could have moved when he fell," Jimmy said.

"True," Austin said, "but..."

"The white socks, too," Jimmy said. "I don't know what the fashion was in 1971, but who wears white socks with a nice black suit?"

"Agreed," Austin said. He thought of the photos of John Johnson he'd seen in the living room on his first visit to the Johnson mansion, then handed the phone to Anna. "I can't remember for sure, but wasn't Johnson left handed?"

"Don't know but..." she swiped a few times, then handed it back. "Check that out, then swipe right a few times."

Austin set the phone in the center of the table so everyone could see. The image showed John in a baseball uniform at maybe sixteen years old. Just like in the one he'd seen earlier, Johnson stood in a left-handed batter's stance. Austin swiped, and the next photo was Johnson at a business function, holding up a glass of Champagne like he was delivering a toast. He wore a similar black suit, and was also using his left hand. In the next photo Johnson was tossing a ball to a little girl of no more than three years old, probably Karen. Also using his left hand.

"Definitely a lefty," Anna said. "That last one was taken not long before he died. It was tucked into one of Eleanor's diaries."

Austin scrolled back to the article. The holster was on the back side of his right hip. "It's not just the position of the holster, it's that it's on the *right* side."

"Could have preferred cross-draw," Lucy said.

"What's that?" Anna asked.

The waiter appeared and set down a platter without saying a word. As bad as the service was, Austin had to admit that the food smelled enticing.

Jimmy waved a hand above the platter like a gameshow host presenting a fabulous prize. "Bánh bèo for everyone to share."

Austin popped one in his mouth. It was an explosion of flavor like he'd rarely experienced. Smoky, fatty and rich, yet tart and topped with fresh herbs. It was a nearly perfect bite of food.

Anna said, "Whoa, these are amazing. I can see Mack coming here, trying them, then trying to recreate the recipe for Eleanor."

"But why recreate an amazing recipe if you're planning to kill someone the same night?" Jimmy asked.

Anna shrugged. "Diversion?"

Lucy cleared her throat. "Can we get back to guns?"

Austin smiled. Lucy loved to talk about firearms.

"Most people wear firearms on their strong side," she explained to Anna. "I'm a righty and I wear my weapon at around four o'clock on my right side. Cross-drawers prefer the weapon on the opposite side of their dominant hand. For example, a lefty who prefers cross-draw would wear the gun on the right side."

Anna nodded. "And 'four o'clock' means?"

"Imagine your belt buckle is twelve on a clock. Six o'clock is your tailbone. Three o'clock is directly on your right hip, and so on."

Anna nodded along. "So four o'clock is just past your right hip toward the back of your body."

Lucy nodded and Anna examined the photo. "So if Johnson was a lefty and wore his gun on his right hip there..."

"That's five o'clock," Austin said. "Maybe five-thirty. But look..." He held up the phone.

"Oh," Lucy said. "Nevermind. That holster is positioned for a righty."

"The retention straps," Jimmy chimed in. "That holster is set up for the butt of the firearm to move from the front of the body to the back. Like a righty would wear. Literally impossible for a lefty to access his firearm with his strong hand."

Anna held up both hands, silencing them. "Okay, okay. I appreciate it, but damn, you three should start a firearms YouTube channel or something." She leaned back in her chair. "I always think about how I'd explain something to an average newspaper reader. Setting aside all the complexities of how he chose to wear his gun, it sounds like you're all saying the same thing: it's quite possible John Johnson didn't shoot himself at all." She glanced around the still-deserted dining room. "Quite possible he was murdered."

Austin nodded. This was the conclusion he'd come to. He couldn't be sure, but the photos made him think someone had shot John Johnson, then attached the holster to the wrong side by mistake, likely in haste, and set the gun next to him to make it look like a suicide.

"Wait," Lucy said. "Can I have the phone?"

Anna handed it to her, and Lucy scrolled back to the photo of the crime scene, the body. "There's something else." She held it up for all to see, then cocked her head slightly. "When was the last time you saw a lefty shoot himself in the right temple? It would be damn near impossible to shoot himself in the right temple, unless of course he decided his final act on God's green earth should be to practice his aim with his off hand."

Austin almost slapped his forehead. He'd been so focused on the holster being on the wrong side that he hadn't noticed the fact that the bullet wound was on the wrong side as well.

Anna was holding her left hand across her face, trying to determine whether it would be possible to shoot herself in her right temple.

"Nice catch," Jimmy said to Lucy. "Can't believe I missed that."

Lucy set the phone on the table. "Remember the whole *way smarter than you* thing?"

Jimmy smiled.

Austin said, "Yes, nice catch." He turned to Anna. "I covered a lot of suicides. Never once saw someone shoot themself in the temple on the non-dominant hand side. It's damn near impossible."

"Secrets," Anna said.

"Huh?" Jimmy asked.

"Eleanor's diaries mentioned secrets. She told me there was a lot she was ready to tell the world about. If John was murdered, and if she knew about it..." She trailed off, her face trembling slightly.

Lucy finished her thought. "That's one hell of a secret."

Austin took another look around the dark restaurant. "A secret that could have gotten her killed."

CHAPTER TWENTY-FIVE

AN HOUR LATER, Austin watched Lucy and Jimmy stroll down the block as he and Anna waited for a taxi.

The main courses had been just as good as the appetizer. The best Vietnamese food he'd ever eaten, all served with a frown in the least hospitable restaurant he'd ever experienced. Something didn't add up. But he was exhausted and needed to get back home, back to Run, out of the city and back to Hansville's clean beach air.

"If Kyon *did* give the oleander to Mack," Anna said, "and if we assume for a minute that Mack killed her, I can't help but wonder, why? Why would Kyon agree to that, and what possible motive could Mack have? He'd worked for her for fifty years!" Austin was about to reply, but Anna was on a roll. "Not to mention, how could it connect to the likely fact that John Johnson was murdered."

The taxi arrived and, as Austin shut the door behind him, he saw two men getting in a black Suburban across the street. He didn't recognize them from the restaurant, but the one getting in the passenger side looked like he might be Vietnamese. He was burly, with short black hair and a perfectly-fitting black suit.

"Downtown ferry," Anna said to the driver.

"Don't look now," Austin said, as the taxi pulled out, "but they're back. The Suburban."

Anna tensed, shot a look through the rear windshield. The Suburban was right behind them.

Austin put a hand on her shoulder. "I didn't notice them following us on the way here. And I was looking. That means they somehow landed on us while we were inside the restaurant."

"But how?"

Austin wasn't sure, but he still believed they weren't in danger, although with the discovery that John Johnson may have been murdered, that belief was starting to waver. "If they wanted to harm us, this isn't how they'd go about it."

Anna seemed unconvinced. "So we're just gonna get on the ferry like everything's normal?"

Austin nodded. "Let's say Mack *was* involved in Eleanor's murder. Maybe he killed John as well and somehow Eleanor found out. Although I have no idea why he'd have killed him."

"Or maybe Eleanor knew all along that John was murdered and she was going to spill the beans."

"That tracks with everything we know," Austin said.

They rode in silence, Austin glancing through the rear windshield each time the taxi took a turn. The Suburban made no move to catch up to them. Simply remained about ten yards back.

When the taxi stopped at the ferry terminal, Austin paid and they got out. "When we get to the door, keep going, okay? Get tickets and wait. I'm going to see if I can find out who's in that SUV."

"But—"

"Please. There's a big crowd inside. You'll be safe." He smiled. "And I'm ninety percent sure I'll be as well." He hadn't mentioned it, but he had his MR 1911 concealed under his blazer.

He strolled with Anna to the door that led to a long ramp into the ferry terminal. As Anna walked through, he turned suddenly and jogged back toward the road. Across the street, the Suburban had stopped at the taxi stand, idling.

He couldn't see so much as a hint of movement through the tinted windows. Halfway across the street he tasted cayenne pepper.

The first time his synesthesia had kicked in during a confrontation, it had scared the hell out of him. The last thing one needs in a fight is the distraction of random flavors entering his sensory experience. But soon after he'd realized that it was just a sign of adrenaline, his body increasing rates of blood circulation, quickening the breath and preparing muscles for extreme effort.

Right hand on his gun, he used his left to offer up a single-knuckled *tap tap tap* on the driver's window.

After a long pause, the window rolled down, revealing a bony-faced Vietnamese man with short black hair. In the passenger seat next to him, another man—the one he'd seen getting in at the restaurant, who looked to be the twin of the driver in face, but the opposite in body type.

The driver's look was neutral. No smile, no scowl. He simply stared at Austin like it was both perfectly natural that he'd knocked on his window, and perfectly irrelevant.

Unable to think of anything better, Austin said. "Why are you following me?"

Neither man replied, and Austin took the moment to scan the car. It was immaculately clean, not even an empty coffee cup or water bottle in the cupholders. The men had no discernible bulges where their weapons might be, but that didn't mean much. If they were the criminals Austin assumed they were, they could carry under the seat, in the glove compartment, or in a well-concealed holster under the flaps of their matching black suit jackets.

Austin smiled and rested his hands on the window. "You're not here to rob me, that's obvious. You're not here to kill me, that's also clear. You're following me because of something about Eleanor Johnson."

He watched the driver's eyes as he spoke, but they were flat, dead, as though nothing Austin said mattered. Everything about these guys screamed "thugs," "hired help."

"Someone told you to follow me, but who?"

Austin heard a vibrating buzz. The man in the passenger seat looked down at his cellphone, then tapped the driver on the knee. Without another word, without even a look, the driver rolled up the window.

Austin moved his hands.

A moment later the Suburban pulled into traffic.

CHAPTER TWENTY-SIX

ANNA'S favorite chair was an overstuffed blue recliner she'd bought at the Goodwill for sixty bucks. She'd found it there on a desperate afternoon the day her divorce had gone through.

In a final blow after nine tumultuous years of marriage, her ex-husband had stolen the leather recliner he'd given her on their first wedding anniversary, a chair they'd agreed she'd keep in the divorce. While she'd been at the lawyer's office signing the paperwork, he'd shown up with a small U-Haul and taken the chair, along with a cord of premium firewood, the stereo they'd picked out together, and most of their nice dishes. Bastard had even taken her favorite leather jacket, probably to sell for a hundred bucks online. It was the only time she'd been thankful not to have any fine jewelry in the house. He damn well would have stolen that, too.

She'd chosen this blue chair because it was the only one in the Goodwill that didn't smell of cigarettes. Now, ten years later, it sat in front of the woodstove. An interior designer would have told her it was too big for her tiny living room, but she didn't care. She did most of her reading and writing in it, and tonight she had a lot of reading to do. The diaries spanned four years and totaled around two-thousand pages. Anna could barely imagine what was in all the diaries she *didn't* have.

She scrolled forward on her phone, scanning pages, looking for John's name. If it was true that he'd been murdered, and if Mack had something to do with it, or perhaps knew about it, there had to be something in the diaries that explained why.

She saw John's name in the middle of a page and scrolled back to the top to read the entry.

December 11, 1970

Today John and I had another row. I truly am growing tired of that man. If I didn't have his son in my belly right now...

But no. Better not to even think about it.

The fight started when I asked John to be a little more discreet about his dalliances. My father saw him at the Gecko Room after midnight, a cocktail waitress on each arm. What daddy was doing there, I shudder to think, but it was an embarrassment to the family, he said.

John accused me of being threatened by the other women in his life. I told him he ought to be threatened by the other women in mine.

Our arrangement seemed so much more simple when we made it. Now... I don't know. It's hard to explain, but I feel as though our story is coming to an end. Mother warned me not to marry beneath myself, and yet here I am.

But the children, they're so lovely. He's not much of a father. Never has been. But he has given me two wonderful children, and soon a third. They are healthy, relatively happy.

Perhaps I should count my blessings.

December 17, 1970

The last week has been hell on earth. It appears as though John is going to be arrested. He is still vague about the specifics, but for the last week he's been passing what money he can over to me.

There was more money at the farm than I knew. Much more. Much of it will remain inaccessible, but I have enough now to begin again if the worst happens. But I know he's hiding more. John will never tell me everything.

Maybe he simply gets off on having secrets. John seems to love keeping secrets, from me, from the children, probably from himself. I guess it's safe to say that the men and women who sell apples and cherries at Pike Place are selling a few other things as well. Things John leaves out of the advertisements.

And it appears as though he's been caught.

Good Lord. He told me he could not survive in prison, not for more than a short while. Then he said he could avoid prison altogether if he told the police things they wanted to know. I didn't understand in the moment, but I think he meant my father.

I know daddy has been involved in some of his dealings, but neither will tell me everything. One thing those two men have in common is that they believe women should be kept in the dark.

Ahh, daddy.

When I was a little girl I overheard him saying that business was like war. There are no good guys, no bad guys, only winners and losers. At the time, I thought he meant he was fighting hard for our family. For success. Now I know he was a crook all along, like John.

And to think, I believed our family fortune was built on hard work, on merit.

At bedtime, John said the saddest thing. He's never talked much about the war, but I knew that's where he'd met Mack. He told me that he owed Mack his life. That his plane had malfunctioned on a mission and he'd been forced to land in enemy territory. Against orders, Mack had taken a helicopter to find him. Said he owed Mack his life and that sometimes he wished Mack had just left him in Vietnam to die.

I'd never seen John cry before last night.

CHAPTER TWENTY-SEVEN

AUSTIN FELL onto his sofa and stared at the ceiling. Run finished the bowl of food he'd given her in the kitchen, then bounded into the living room and launched herself onto his lap.

"I'm sorry I've been gone so long," he said. "Tomorrow we'll go to the beach."

When she heard the word 'beach,' Run leapt off him and bolted for the door.

"No, sorry," Austin said. "*Tomorrow*. Beach."

She stared at him expectantly, wagging her tail. She knew the word 'beach,' but 'tomorrow' was not yet a concept she could grasp. Eventually she got the message and lay down on the floor by his feet.

Austin grabbed his laptop from the side table and opened his email. His buddy from the NYPD had responded.

Austin,

Great to hear from you. Writing in a rush as I'm on a big case and have to testify tomorrow.

You know I'd love to help, but I can't share anything now that you're not in the department. I think you know that.

Take care, man. We miss you out here.
DMJ

His phone had finally found a signal and it dinged with a new voicemail. A New York City area code.

"Hey Austin, DMJ here. Don't know if you saw my email, but better we don't do anything in writing. Calling you from a pay phone, so don't call back and please erase this message after you listen to it. Short answer: no record of any homicide victim by the name Michael Lee between 2018 and 2021. No missing persons reports with that name either. And, no surprise here, there are forty Michael Lees living in the five boroughs. Three have records, but nothing jumped out at me. No obvious connection to Fiona. I'm sorry."

Austin walked into his office and read Fiona's paragraphs, illuminated by the soft glow of a desk lamp. If DMJ was right, which was a safe assumption, then the paragraphs weren't the first part of an opening statement for a trial.

Michael Lee strolled into the parking lot of his favorite Korean restaurant in Brooklyn at 7 PM on a cold Tuesday in February. He'd never lived in Korea, but he went to Mama Dae's BBQ once a week for their famous galbi and kimchi. The meal made him think of his grandma, who'd raised Michael and passed away when he was ten.

He was at Mama Dae's to meet Megan, a woman he'd connected with in a dating app. He'd worn his lucky outfit—black jeans and an authentic t-shirt from David Bowie's Serious Moonlight Tour.

His lucky restaurant. His lucky outfit.

The unluckiest day of his life.

His "date" turned out to be a stand-in for the Namgung crime family. Megan had come to steal his identity, then lure him to his death.

. . .

"Lure him to his death," Austin whispered.

Every time he'd read it, he'd assumed that meant Michael Lee had been killed. But it didn't actually say that. Taken literally, it only meant that Megan had come to attempt to lure him to his death. Whether or not she'd been successful in doing so, Austin assumed, would have been revealed later in the book.

Austin returned to the couch and ran a few searches for "Michael Lee." He was quickly able to determine that there were two Michael Lees serving time in the New York prison system, but one was white and one was Black. Fiona's writing implied that her subject was Korean, likely a second-generation immigrant from the phrase "never lived in Korea."

Next he did a standard Google search for Michael Lees living in the five boroughs of New York. DMJ said there were forty, but his search indicated that there might be more.

A CEO at a tech startup. A photographer who specialized in documenting the birds of Central Park. A barista at a Starbucks who posted his every moment on Instagram.

Austin shut his laptop and let out a long breath. This was getting him nowhere.

Actually, it was worse than that.

The revelation that the writing may have been nonfiction, or possibly even the beginning of an opening statement, had gotten his hopes up, had made him feel the possibility of resolution dangling before him. Now he felt worse than ever.

He kicked his shoes off and lay down on the couch, his long legs dangling over the side.

Run leapt onto his belly and, before he knew it, they were both asleep.

Still on the couch, Austin woke early the next morning and headed to check on his café. He'd been dreaming about secrets.

Sipping black coffee and trying to shake the cobwebs from

his brain, he wandered through the cold, empty kitchen. The renovations were going well. New stainless-steel counters had been attached to the walls and the new sink lay on the floor, unwrapped and ready to be installed. He didn't want to jinx it, but it was looking like it might be the first time in recorded history that a contractor had completed a job early and on budget.

Austin grabbed his fishing pole from the closet and headed to the beach, Run leading the way. He didn't have much hope of catching anything at this time of year, but he'd heard of an occasional blackmouth salmon being reeled in from the shore during high tide. And, for him, it was never really about the fish.

He attached a lure and cast far out into the Sound, reeling the line slowly in between tosses of the ball. Run was in rare form, taking off at a full sprint, skidding to a violent stop in the sand, and returning at a thoroughbred's pace to drop the ball at his feet.

Austin's mind kept returning to a single word: secrets. Eleanor had told Anna that her family had plenty, and the diaries had hinted at even more.

He'd always been sure that he and Fiona didn't have any. Not that they told each other every little thing. They didn't. They'd never been that type of couple. But that was because they had trust between them, and neither was the type to discuss every detail of their lives.

So why had she told him she was writing a novel when the passages on her typewriter appeared to be something else entirely?

As he fished aimlessly and tossed the ball for Run, he pondered this. It could be a hundred things, most of them benign, but somehow his mind kept searching for the worst possible explanation. Austin had always known that losing a loved one to an act of violence not only brought on grief, it messed with people's minds. And he'd always assumed his mind was too strong for that.

But on the deserted beach, the sky grayer than gray and a chill creeping through his jacket, his mind started doing strange things. Maybe Michael Lee was part of a huge case she'd concealed from him. Maybe Michael Lee was an old college boyfriend. Maybe Michael Lee had been a *current* boyfriend. An affair. Maybe Fiona was actually the "Megan" in the story, a secret killer.

He laughed out loud. His thoughts had gone well past paranoid into pure delusion.

He made another long cast, then turned as he heard gravel kicking up under car tires. He tensed as he turned, anticipating the black Suburban for a half second before seeing Anna's white SUV.

She leapt out and jogged down the beach, greeting him with a wave. Run dove at her feet, rubbing her face against Anna's ankles.

Anna kneeled in the damp sand and scratched her, then looked up at Austin. "Secrets."

Anna's presence had brought him back to the present. "What?"

"I gotta tell you what I just read."

CHAPTER TWENTY-EIGHT

AUSTIN LED Anna to a cracked wooden bench just up from the beach.

She handed him her phone. "I was up most of the night reading the diaries. Read this."

Christmas Day, 1970

It is the darkest of Christmases. What I thought was a subtle threat has now become a promise. John intends to cooperate with detectives. To give them all my father's secrets.

He assures me that my father is a terrible man, that my family's money comes from dark, nefarious dealings, that he is no worse than my father. He may be right, but...

I spent the morning opening presents with the children, pretending everything was normal, then left them with the nanny and met my father.

Daddy assured me John had nothing on him, that John was making up stories to attempt to save himself. I implored daddy to come clean, to tell me everything so I could help him, help the family. He wouldn't. He is still determined to lie to me, to pretend that he's never done anything wrong.

He also told me that he does not know the extent of John's illegal deal-ings, though he has heard rumors that he is acquiring heroin from South-east Asia and selling it at the market.

Lied to by my father my whole life, lied to by John since the day I met him. Sylvia Plath had it right: "Men are dirty rotten lying bastards."

Then I realized what this means: John is going to prison for a long, long time. Either that, or my father is.

Maybe what John said is true. Maybe he'd be better off dead.

Austin handed her back the phone. "You think Eleanor killed John?"

"Or had him killed, yeah."

"No way." Austin shook his head. "It's a diary, people write all sorts of stuff in their diaries."

"Think of it from her perspective. She's a woman with two kids, about to be three, born rich, who married a man her family saw as beneath her. John gets caught importing heroin and dealing through a fruit stand at Pike Place Market, then tries to offer the detectives some dirt on her father—who's quite liter-ally a pillar of the community—to avoid prison time. I mean, there are parks named after her father and grandfather. Even if it's true that her dad was a crook, he's got a better shot of getting away with it than her rags-to-riches husband. And if John goes to prison, she's attached to him still, legally anyway. He owns the house, has control of finances." Anna stood and walked a circle around the bench as Run playfully nipped at her heels. "If he's dead, it's a clean break. She's the grieving widow with control of the money. Not to mention, she was gay, it would appear. Given the time period, likely she felt she had to marry, to have children. But the diaries make it clear they had an arrangement."

Austin stood, shoving his hands in his pocket to stave off the chill. "Eleanor's father. Is there any truth to what John was threatening?"

"That's why I look like hell," Anna said. "Only slept two hours because I was researching that all night."

"You look fine. Want a cup of coffee?"

She nodded and they walked across the driveway and into his apartment. Austin leaned the fishing pole in the corner. "Shall I just give you a cup of sugar with a splash of coffee?"

She was clearly unamused. "Ha. Ha. Ha."

Austin poured her half a cup, then handed her the milk and sugar.

"So," she said, "my sense of Eleanor's father is that he is like a lot of old-money guys in big American cities. Shady, ruthless, but not exactly a criminal. Not the kind the police investigate, anyway. There's no way he was involved in dealing heroin. He was more the type who made deals with the local government to open up a hundred thousand acres for foresting, then profited off it. Or got zoning laws changed after buying up properties."

"So, fraud?"

Anna sipped her coffee. "Yeah, and corruption, bribery. In the early days of Seattle, corruption and business development went hand-in-hand."

"So, we have Kyon in jail for procuring the oleander. We suspect Mack actually poisoned her, and now we suspect Eleanor herself of killing John."

"Best theory I have," Anna said, "is that Mack and John were war buddies, brothers almost. Somehow Mack found out that Eleanor had killed him and he lost his shit. Revenge."

Austin was skeptical. "He found out after fifty years?"

"Maybe it was the memoir that triggered it. Maybe he found her diaries, maybe..."

Austin shook his head. "We're close, but we're missing something."

Anna sighed. "It's like a puzzle where we know all the pieces are there, but they're scattered everywhere in the room. How the hell did you do this for a living?"

Austin laughed. "Don't forget, we failed to solve around half of the cases we caught. You get used to living with frustration."

Anna flopped into her chair and pushed the coffee to the middle of the table. "So, when you *did* solve a case like this, how did you usually do it?"

Austin tasted lemon-lime, just a hint of sweetness, like a fresh-cracked Seven-Up. It was the sense he got just as a light-bulb moment struck, usually *as* it was striking but before he could articulate it.

Then his mind caught up with his senses. He sat across from Anna. "If you know the puzzle pieces are all there, but they're strewn across the room, what's the very first thing you do?"

"Gather them all on the table?"

Austin stood and grabbed his phone from the counter. "Call the sisters, Karen and Susan. Get them to agree to meet at their mansion tonight. They need to get John Junior and Mack, Brenden, and Andrew. I want to recreate the night Eleanor died. I'll get Jimmy, Lucy, and Ridley to show up."

"Why would they do that? I mean, why would the family agree to meet?"

"Tell them I've solved the case."

CHAPTER TWENTY-NINE

"WAS this the setup on the night in question?" Austin asked, scanning the people gathered in the giant living room.

Karen nodded. "Other than the additions, and the absence of my mother, yes. This is where everyone was."

Austin stood in the front of the room by the fireplace, exactly where Eleanor Johnson was standing as she delivered her verdicts about the year's charitable donations. Karen and Susan sat on the couch before him.

Andrew crossed and uncrossed his legs from an armchair to Austin's right. Mack sat by the bay windows that faced the street. John Junior leaned on the billiard table, and Brenden stood against the wall in the back, arms crossed, a skeptical look across his face.

Austin waved a hand toward the far corner, where Anna stood with Ridley, Jimmy, and Lucy. "Karen, if it's alright with you, Detectives Calvin, Jule, and O'Rourke will act as the jury, or simply as neutral observers. None of them have a stake in this, besides getting to the truth. And Detective Calvin hasn't heard anything about what we've discovered, so I'll be counting on him to interpret certain things neutrally for your benefit."

Karen nodded. "That's what we're here for. And we trust Detective Calvin."

"Can we get on with it?" Andrew asked. "I have a date later."

Junior sipped his drink and huffed. "Didn't know Tinder had a *seniors* section."

Andrew ignored the quip but Susan shot Junior a judgmental look.

Austin moved on. "Anna, the evidence, please."

Anna came to the front of the room, pulling a stack of printouts from a folder. "I have to warn everyone, there will be some disturbing images. It's necessary to show you all what we have learned." She handed the papers to Austin.

Junior rattled the ice cubes in his empty glass and shot an angry look at Karen. "Can't believe you agreed to this. I'm paying eight-hundred bucks an hour for a lawyer for Kyon, and now I have to sit through this?"

Andrew turned, scowling. "Maybe if you'd ever been a father to the boy he—"

"Please," Austin said, "can we stay on track?" He cast a stern glare on Junior. "You're going to want to hear what we've discovered. I promise."

Andrew waved a hand at Junior dismissively. "If my brother saw what his patriline had generated, he'd roll over in his grave."

Every family had their issues, but Austin would be glad when this case was through and he could leave the Johnson family in the rearview mirror on his way back to the beach. He held up the first printout, an enlarged version of the grainy photograph of Johnson from the newspaper clipping—sprawled on his stomach, only one side of his face visible, a pool of blood near his right temple. "I'm sorry to bring up the past, I really am. I know this can be painful. But I imagine you've all seen this image before."

He looked from person to person, paying special attention to Mack, who'd been silent and stone still the entire time. Mack showed no reaction. The others either looked away or nodded sadly.

"And I'm sorry to subject you to this again, Karen. Can you tell us what you remember about your father?"

She closed her eyes briefly, then ran her hands over the crease in her designer pants. "Very little. He played with me some, but that might just be memories I've made up based on photographs I've seen." She looked at Susan. "Mother told us he liked to play ball with us." She shook her head. "I really don't remember much."

Susan huffed. "I can't see what our father taking his own life has to do with our mother. Why, Mr. Austin, would you subject us to this?"

"He gets off on other people's pain," Junior spat, "all cops do."

Austin took a deep breath. "I assure you I don't. And I'm no longer a detective." He met Junior's look with one of his own, his hardest *shut-the-hell-up-before-I-make-you* stare. It almost always worked on weak men pretending to be tough. The drunk in his ill-fitting suit dropped his eyes. "And please don't interrupt again. You'll understand in a moment." Austin paced back and forth, two steps left, two steps right, hands in his pockets. "Anna, can you explain what we learned about the position of the firearm and the holster?"

Anna handed the photograph to Susan. "Please take a look and pass it around." Stepping back in front of the fireplace, she said, "As you likely know, your father was left handed." She pointed at the photo of John Johnson on the wall, in which he held a baseball bat in a left-handed stance.

As she continued with the explanation, doing an excellent job of summarizing it for everyone to understand, Austin watched Mack out of the corner of his eye.

Being a detective was roughly seventy-five percent investigative work, twenty-five percent poker. Sure, he had to follow leads, interview witnesses, and comb through files, but rarely did that lead to a conclusive *gotcha* moment. More often, all the evidence pointed in a direction, but it took a bluff or two to turn that into a confession.

As Anna explained the clock face positioning of the holster, Mack showed no emotion, nothing. Even when Junior walked the photograph to him, his eyes betrayed nothing. He stared down at it for a moment, then passed it over to Andrew without so much as a flinch.

Anna said, "Detective Calvin, you are widely respected and have zero stake in this case. Having examined the photo, what would you conclude about the position of the holster?"

Ridley cleared his throat, walking to the center of the room. "It's a fifty-year-old case, and I'd want to look more thoroughly into it before declaring it a homicide. But..." he looked from Karen to Susan, from Susan to Junior... "I can say it's very unlikely he took his own life, given the evidence. For me, the definitive piece is the bullet hole in the right temple. Please, each of you, hold your left hand as though holding a firearm and try to place it flush with your right temple."

He waited as they tried this, then continued. "You'll see that, unless you're a yoga master, the best you can do is place the imaginary firearm on the right temple at an angle. Now, if you imagine pulling the trigger, you might be able to hit the temple, but the bullet would be moving from the front at a slight angle toward the *back* of your head."

"And," Anna said, "is that the direction the bullet moved?" She pulled another set of papers out of her folder and handed it to Karen. "A source within the Seattle Police Department was able to pull this from the records."

In fact, Anna had traded her sit-down interview with Chief Jackson for a copy of the autopsy that had been performed on John Johnson. Jackson had been happy to get out of the interview, and had no problem sharing a small piece of a file from a fifty-year-old case. Like the investigators at the time of Johnson's death, she had no idea it was anything but a suicide.

"Detective Calvin," Anna continued. "What did the autopsy find?"

"I examined the report, and it shows that the bullet moved from the right temple and exited out the top right side of the skull. The exit was only a few inches from the entrance, consistent with a shot from the right temple with the firearm angled slightly forward. A shot consistent with a right-handed person holding the weapon to the temple."

Austin cleared his throat and made eye contact with Karen, whose eyes were wide. She was beginning to understand. "So, unless your father's last act on earth was deciding to use his off hand, we can conclude he was murdered."

Susan gasped.

Karen's eyes closed, her face went blank. Junior stood and poured himself another drink.

Andrew's mouth was hanging open like he'd seen a ghost.

Mack shook his head, as though in disbelief. If he was acting, he was good at it. But if Austin was right, he'd been acting for fifty years, and the longer someone practices a lie—lives a lie—the more they believe it. And the more they believe it, the better they are at convincing others.

He'd convinced a lot of people, but that was about to come to an end.

CHAPTER THIRTY

KYON LAY his head on the table as his lawyer shut the door of the interrogation room behind him. They'd been at it all day. Detectives, lawyers, more detectives.

He finally had a moment alone.

Before he could take a breath, the door opened and shut with a few clicks and the hiss of the hydraulic door closer.

An officer entered briefly and dropped a brown paper sack on the table, smiled a sarcastic, yellow-toothed smile, then left.

The door hissed and clicked closed. The sound had been grating on him all day. Alone in the room, he realized why. His middle school had used the same type of hydraulic closer. Silver and protruding about six inches off the top of the door, it ensured that the door was never left open by accident. Each day when the nanny dropped him off at school, he'd heard that sound like the final nail going into a coffin.

Kyon opened the sack. His lawyer had asked for Din Tai Fung, Kyon's favorite Cantonese restaurant. What he wouldn't give for a basket of their famous soup dumplings? The detectives had called him a "spoiled little rich kid" and offered to get him something from the place on the corner.

The sack contained a turkey sandwich and a Coke. Kyon

examined the sandwich, which was dry and sad. He cracked the Coke.

His lawyer had assured him that he had little to fear, and Kyon had seen enough TV to know how it worked. As long as he gave them someone who'd done something worse than him, he wouldn't catch all the blame. As long as he told the truth, he'd be alright. The worst he'd get was a few years. Most likely he'd be out in a year, assuming they caught Mack and his story checked out.

His lawyer had left to make a few calls, then he'd return for a final consultation with Kyon before offering up the full story to the detectives. All he had to do was wait.

The Coke wasn't even cold. Could he sue them for serving him a warm Coke? Kyon laughed bitterly. He *was* a spoiled rich kid, but at least he knew it.

Not like Nassar, who was even more spoiled because of the oil money from his Kuwaiti relatives. Kyon would never forgive that bastard. Not only did he have the stupidest stage name ever —*DJ NormalHair*—but now he'd sold him out. Kyon remembered the night they'd worked for hours to come up with Nassar's signature stage call. Right at the beginning of every set he'd hop on stage, start a track and scream, "I AM NORMAL!!!" The line always got the crowd hyped. And now Nassar had told the detectives everything they wanted to know to save his own ass.

Kyon sipped the Coke, which made him realize how empty his stomach was. As pissed as he was at Nassar, he had to admit, he was about to sell Mack out in the same exact way.

What he couldn't understand was why Mack would want to kill his grandma in the first place. Boomers were all nuts, of course, so who knew why they did what they did? Maybe Mack had a thing for her. Wasn't unrequited love the most common reason for murder? He didn't know, but he'd heard that in some show.

Soon, none of this would matter anyway.

His lawyer entered the room, followed by the two detectives. The bald giant of a man had been the main detective questioning for most of the day, but this time the other guy led the way. He was an older Black guy, late sixties, with a pleasant face and bright white teeth.

Mike sat across from him. "I'm going to ask you a few more questions before we go over your official statement and have you sign it."

Kyon nodded, then swigged the Coke. If he was going to go through with this, at least he could be on a sugar high.

Mike lowered his glasses and looked into Kyon's eyes. "What we want to understand—what your lawyer couldn't tell us—is how Mack convinced you to acquire the oleander in the first place."

"Cancer," Kyon said. "He told me he had terminal cancer and didn't want to deal with doctors. I even looked up assisted suicide to see if it was legal. Check my browser." He sighed. "Mack said he didn't want to be a burden on his family, on *my* family. So when there were no more treatments, he would, you know…"

His lawyer had told him to be honest and there would be nothing to worry about. But as he answered, he didn't begin to feel better like he thought he would.

With each word, he felt worse. The giant bald detective glared at him like he was the lowest scum on earth. He imagined the detective wearing a prison guard uniform, locking him in his cell at night.

He was going to get a few years in prison. With good behavior, maybe that would only end up being a year.

The bald detective glared at him like he either wanted to screw him, or kill him. Maybe both. What could a guy like that do to a spoiled little rich kid alone in a prison? For a year.

His stomach hurt.

He didn't want to be here.

CHAPTER THIRTY-ONE

"WE BELIEVE that whoever knew that John Johnson was murdered," Austin said, looking at Karen and Susan, "is connected to the murder of your mother."

The sisters were too stunned to speak. For now, he was not going to raise the possibility that Eleanor herself had something to do with John's death. One thing he'd learned is that people were slow to accept the truth about people they loved, and it was much better to have them come to the conclusion themselves, rather than having a life-shattering truth dropped on them by a detective.

He said, "We know that Kyon procured the yellow oleander that ultimately killed his grandmother. And—"

"There's no way," Junior interrupted. His voice was near a shout, but full of pain. As far as Austin could tell, it was real pain. Bordering on anguish. Even absentee fathers, even terrible fathers, wanted good things for their children.

Austin held up both hands. "I believe he did so without knowing how the poison would be used. Detective Jule—Jimmy —is it true that people sometimes use yellow oleander recreationally?"

Jimmy walked to the center of the room. "Idiots do, yeah.

Everyone knows there's an opioid problem right now, and sometimes people who get hooked turn to heroin and fentanyl when they run out of pills. Sometimes they turn to oleander in very small amounts."

"We believe," Austin said, "that Kyon acquired the oleander for someone in this room. But not because he thought it would be used to murder his grandmother."

This is where the evidence ended and the bluff began. Austin was fairly sure Kyon had met with Mack. And he was fairly sure Mack had killed Eleanor, but he still had no idea why, or exactly how he'd delivered the fatal dose.

"Wait," Andrew said, standing stiffly and pulling a cigar from his inside pocket. "What makes you think Kyon didn't know how it would be used?"

Austin cast a look to the back of the room. "Brenden, do you happen to recall what was on the menu the night Eleanor died?"

The reporter was dressed in a blue suit, slim cut so it almost looked too small. His jaw popped as he prepared to speak. "*Of course* I do." The guy couldn't even answer the simplest of questions without sounding full of himself.

Anna sighed loudly enough for all to hear. Austin couldn't help but wonder whether her sigh carried some disappointment that Brenden was not, in fact, the murderer.

Austin said, "And would you remind us?"

"Vietnamese food. Little rice crepes topped with pork and shrimp. Bánh bèo, I believe they're called."

"As a reporter," Anna chimed in, "what would you make of the fact that Kyon Johnson ate at a restaurant specializing in bánh bèo only a few nights before Eleanor died?"

Brenden's face tightened, like he was pained by the fact that Anna knew something he didn't. "I'd need more information."

This was the moment.

Austin stepped forward, then turned on Mack, who still sat at the bay window, face neutral. "Information like whether the chef responsible for the menu that night had ever been there?"

Mack met his eyes, unblinking. "I've cooked Vietnamese food many times."

Austin raised his voice. "We found evidence on Kyon's laptop that he'd been to a restaurant specializing in the exact food you all ate that evening. We believe Mack met him for dinner. In addition to acquiring the poison used to kill Eleanor Johnson, he discovered a delightful new dish."

Mack stood. "Lies." The word came like a gunshot, followed by a long silence.

Austin looked around the room. This was where he hoped someone would say something. A memory would be jostled loose. A little comment—long forgotten—would resurface to provide the missing link in the case.

Instead, all that emerged was a yawning chasm of silence.

He had one more card to play, "Of the people in this room, only Andrew and Mack were in a position to know that John was murdered. Everyone else was either too young or not yet born."

Andrew stood and got in Mack's face. Something that had been simmering exploded all at once. "If you knew my brother was murdered I will strangle you right now."

"I... I didn't..." Mack stammered. "I didn't know anything." He was shaken. His face turned a bright red to contrast with his bright white hair. "This guy is nuts."

Austin pulled Andrew back by the shoulders. "Please, sit."

As Andrew sat, Mack collapsed back into the seat in the bay window. He looked away, out across the lake, where the gray of the sky matched the gray of the water.

"You saved his life in Vietnam," Karen said. "That's what mother told me once."

"He was like a brother to me," Mack said. "I would do anything for him, for his family. I've served you all well. Eleanor above all. She wanted the whole world served to her on a platter. And I gave her that." His voice had turned melancholy, like he was at his own funeral.

Austin almost felt bad for the guy, but this was no time to let up. "Mack, how'd you do it? How'd you deliver the oleander?"

Mack said nothing.

"Did you meet Kyon at the restaurant Little Huê?" Austin demanded.

Silence.

Austin shoved his hands in his pockets, turned away from Mack, and took in the room.

Susan and Karen sat next to one another—as always—looking shaken. Susan had tears in her eyes.

Junior drank angrily, still leaning on the billiard table. Brenden leaned against the wall, an *I-could-care-less* look across his face, which Austin knew was an act. He was riveted. Andrew had his head in his hands, mumbling something inaudible.

The room was silent, except for the sound of Anna's footsteps.

She was rushing toward the door.

CHAPTER THIRTY-TWO

"ANNA, WHERE ARE…" Austin called, but she'd already burst through the door into the hallway. A moment later she returned carrying a small picture frame.

Everyone's eyes landed on her.

Anna held it up for Austin to see. Although he recognized it, he had no idea why she'd brought it in. It was the photograph of Mack's granddaughter, the one they'd seen hanging in the kitchen on the day of the memorial. In the photo, a pretty girl of no more than twenty stood leaning on a palm tree beside what looked like a big library or academic building.

"Mack," she said, sitting next to him at the bay window, "is this your granddaughter?"

Mack turned back toward the large room, a surprised look on his face like he'd just remembered there were others there. "Yes."

"She's in college?"

He nodded.

Anna held up the photo for all to see. "Austin and I noticed this photograph when we came for the memorial. I thought about it a few times since then because my son—who's at UW— looked into all the Los Angeles and San Diego colleges before I told him I could only afford an in-state school. So I kept thinking about this photo, assuming it was an LA school because of the palm trees. Then it hit me, it's not LA."

Mack looked unperturbed. "It's Vietnam. And it's no secret. Eleanor even helped me pay. Gave me a ten thousand a year bonus, promised for the four years Evie was planning to be over there. Schools are cheaper there, but they tack on all sorts of fees for Americans."

"Vietnam," Anna said. "You saved John's life there. You served there. Had friends who never came home."

Mack nodded.

"Now your granddaughter is there."

He nodded again.

"Please!" Junior burst out. "Where are you going with this?"

Anna ignored him. "Vietnam is very important to you. The bond between you and John was unbreakable, forged in war in a land you came to love."

"That's all true," Mack said, his voice flat.

Austin swallowed hard. As usual, Anna was going to come right out with it. And he couldn't blame her. His method had gotten them nowhere.

She pointed at him like a prosecutor delivering the knockout line in a high-profile trial. "And you could never forgive the woman who killed him. Eleanor."

The room was still as death. The moment seemed to go on and on, though Austin knew it was only a few seconds.

Andrew broke the silence. "Anna Downey, you are insane, even for a reporter."

"Karen," Junior spat, "can we end the charade? This woman is so desperate for the money that—"

"It's in the diaries," Anna said defensively, "sort of."

Karen stood, "But you don't *have* the diaries anymore."

Anna's eyes dropped.

Austin moved between them. "Everyone, please. Let me explain."

Karen sat.

"It was necessary that Anna make scans of the diaries, only to use to solve this case. Not one shred appeared—or *will* appear—in the paper."

This seemed to calm Karen down, at least for the moment.

"The much more important thing is that she's right," Austin continued. "I read multiple passages in which Eleanor hinted, very strongly, that John was not only in bad legal trouble, which you already knew, but, and I am sorry to say it, she thought the world might be better off without him. Detective Calvin..."

Ridley stepped forward. "I am deeply sorry Karen, Susan, all of you. I should say, it's not definitive, but I read the pertinent sections. The selections Anna showed me end before John's death, but if I were a prosecutor, I'd say it comes close to a confession that she intended to kill her husband. Or perhaps have him killed. Combined with the fact that John's suicide appeared staged..."

Susan let out a soft sobbing noise. Even Junior fell silent, just staring into his drink as though it might contain the remedy for whatever he was feeling.

Mack stood and looked slowly around the room, making eye contact with each family member one by one. "One thing I can tell you all for certain is that Eleanor did not kill John, or have him killed." He sank back down into his seat. Defeated. "But I did it. I killed her. I had to. The family name was on the line—John's name, all of your names—and I love you all too much to let her get away with that."

CHAPTER THIRTY-THREE

KYON EYED the gleaming silver on the hydraulic door closer, wondering whether the police got theirs from the same place as the school system.

There was probably some company that provided them to all the institutions of the state, he thought, morosely.

Mike asked, "Did Mack say anything else?"

"He had a whole story about how, when he'd been serving in Vietnam, he'd been prepared to take his own life. Like if he was ever being tortured for secrets. The old man told a convincing story. I always liked him. Wanted to help. He was old and said he had cancer." He tugged at his nose ring. "I think I already told you that."

"We know you wanted to help him," Mike said. "But was there another reason?"

Kyon finished the Coke. His brain buzzed and, suddenly, he was hit by a wave of rage. The real reason he'd agreed to get the old fart the oleander was because he'd offered him twenty-five hundred bucks. The money made him think of his dad, the asshole, or 'Junior' as everyone affectionately called him.

"Twenty-five hundred bucks," Kyon said.

Mike jotted a few notes.

As quickly as Kyon's rage came, it vanished, blown away by a storm of sadness. Every time he thought of his father, this is what happened. It was why he tried not to think about him.

Mike looked up. "When you gave him the oleander, it was in what form?"

"Tiny baggie. Powder. Looked like sand-colored coke."

"The drug, not the soda, I assume?"

Kyon nodded.

His father made him feel like he was the lowest scum on earth. As a teenager, he thought he'd become a famous DJ, tour the world, get rich and amass millions of followers on Instagram and YouTube. That would have shown 'Junior.' But now he knew none of this would happen. He was going to jail.

His next thought was worse than all the others combined. He was going to jail, and he was bound to become just like his father, if he even made it out alive. Even if someone like the giant bald cop didn't rape him to death in his cell.

His breaths quickened. His heart thumped in his chest and he began shivering.

What was happening to him?

"You cold?" Detective Mike asked.

Kyon nodded. He felt like he was freezing from the inside. He'd had a panic attack before his first set at a club, but nothing this bad.

The bald detective disappeared, then reappeared a moment later and tossed a thin blanket over him. "You're lucky we have this. Now answer the rest of my partner's questions."

Kyon pulled the blanket up around his chin. It did little to warm him. He couldn't stop shaking.

As he answered the rest of Detective Mike's questions, a thought played itself over and over on repeat. It was a familiar thought, as though it had been playing quietly in the background of his mind for years and only now—only finally—had it reached full volume.

I don't want to be here anymore.

He pulled the thin blanket up to his chin, noticing how it frayed at the edges.

He tuned out Detective Mike and let his eyes fall again on the hydraulic door closer, jutting out from the door at the perfect height.

CHAPTER THIRTY-FOUR

MACK PEELED off his chef's coat and put it on the cushioned seat of the bay window. It was odd, Austin thought. Almost as though he was resigning his position as chef of the family after fifty years.

He walked over to John Junior. "I knew Kyon dabbled in drugs. I thought oleander was untraceable. I met him for dinner and he gave it to me."

"You son of a bitch," John said. "How dare you involve him in this?" His phone rang and he pulled it out of his coat pocket angrily, tossing it on the billiard table. Next he smashed his drink down onto the billiard table and grabbed Mack by the arm, cocked his fist, and threw a wild punch that glanced off Mack's cheek, knocking him back slightly.

In half a second, Ridley was on Junior, holding him back. "Junior," he said. "It's understandable you're upset, and he probably deserves it, but this isn't the way."

Junior struggled, but had no chance against Ridley, who had fifty pounds of muscle on him.

Mack rubbed his cheek, checking for blood. It hadn't been much of a punch.

Mack walked slowly to Karen and Susan, standing before

them. "I paid a tech at your pharmaceutical company five thousand dollars to turn the oleander into a pill that looked like Eleanor's heart medication. I swapped it out. She popped it at the end of the night with her regular pills."

Susan's face was a mix of rage and horror, her cheeks shaking as the tears ran down.

"At two in the morning," Mack continued, "I crept into the room and cleaned up the vomit. I made sure it would look as though she'd died peacefully in her sleep."

Karen's glare was pure ice, as though she could kill the old man standing before her with the strength of her rage. "At our company? Who?"

"His name was Ahmed. Nice guy. And please don't blame him."

Karen stood, rising on her tiptoes to get closer to Mack's face. "Oh, I'll blame whoever I want. You bastard!"

"I told him it was for me, that I have terminal cancer, same as I told Kyon."

Karen's face quivered. "Why would you say that, you sick, twisted—"

"I *do* have terminal cancer," Mack said. His voice was resigned. "They're giving me three to six months."

"So..." Karen was confused.

Mack said, "If you only knew everything, you'd know I did it all for you, to protect you. Eleanor was going to ruin everything with that damn memoir."

Austin glanced at Anna.

The memoir. The secrets.

Anna said, "If she had nothing to do with John's murder, what was she going to reveal in the memoir? What were you trying to protect the family from?"

Everyone stared at Mack, who ran a hand through his hair. His face went through a series of contortions, as though he was living a dozen different possibilities all in a row. Then his face hardened again, and he said nothing.

Austin's phone vibrated in his pocket. Through his pants he pressed the silence button.

Then John Junior's phone rang again. This time he checked the caller ID and shoved it back in his suit pocket. All of a sudden, two other phones began ringing. Karen and Susan reached for their purses.

"It's the police station," Karen said, staring down at her screen.

"Well, answer it," Susan said impatiently, her glare still fixed on Mack.

Karen swiped angrily at her screen. "Hello?"

Austin had a bad feeling, and it only grew worse as he watched the look on her face darken, her eyes close. She staggered over to John Junior, handing him the phone. "They've been trying to reach you."

John had gotten himself another drink. He sipped it and took the phone. "Yeah?"

Junior listened, his eyes going wide as Karen sat back down.

Susan asked, "What was it?" as quietly as she could.

Junior dropped the phone and fell to his knees, then let out a scream that pierced the heavy quiet hanging in the room. The scream seemed to last forever, the pent up pain of decades. He collapsed into sobs on the floor.

Karen looked at Susan, her face a hard mask. "Kyon hung himself. He's dead."

Austin was struck by a wave of nausea, the taste of popcorn and licorice jelly beans eaten at the same time. Dread mixed with guilt, mixed with the compounding sorrows of human pain and suffering, both his and everyone else's.

For a moment, everything went blank.

He only came to his senses when he heard a door slam. When he looked up, he realized Mack was gone.

He glanced out the bay windows toward the lakefront road. The black Suburban was idling out front. Mack was walking toward it.

Hurrying over to the window, he watched as Mack walked up to the passenger side. The window cracked, but not wide enough for Austin to make out a face.

A man emerged from the back of the car, grabbed Mack from behind and shoved him in the back seat.

A few seconds later, the Suburban peeled down the block with a screech that made the pigeons rise from the trees shading the street.

CHAPTER THIRTY-FIVE

"ANYTHING else you can tell me about your father?" Austin asked.

Karen looked at Susan, who shrugged as she wiped tears from her eyes with a handkerchief.

Jimmy and Lucy stood against the wall, scrolling on their phones, looking for more information about John's suspected crimes in the police databases. John Junior was in the next room, still on the phone with the police. Ridley had accompanied him, saying he could help communicate with the police. But Austin knew Ridley was probably thinking the same thing he was. John Junior was a suicide risk and needed to be watched.

Austin had called Chief Jackson and told her about Mack's confession. She'd been pissed that he'd been questioning him, even though he hadn't broken any laws. And she'd been even more pissed when he told her how he'd fled, or been kidnapped. It still wasn't clear exactly what had happened. All Austin knew for sure was that Mack's phone had rung, he'd voluntarily gone outside, then involuntarily been shoved in the back of the same Suburban that had been following him all week.

Karen spoke through tears. "We had a little game I remember. Or it may be that my mom told me about it enough that I only think I remember it. I was three when he died."

"I can't believe Kyon is gone," Susan said softly. She looked as though she'd checked out, as though her body was still there but nothing else was.

"What was the game?" Austin asked.

"When dad would leave, he'd say, 'Guess when I'll be home.'"

"I'd always say a long time, like a year, or a month, or a week." She smiled sadly. "I don't know where the hell that game came from. I think even back then I was the kind of person who wanted to imagine the worst so I could be pleasantly surprised. So I'd say, 'You'll be home in a month,' and he'd say, 'No, less.' Then I'd say, 'You'll be home in a week.' And he'd say, 'No, less.' And we'd go down and down until finally we'd land on whatever it was, three hours or whatever, and he'd say, 'That's right. I'll be home in three hours. See ya later alligator.' And I'd laugh and that would be that."

"And," Anna interjected, "did he say that on the day he died?"

Karen nodded. "I don't think he would have said that if he was planning on killing himself. I don't know why I never thought about that until now."

Susan wiped her face. Her eyeliner had run, leaving a dark trail down her right cheek. "I think when you're told a story your whole life—never given a reason to question it—you just go with it."

"Now that you know he didn't take his own life," Austin said, "can you think of anything that might help us?"

Anna reached out and took Susan's hand, which was shaking. "I'm sorry, I know this is a lot. Too much. Way too much to happen in one day, in one week. But I'm stuck particularly on what Mack said. About him doing it to protect you, to protect the family. What could he have meant?"

Susan shook her head slowly. "I have no idea. Probably just covering his own ass."

She was angry, not thinking straight. Whatever he was, Mack

was no fool, and he wasn't a sadistic serial killer, either. He didn't kill for the fun of it. However twisted his reasons for poisoning Eleanor, he *did* have reasons.

Anna stood up, walked a lap around the room, then stopped in front of Karen. "Would it be alright if I poured myself a drink?"

Karen nodded.

"Anyone else want one?" Anna asked.

No one did, so Anna poured herself a cognac and, like John Junior, she poured it in a whiskey glass.

When she returned, she sat across from Karen. "The diaries. Is there any chance there are more diaries somewhere? Eleanor had said that there were, or at least *hinted* there were. If John was murdered, and if she had nothing to do with it, I can't help but think she knew about it, or knew why. Something very strange is going on here, and her diaries might go a long way in helping us find out."

"We've already been through her belongings," Susan said. "Every drawer, every box, even the attic. Trying to decide what to do with all her belongings. We didn't find any more diaries."

"Did she have any safe deposit boxes or storage containers?" Austin asked.

Karen perked up at this. "She has a lock box at the bank. I know she kept a little jewelry there, but I doubt there are any diaries."

Austin glanced at Anna. Like her, he was sure that somehow Eleanor was involved in John's death. The hints she'd left in the existing diaries were too strong to believe anything else. But Mack's insistence that she hadn't killed John had been forceful, and convincing. Either he was being duped, or he was missing something big.

"Could we head down there and check it out?" Austin asked.

"After the police leave," Karen said, pointing out the window.

Two police cars had pulled up, followed by a silver SUV. They were coming to take statements regarding Mack's confession and disappearance. At first, he saw three uniformed officers making their way up the walkway, but soon after, Chief Jackson wedged her way between them, marching up to the door like she was coming to haul Austin away to prison.

She was pissed, and she had every right to be.

At the front door, Chief Jackson didn't make eye contact with Austin, instead offering the family condolences about Kyon and asking to see John Junior.

When a suspect dies in police custody, it's a problem on more than one front. Not only is it devastating for the family, it's devastating for the officers on duty who let it happen. For Chief Jackson, it would likely be all of those things, not to mention a massive financial liability and a PR nightmare for the city.

As she walked past him in the hall, she stopped long enough to touch Austin on the shoulder. "I'd like to chat with you and the detectives after we speak with Kyon's father."

Her voice was fairly neutral. After all, she was a professional.

But Austin had pissed off enough bosses to know that she was not pleased, and he was about to hear all about it.

CHAPTER THIRTY-SIX

AN HOUR LATER, Austin and Anna sat on the couch in front of the fireplace, waiting for Chief Jackson.

Austin let out a heavy sigh.

"You okay?" Anna asked.

"Yeah. I'm just thinking about Kyon. Maybe if I hadn't pressured him like I did he wouldn't have..." Austin tasted pennies and pencil lead. He recognized the familiar taste of regret.

"That kid had a lot more going on under the surface. You met his father, remember. Not exactly a model for excellent parenting."

She was right, but still, Kyon's death stung. "'Suicide is painless.' You know that song from *MASH*?"

"Only you would reference a hit television show that aired before you were born. But yeah, I know it."

"I used to watch reruns with my dad." Austin stood and began walking around the couch. "It says a person can take it or leave it if they please. I know it's never one thing that drives someone to do it... I'm just thinking how much pain that kid must have been in before I came along and pointed a finger at him. That's all."

"It's not your fault, Austin."

"I know. I know." He sat next to her again. "We should focus on the case, Anna. Thanks for listening."

They were silent for a few minutes.

"What I keep coming back to," Anna said at last, "are the diaries and something Karen said a while back."

"The thing about wanting to talk to Eleanor about a donation?" Austin asked. He'd been wondering about this as well. One of those little loose ends they'd never tied up.

"Yeah," Anna said. "Of course, it could be a coincidence. But—"

The door swung open and Chief Jackson marched in, trailed by Ridley, Lucy, and Jimmy.

She stood in front of Austin, hands on her hips, as the detectives stood along the wall.

"Before you say anything," Anna said, already on defense, "we got a confession. Half a dozen people saw it."

Austin tapped her foot with his own. He'd been chewed out by enough superiors to know that trying to defend yourself usually made it worse. In this case, none of them worked for the Seattle PD, but Anna needed a good working relationship with them, and Austin did as well.

"We didn't *need* a confession," Jackson said. "We would have gotten one ourselves. Kyon had just pointed the finger at Mack. We would have been here to arrest him within the hour. And you two scared him off."

Austin said, "That's my fault. I can't believe I let him escape. I was distracted and, honestly, he seemed like a beaten old man. He has terminal cancer and... I don't know. He's not some cold-blooded murderer." Austin let out a long sigh. He knew how stupid that sounded. Mack had confessed to premeditated murder, so a cold-blooded murderer was exactly what he was. And yet, Austin was sure Mack's insistence that he was helping the family by killing Eleanor was sincere. He didn't explain any of this to Jackson, though. He knew it wouldn't do any good.

"My job," Jackson said, "and the job of my detectives, is to solve crimes. In this case it was to figure out who killed Eleanor Johnson. We figured that out. And just before we were going to come arrest him you let him escape. And not only that, now he knows that everyone knows. He could be out of the state by now."

"He's not," Austin said.

"And how do you know that?"

Austin shook his head, standing. "I don't know. I just... look, something is strange here."

Jackson scoffed. "You mean other than a former detective and current reporter being a pain in my ass?" She glanced up at Ridley and the other detectives, who stood against the wall silently. Jackson wasn't their boss either, but they all had the look of kids who'd forgotten their homework.

Austin said, "How can we make it up to you?"

That threw her off guard. "Get on the next ferry back to Kitsap County. Stay on your side of the water. And if you learn anything else about this case, call me before you do anything stupid."

Jimmy let out a little laugh and Jackson spun in his direction. "What's funny?"

"It's just that, *when lives are on the line, he makes the rules.*"

Lucy and Ridley both cracked smiles. Austin was never going to live that moment down.

Jackson frowned, more frustrated than ever, and stepped toward Jimmy. "A kid is dead, JJ."

Jimmy didn't like to be called JJ. "And I take that seriously. We all do! We were here helping to solve this thing. And we did. New York and Anna have been a step ahead of your people all week."

Jackson let out a long, slow breath and opened her mouth, ready to unload.

Ridley stepped between them. "This isn't helping. Chief, look... we'll head back to Kitsap. No more interference." He cut a sharp look in Jimmy's direction, which made him back off.

Jackson stepped over to Austin. "And you'll call me if you get anything on Mack?"

Austin nodded.

Standing on her toes to meet his eyes, she said, "If you go home and Mack is cooking spaghetti and meatballs in your kitchen, a signed confession sitting on the table, you call me before reading it. Got it?"

Austin smiled. "Wouldn't even taste the sauce, Chief."

Jackson ignored the comment, marched out, and slammed the door behind her.

"That could have been worse," Austin said.

Ridley approached him. "She's not as mad as she sounds. That was her friendly voice."

Austin waved him off. "She has every right to be pissed."

"So," Anna said, "You gonna do what she says? Make it right by heading back across the water? We could still catch the six o'clock ferry."

Austin stacked the photographs of John's body and the printout of the autopsy report, shoving them into the folder. Next he retrieved the photograph of Mack's granddaughter Anna had brought in from the other room.

"I should hang that back up," Anna said, reaching for it.

Austin paused. "Vietnam."

"Yes," Anna said, "we've established that it's Vietnam."

Austin locked in on the photograph. A young woman leaning on a palm tree and smiling, a large academic building behind her. "Does it seem like a big coincidence that he and John served in Vietnam together, that he met Kyon at a Vietnamese restaurant, served Vietnamese food the night he killed Eleanor, and that his granddaughter goes to college in Vietnam?"

Lucy said, "When I was in college, before I decided to be a cop, I used to stay up late watching Ancient Aliens with my friends drinking beer. My friends were super into it, believing every wild thing that the show threw out. You know how that show does a thing where they'll be like..." She made her voice spooky and mysterious... *"Three cows disappeared from this Idaho farm the same night an odd light was seen in the sky eighty miles away. Coincidence, or aliens?* I would always be the one to scream at the TV, 'Coincidence!'"

"Lucy-O-Buzzkill," Jimmy said. "I could see a connection."

"You never struck me as the conspiracy theory type," Lucy said. "Sure it's possible there's something there, but Mack may just be fond of Vietnam. A lot of GIs who went over there hated the war, but loved the people, the food, the culture."

"Maybe," Austin said. There was something else there, something beyond coincidence, but what? Then he had an idea. "Samantha, your tech guru, is she in the office?"

"I just spoke with her," Jimmy said, "she's simultaneously running the department's new social media and playing with various crime-fighting AIs she learned about in school."

"Does she do any of those facial recognition programs?"

Ridley gave him a skeptical look. "Sure she does, but..."

"Any chance you can do me a favor and ask her to look into something for me?" Austin pulled the crime scene photo of John Johnson from the folder and handed it to Ridley. "Would you send her a copy of that—tell her she can pull it up online if she needs a cleaner digital version. Tell her I'll call her in a little bit."

Ridley raised an eyebrow, asking for an explanation.

"Trust me," Austin said. "I'll explain later. Karen should be done by now and we need to get to the bank before it closes."

Ridley raised a finger as though he was about to object, but Austin was already heading toward the door, Anna close behind.

She caught up to him in the hallway. "What was that about? Why do you want Samantha running facial recognition on a dude who died fifty years ago?"

Austin opened the wide front door, which was so heavy it required a genuine shove to open. "How sure are we that's John Johnson in the picture?"

PART 3

THE RETURN OF THE PAST

CHAPTER THIRTY-SEVEN

KAREN CRACKED a bottle of Champagne the moment she slid into what appeared to be her usual spot in the back of the limousine. "As bad as things are," she said, "and they've never been worse, my mother would want me to keep drinking." She poured a glass for Anna, offered one to Austin, who waved it off, and then poured one for herself. Placing the bottle in an ice bath secured to the wall, she said, "Celebrate every day, mother used to say, you never know when it will be your last chance."

"Where to?" the driver called, lowering the glass divider between the front seat and the back, which had seating for six.

"Our bank, Brian."

The driver flashed a grin. He was in his fifties, Asian, and had the whitest hair Austin had ever seen. Even whiter than Mack's.

He noticed Austin noticing it. "It was going gray anyway. I figured, why not make it stand out? I used to be 'Brian.' Now I'm *Whitest-Hair-Ever* Brian."

Karen laughed. "Brian used to drive limousines in Washington D.C."

"Two senators I worked for," he called as he pulled out, "not to mention a congressman and a few lobbyists. And I'll say this in all honesty, I had planned never to drive again before I met Eleanor."

"Why? Anna asked.

"Mostly they treated me like garbage. Eleanor treated me great."

"How long did you drive her?" Austin asked.

"Ten years."

"Tell them what you told me the other day," Karen said, sipping Champagne.

Brian laughed, glanced at them in the rearview mirror. "I worked for Democrats and Republicans—and you have to understand, in China, where my parents were born, we don't exactly have political parties like you do here. Anyway, I worked for Democrats and Republicans, and they were both jerks. At least to me." He laughed. "Sign me up for Rich Karen political party."

Karen laughed loudly. Too loudly. Austin thought that between the Champagne and the interaction with Brian, she was doing her best to avoid the recent horrors that had befallen her family. At that moment, Junior was on his way to the morgue to make a formal ID of Kyon's body. "Rich Karen Party," she said to herself, refilling her glass.

Austin didn't get it.

Anna noticed the look on his face. "You'll have to explain," she said to Karen. "He's never seen the internet."

"You don't know what a 'Karen' is?" Karen asked.

Austin shrugged.

"It's a thing online," Brian said. "My kids explained it to me once when my wife was complaining that we couldn't bring our own food into a movie theater."

"It's a middle-aged lady like me," Karen said, "who is entitled and complains to service workers like waiters—"

"Or limo drivers," Brian chimed in.

"And has no self awareness about it," Anna added. "There are whole websites dedicated to the meme online. 'Karen's Gone

Wild' and stuff like that. People capture videos of them complaining and post them online."

Austin shook his head. "That sounds really mean. So everyone with the name 'Karen' is just painted with this insult or meme or whatever it is?"

Karen smiled. "It's all in good fun. Millennials need Baby Boomer targets because we have most of the money."

Austin looked out the window as the limo eased up a steep hill, passing a park. He felt better than ever about his decision to avoid the internet as much as possible.

Karen relaxed into her seat, her eyes half-closed. It appeared as though the Champagne was taking effect. Austin wondered if she might have popped a pill or two as well.

"There's something I want to ask you," Anna said.

Karen closed her eyes all the way. "Go for it. Not like today can get any worse."

"A few days ago you said that you had stayed over that night to talk to your mom about a small financial issue."

She opened her left eye slightly. "Doesn't have anything to do with Mack, or her death. Really, it was a tiny thing. I don't even know why I mentioned it."

Brian half-turned, winking at them. "Don't be such a Karen, Karen."

"That's not being a Karen," Karen said. Her words had grown a little loose.

Anna said, "Karen, can we get back to—"

"Money," Karen said, waving a hand dismissively. "It was about money she was sending to a charity."

"What charity?" Anna asked.

"East Saigon Farmers Alliance."

Austin froze. East Saigon. In *Vietnam*. Anna was already tapping on her phone.

"As she aged," Karen continued, her words sloppy but still coherent, "mother asked me to take a closer look at the family finances. Each year I checked out all the charities we gave to, you see. You have to remember that, in addition to all of the large, yearly donations, mother gave to dozens of smaller organizations around the world. Thirty thousand here, ten thousand there."

Anna didn't look up from her phone. "So what was so special about the East Saigon Farmers Alliance?"

"Nothing, at first. Mother had been giving to them for decades, long before I got involved in the family finances. I just wanted to question why we gave a quarter million a year to a small non-profit farming cooperative halfway around the world."

Anna handed her phone to Austin. "A quarter million a year, you say?"

Karen waved her hand again, as though she was done with the conversation. "Brian, dear, please wake me up when we reach the bank."

Anna's phone was open to a simple website with a logo at the top in bright green:

East Saigon Farmers Alliance: Sustainable Farming From Our Hearts to Your Table

He scrolled down, scanning the text. It was only a few paragraphs, and there were no links or additional pages anywhere on the site.

Anna eyed Karen, who'd gone still, and leaned in to whisper in Austin's ear. "I did a report a few years back on how rich people use fake charities to hide money away. In some cases, they set up charitable organizations in other countries with looser laws, then donate the money through a U.S. shell corporation to essentially hide it overseas."

Austin nodded. He didn't want to say it out loud because he wasn't sure Karen was asleep. But this web page was a lot like the Vietnamese restaurant they'd been to. Well beyond minimalist. Not the kind of place you donate a quarter million dollars a year to. Austin had no doubt the donations were being used to hide something nefarious.

And he thought he might know what that was.

They made it to the bank five minutes before it closed.

Anna walked arm in arm with Karen to keep her steady. If she appeared to be under too much duress, the bank might not give her access to her own vault. Luckily, the guard recognized her right away and led them into the room containing the lock box. Anna and Austin were not allowed to enter, so they waited in the lobby.

"Being in a bank at night is strange," Anna said.

Austin nodded. "Are you thinking what I'm thinking?"

Anna stared at him and put a single fingertip dramatically to her temple. "Oh no!"

"What?"

"Turns out I'm not psychic. What are you thinking?"

Austin frowned. "The tiny charity in Vietnam receiving huge money. John not committing suicide, the least inviting Vietnamese restaurant on earth, with zero customers, that happens to serve amazing food."

"That's why you wanted Samantha to run facial recognition AI on the crime scene image?"

"I don't know how that software works, but can't they run two photos against each other to tell if they match?"

"Sure," Anna said. "That software has been around for a decade, at least. The crime scene photo, though... it's old, low resolution, and only a profile view. Plus, it looked enough like John Johnson for me."

Footsteps echoed through the large, empty, bank, heels striking marble as Karen emerged with the security guard. In her arms she held a small stack of diaries.

Back at the limo, Karen handed them each half of the diaries, all the same style as the ones Anna had been given by Eleanor. Blue cloth marked with a range of dates on the front.

"I'm gonna pass out," Karen said. "Took half an Ambien before we left. Wake me up when... well, never. Just let me sleep."

Austin flicked on the overhead light as Anna opened a diary.

CHAPTER THIRTY-EIGHT

"WHERE TO?" Brian called.

"Can you just drive around a little?" Austin asked. "We're not sure yet."

"Driving around is my specialty. Just press that black button if you need anything." He rolled up the divider.

Anna flipped a few pages. "Found it. The week John died."

As Brian drove through downtown Seattle, the car's interior fell in and out of shadow as the limo passed under street lamps and passed neon signs.

Anna held the diary on her lap and they read together.

January 17, 1971

Today, John took his final trip home. He won't be returning.

Sometimes I reflect back on the times we had together. I wonder, do I regret marrying a man I wasn't attracted to, a man I didn't love? Or did I love him? I've asked myself this question a hundred times and, now that he's gone, I have to admit, I never did.

He was fun, like a cool brother. And marrying him pissed off my family, which I'm beginning to think was part of the point.

But I never loved him.

Now that John is gone I can do whatever I want.

Only three people know. Only three people can ever know. John himself, Mack, and me.

While he was still here, John told me that Mack would be forever loyal. That it's a part of his personality, like a dog. I hope that's the case, and I believe it is.

I do not like how this had to happen. I wish that Simon had not been part of this, but there was no other way.

It's a sad world we live in where no one will miss a farmhand, where the police will look no further because he has no one to miss him, but I did not make the world.

Here I am, lying, even to my diary.

The truth is, I'm devastated Simon had to die. I did not love him either, but I enjoyed him. He was good to me. John said I did it just to get back at him, but there was more to it than that.

It's all over now. John is gone, and he'll never return.

All I can do is try to make amends for all he did, all that I did.

And never speak of it again.

CHAPTER THIRTY-NINE

AUSTIN FLICKED off the overhead light as Anna closed the diary.

"I'm so confused," Anna said. "It reads like a confession of murder, and yet..."

"Any idea who Simon is?"

"Sounds like she had an affair with him, but I don't think his name has come up in any of the other diary entries I read."

Austin considered this. "Hungry?"

"Kinda. Why?"

"How about some Vietnamese food?"

"You're not suggesting we go back to—"

"The food *was* delicious."

Anna closed the diary. "But why there?"

"I have a feeling about something, and..." Austin tapped on the divider. "Karen seems to be fast asleep back here. Any chance we could drop her off, then you could take us somewhere else?"

"I'm not asleep," Karen mumbled, her first words in a long time. She yawned. "Take me to my mother's house, then take these two wherever they want to go." She sounded like her mouth had been stuffed with wet marbles. "I'm generous, like my mother. I'm no *Karen*."

They rode in silence as Anna flipped through the diary, reading by the light of her cellphone.

Austin puzzled over the entries they'd already read. He couldn't shake the thought that the dead man in the photograph wasn't John Johnson at all. He kept coming back to the white socks worn by the dead man in the crime scene photo. Perhaps someone else had been killed, then dressed in one of Johnson's fancy suits, but the socks had been overlooked. And if he was right about that, perhaps it was the 'Simon' Eleanor had mentioned. But if that was true, where was John?

As they pulled up to the mansion, Austin's phone rang.

"Austin, it's Samantha."

"Hold on a sec."

Karen was trying to gain her footing after stepping out of the car. Brian hopped out of the driver's seat and began leading her up the walkway to the house. Austin tapped the phone to put it on speaker.

"Samantha, I'm here with Anna."

"Hi Anna."

"Tell me you found something interesting." Austin held his breath.

"I ran three different AIs on the photograph from the newspaper. It's old, black and white, and not especially high res. And things are always more difficult when you don't have a full-on face. When you only have a profile view, these things are less accurate. But the nose and jawline are usually enough to provide key match indicators."

Anna looked at Austin and mouthed, "What is she talking about?"

Austin shrugged.

"Okay, I can tell I'm losing you. Here's the point. I ran that photo against five others that we are sure are John Johnson. The dead guy in the picture is someone else."

"Any idea who?" Anna asked.

"None. I ran his photo against various databases and came up with nothing. Looks like Johnson, but it ain't him. Jawline in particular."

Brian returned to the driver's seat. "Karen made me promise, not a scratch. Her mom had a thing about pets, she's got a thing about this limo."

"Little Huế restaurant," Austin said, before rolling up the divider. He didn't want Brian to know what they'd discovered. Someone would have to break the information to Karen and her family, and Austin thought he owed it to them to do it himself.

"There's more," Samantha said. "Check your email. I ran the known images of Johnson into a composite image creator, then aged him up. I sent you three different versions of what he might look like now."

Austin hadn't asked her to do that, but he was glad she had. "You're amazing, Samantha."

"Those programs are fun as hell. I can make him bald or bearded, skinny or fat, tan or pale. It shoots out dozens of different versions. It would have crashed your inbox if I sent them all."

"Did you run those aged-up photos against—"

"Already did. Nothing. We've got the LightningClick system that even matches against existing social media databases. If there's a photograph of an adult John Johnson on the internet, he's likely done things to change his appearance."

Austin thanked her and they hung up.

"Or it's possible he's been hiding out in a foreign country," Anna said, "avoiding photographs altogether."

"A country like Vietnam," Austin agreed.

"Secrets," Anna said. "Reporters always have double loyalties. On the one hand, they want to report everything they know in their paper, magazine, or TV show. Sometimes on Twitter. On the other hand, they like to hold back nuggets so they can use it to sell books later. Eleanor Johnson was certainly holding back a bombshell for her memoir."

Austin nodded. "You think she was going to tell you?"

Anna considered this. "My guess is that she was easing me into it. There's a reason certain diaries were in a lock box. You can tell from that last diary entry that she felt bad about what happened. Assuming Simon is the dead guy in the picture, she lived with the secret that John was alive and... wait, why're we going to Little Huê?"

Austin had come up with a theory that explained everything. "If you were John Johnson, alive and well when the whole world thought you were dead, and only two people from your old life knew you were alive—Eleanor and Mack—and if your image had been rehabilitated because of your wife's efforts..."

Anna snapped. "He's got libraries named after him, public parks..."

"Exactly. You're older now...he'd been in his late seventies or so. And all this time you're living in Vietnam, reading the Seattle papers, watching your kids grow up, watching your wife become a beloved member of Seattle high society."

"What *passes* for high society," Anna interjected, "but go on."

"Anyway, then you hear that your darling former wife is working on a memoir, that she's planning to come clean about everything—"

"But how could he have heard that?" Anna asked.

"Mack. He obviously had a bond with John. And the diary says that he was the only other one who knew. So John and Mack could have been in touch all along."

"So Mack tells John that Eleanor is writing a memoir. That she's going to come clean."

Brian rolled down the divider a crack. "Almost there. Shall I just drop you out front?"

Austin nodded. "Thanks."

Anna touched his shoulder. "But how could he convince Mack to kill Eleanor? I get that Mack might be loyal, that they have a *bond forged in war*, or whatever men say, but he worked for her for fifty years."

"But remember what Mack said? He said he was doing it for the family. I think, in his mind, he wasn't only protecting John, but the kids. If Eleanor came clean about John being alive, that leads to the dead guy in the picture. Simon. Who was he? Who killed him? Not to mention, John was being investigated for another murder already, right before he died. No statute of limitations on murder. It could have ruined the family."

Anna seemed skeptical. "Okay, but..."

"There's something else. Remember the photo of Mack's granddaughter?"

"In Vietnam. John may have threatened Mack? Threatened her?"

"It's a theory."

The limo slowed and Austin rolled down the window. The restaurant was deserted except for a Black Suburban, idling out front. Austin pointed. "And now we know who's been following us, too."

He rolled down the divider. "Brian, any chance we could hang out here for a bit?"

CHAPTER FORTY

PULLING OUT HIS PHONE, Austin kept his eyes on the Suburban.

Opening his email, he found the message from Samantha and handed it to Anna. "Check out the images. Maybe we'll get lucky and you'll recognize him."

"How would I recognize him?"

Austin considered this. "I don't know. Figured you were doing research into Eleanor, her businesses and charities and all that. Maybe he snuck back into the U.S., maybe she flew over to Vietnam and..."

"The donations. East Saigon Farmers Alliance."

It hadn't made sense to Austin why John would agree to leave his life, his family, his home country. But now it did. "He was likely going to jail if he stayed in the United States."

"And what's better," Anna asked, "jail in the U.S. or living it up in Vietnam on the money your former wife sends to a phony charity for the rest of your life?"

Austin rolled down the divider and moved to the seat closest to it.

Brian looked up from his phone.

"Brian, can I trust you?"

"Sure you can."

"I mean, I'm going to tell you a few things and I don't want you to tell any member of Karen's family, or Karen herself. Not because they don't get to know, but I need to be the one to tell them."

Brian nodded, thinking. "Okay, but if it's anything that puts her in danger..."

"It's not," Austin said. "But it may get a little dicey. See that restaurant?"

Brian rolled down his window. "Barely. Not much of a street presence, huh?"

"I believe Mack is being held there by a gang of criminals."

"I worked in Washington, D.C." Brian smiled. "I'm used to criminals."

Austin liked this guy. Eyes dancing from the door of Little Huế to the SUV, he explained the situation to Brian. He nodded along as though it was perfectly normal that his boss's father—presumed dead for fifty years—was alive and well and possibly running a criminal enterprise from a hole-in-the-wall Vietnamese restaurant.

Next, Austin took his phone back from Anna and called Chief Jackson. The call went straight to voicemail, so he began tapping a text instead.

He was about to send the text when his phone rang.

"Austin," she barked, "you called me?"

"Hello, Chief Jackson. I have some news."

"So do I."

He paused awkwardly, eyes still on the idling Suburban. "Um, how about you go first?"

"I'm busy, New York, running a city. Why did you call me?"

"We think John Johnson is alive. They faked his death."

There was a long pause.

Austin put the call on speaker. "Chief Jackson, are you still there?"

"I'm here, just trying to figure out how much to tell you."

Austin glanced at Anna, who raised an eyebrow. "Tell me about what?"

Jackson sighed. "Ridley said I can trust you, so I will. First, how did you find out Johnson was still alive?"

"Find out? So you *knew*?"

"My people figured it out earlier today."

"Facial recognition artificial intelligence software. One of Ridley's tech people ran the photo from the crime scene. Definitely looks like him, but that's not his body. I assume you found out the same way?"

"Not at all," Jackson said. "I can't tell you everything. But let's just say that my department has been looking into a fentanyl smuggling ring in Seattle for a year now. We knew it was coming through China's southern border into Vietnam and from Vietnam into the Port of Seattle. Vietnamese import company owned by a man named Min Hui who lives in Vietnam. We're not talking about Pablo Escobar here, but it's like a mini Vietnamese drug cartel, right here in Seattle. Long story short, my officers picked up a guy last week on an unrelated matter. Told us he could get us Min Hui. That Min Hui was in town right now. He told us that John Johnson—dead for fifty years—*was* Min Hui. He's been smuggling fentanyl into my city for years. Before that, heroin. Before that, opium. All the way back to the seventies."

Austin swallowed hard. The Suburban idling across the street had suddenly become a bit more intimidating.

"We believe that it was his people who picked up Mack, and it's likely he had some hand in Eleanor's death."

"He did," Austin said, "and..." He trailed off as the driver's door of the Suburban swung open. A man in a black suit got out and walked slowly around to the rear and opened the door. Leaving it open, he got back in the front.

"What we don't know," Jackson said, "is where the hell he is. Min Hui. John Johnson."

"I might be able to help you there. I'm texting you an address."

Austin ended the call and began tapping out the name and address of the restaurant.

"Austin," Anna said, "remember how you hoped I might recognize some of the aged-up images of John Johnson that Samantha sent?"

Austin typed slowly. His thumbs weren't any larger than normal, but he'd never adjusted to typing on such a tiny screen. "Yeah," he said, sending the text.

"Well, look up. He just walked out of the restaurant."

CHAPTER FORTY-ONE

BY THE TIME Austin looked up, all he saw was a bald head disappearing into the Suburban. He reached for the door.

"Don't," Anna said.

Before he could respond, another Suburban pulled up behind the first. This one was silver, with the same tinted windows as the first. Mack emerged from the restaurant, two men behind him, each gripping one of his arms. They shoved him into the back seat of the silver Suburban.

"Wait here," Austin said, swinging open the door.

He jogged across the street, cutting off the black Suburban before it could pull away. It came to an abrupt stop a few inches from his chest. Through the windshield, he saw the two men he'd seen before. They looked at him quizzically, like they'd just spotted some rare animal in the jungle.

Hands pressed into the warm hood, Austin stood for what seemed like forever. Likely it was only five seconds. If that had been John Johnson getting into the back seat, there was no way he was letting him get away before Jackson and the SPD arrived.

The driver turned slightly, listening, it appeared, to someone speaking to him from the back seat.

Then the rear window rolled down.

Austin eased around the side of the SUV, where he was greeted by the tanned face of John Johnson.

At least, that's what he assumed. John's nose had been flat and wide, but this man had a sharp, bony nose like something out of a cartoon. Likely a poor cosmetic surgery done soon after his disappearance. John had been fairly pale, typical in the Pacific Northwest. This man was deeply tanned. And even in the skinnier versions of the aged-up images Samantha had created, Johnson wasn't this lean. His face looked like it had been chiseled out of granite and he appeared ten years younger than he was.

"Mr. Austin," he said, his voice carrying that strange accent of an American who'd spent decades living abroad. It was as though English had become his second language and, when speaking it, his voice sometimes reverted back to the patterns he'd learned as a child, but sometimes took on the tones and patterns of Vietnamese.

"Min Hui," Austin said.

He didn't flinch. "Please, call me John. I'm curious, though, how did you know my name?"

"How did you know mine?" Austin asked.

"You've been meddling in my affairs for a week now." He looked Austin up and down. "I don't know if you're carrying a weapon, Mr. Austin. But I assure you that my men are. I could have had them run you over, but you're smart enough to know not to attack a man with five armed guards."

Austin didn't watch a lot of movies, but from time to time he enjoyed an action flick in which a single cop or military man took out an entire armed gang. He enjoyed them because they were fantasy, without much connection to real life. Sure he had his weapon concealed under his jacket, but at this moment the best thing he could do was stall long enough for the SPD to arrive.

"Let Mack go," he said.

Johnson smiled. "What makes you think he doesn't want to be here?"

"I saw your men shove him into the SUV. My guess is that you forced him to kill Eleanor, blackmailed him. Threatened his granddaughter."

"You know less than you think."

"Am I wrong?"

Johnson didn't reply. Instead, he scratched his boney chin, as though deep in thought. "I have heard that you are a dogged detective, Mr. Austin. So let me give you a piece of advice. You might want to spend less time meddling in matters that don't concern you, and more time managing your own affairs."

This caught him off guard. *What the hell was he talking about?*

Johnson read the look on his face, which he'd tried to conceal. "Your wife," Johnson said. "Fiona. I would think that a detective as good as you would be working day and night to find out what happened to her."

Austin smelled hot tar. It filtered down into his mouth, as though his face were being pressed into fresh blacktop on a hundred-degree day in Virginia. It was pure hatred. "What the hell are you talking about?"

"Oh don't be so upset," Johnson said. "I promise I had nothing to do with it, personally. But word gets around. An up-and-coming DA doesn't get killed without people wondering who did it. People on your side of the fence, and mine."

Austin shoved his hands through the window and grabbed the lapel of Johnson's tan linen suit. An instant later, the guard sitting next to him pulled a .45 out of his belt and pointed it at Austin's head.

Johnson laughed, "We both know you're not going to do anything. Lucky for you, I abhor violence of any kind."

Austin glanced at the man with the gun, who did not appear to share Johnson's aversion to violence. Austin couldn't be sure, but the scars on his cheeks and the scowl on his lips made Austin think he was the kind of guy who'd pull the trigger with glee.

Austin let go of Johnson's lapel, eased back onto the side-walk. He was dizzy, close to passing out. He wobbled backwards, steadying himself on a street sign.

Johnson's window raised slowly, leaving Austin staring at his own reflection in the glass. He barely recognized himself. Hearing his wife's name on the lips of a drug dealer who'd been presumed dead for fifty years had shaken him in a way he didn't know possible.

The black Suburban pulled away. The silver one followed.

CHAPTER FORTY-TWO

AUSTIN CAME to his senses and bolted across the street. Anna swung open the door as he reached the limo.

"Brian," Austin said, slamming the door, "you ever been in a chase?"

Brian ran a hand through his whiter-than-white hair. "No, but I'm not opposed to the idea."

"Then let's go."

"Those the bastards that killed Eleanor?" Brian asked.

"They are," Austin said.

The limo lurched forward as Brian peeled out and took a sharp turn, following the path of the Suburbans.

Austin said, "I think Mack is more of a hostage than anything."

"You look shaken," Anna said. "What happened?"

Austin didn't want to tell her what Johnson had said about Fiona. Half of him wasn't sure what it meant, the other half didn't believe it had happened.

"I'll tell you later," he said. "For now, call Jackson, tell her where we are and describe the vehicles we're after. This is not something we're equipped to handle."

"They were armed?" Anna asked as she pulled out her phone.

"Heavily. Put it on speaker when you get her."

Brian was weaving in and out of traffic deftly, especially considering that he was driving a limo. He pointed. "That's them, right?"

The top of the silver Suburban was visible above the cars ahead.

"Yeah," Austin said. "Don't get too close. A few cars back is fine. Let's just see what they do."

Jackson answered Anna's call. "Chief Jackson, it's Anna Downey. I'm here with your favorite former detective."

"What is it?"

"Suspects have left the restaurant and are headed northwest, out of Little Saigon toward downtown. John Johnson is in a black Chevy Suburban. Mack is in a silver Suburban that's tailing them."

"We just pulled onto Alaskan Way," Brian called from the front seat.

"Hold on," Jackson said. Her voice muffled, Austin could hear her speaking to someone else, likely calling in the location of the Suburban to nearby patrol. "What else?" she asked.

"Is that for me?" Austin asked.

"Yes, talk!"

"I believe Johnson blackmailed Mack into killing Eleanor."

"Save the story," Jackson said, "what about the men in the vehicles? Any more on them?"

Austin cursed under his breath. He'd been so distracted by Johnson's mention of Fiona, he hadn't memorized the position of each of Johnson's men. "They're heavily armed, I believe. Safe to say two or three thugs in each vehicle."

"We're on it," Jackson said. "And, for the love of God, I shouldn't have to say this, but I know I do: *do not* approach them. Do not do *anything*. If you cause a shootout in my downtown..."

"We're about four cars behind the second SUV. I don't have a license plate number but—"

"Don't get any closer. I've got people on the way. And call me back if they turn off Alaskan Way."

Austin ended the call. Through the front windshield he could make out the silver Suburban. And, every once in a while, he saw the black one carrying Johnson peek out in front of it. They were not speeding, not driving aggressively. Simply heading north along Alaskan Way as though they were heading downtown, or possibly to the ferry terminal.

Brian asked, "I should just keep following?"

"Yeah," Austin said.

He glanced at Austin in the rearview mirror. "You said they were armed?"

"Hope that's not a problem."

Brian considered this for a moment. "You sure they killed Eleanor?"

"Sure."

"Then nah, it's not a problem. Low speed chase I can handle. Only ever been in one high-speed situation, and that time the roles were reversed." He changed lanes to pass a truck that had temporarily blocked their view of the Suburbans. "Funny story. The Senator I was working for was having an affair. Couple of them, actually. Papers found out and the paparazzi were after him day and night. Not that I condone the affairs, but I don't give a damn who a politician sleeps with. Long story short, I led a high-speed chase through D.C. with a pack of journalists on my tail."

Anna laughed. "Did you win? I mean, did they get the photos they were after?"

"Hell yeah I won."

"There," Austin said, pointing. Two cars had pulled between them and the Suburbans. Austin could tell they were unmarked police cars from the multiple radio antennas and special, numbers-only license plates.

"Why aren't they blaring sirens?" Anna asked.

"Likely waiting for backup. Maybe waiting to get to a more secure spot, less foot traffic."

"Stadiums are ahead," Anna said. "No football or baseball tonight. Kind of a dead, post-industrial neighborhood when there are no games. Now might not be a bad time."

Austin agreed. The hulking frame of CenturyLink Field, home of the Seattle Seahawks and venue for the city's biggest concerts, loomed before them, but the wide streets were dark. The silver Suburban trailed the black one by about forty feet and the two unmarked police cars tailed it.

The car directly behind the silver SUV lit up suddenly, not with the typical light on the top of the car, but hidden blue and white flashers on the front.

"They don't have enough people," Austin said. "Damn. Unless they have a few more cars fronting them..."

"They don't," Brian said. "I can see. Unless they're fronting them from a few blocks ahead, which is impossible."

The Suburbans didn't adjust course. Didn't speed up. And they definitely didn't slow down.

They passed the stadiums and, a block later, entered the more touristy section of Seattle, only about half a mile from the ferry and the waterfront.

Traffic was still light, but the wide streets of the industrial area had given way to narrower ones. Ahead, the beginnings of ferry traffic was starting to appear. Both police cars now flashed their lights, but the Suburbans continued ahead.

"This is going to end badly," Austin said.

"What is the protocol in a situation like this?" Anna asked.

He didn't have time to answer. The silver Suburban reached the section of backed up traffic and took a sudden left turn down an alley that headed toward the water. It appeared as though the black Suburban had already made the same turn.

The police cars followed, lights reflecting off the alley walls.

"Follow," Austin said.

Brian was already on it. He floored it into the alley and,

making a wide right turn, skidded out of it. They'd fallen behind the smaller cars, but they were still in sight.

"We're about to run into the ferry line," Anna said. "And foot traffic. This is about to get bad."

It was already getting bad. Under the glow of the street lights, Austin saw the black Suburban with the silver one right behind it. They were both slowing as they approached a long line of cars, but instead of stopping, they pulled to the left onto a sidewalk, then weaved through a section of unfinished sidewalk blocked off by orange tape.

The two police cars followed.

"Don't follow," Austin said. "The limo won't make that—"

Brian already knew, but instead of giving up, he swerved to the right, into traffic heading the opposite direction. Horns blared and lights flashed, but the cars heading straight for them made it over and out of the way.

Austin watched the Suburbans.

Still weaving through construction vehicles and blasting over traffic cones, they made it past the ferry terminal. Traffic thinned and the lead Suburban peeled back onto the main road.

Just as the silver one did the same, the police car sped up, passed the Suburban, and cut in at a sharp angle to block it. The Suburban swerved, but clipped the police car, spinning out and colliding with a giant concrete pillar head on. The police car slammed on its brakes and swerved to avoid it, causing the trailing car to rear end it.

Now on the open road, the lead Suburban was on its own.

Brian veered into the far right lane, then shot across an intersection. Crossing the center divider, he peeled into the left lane again, only a hundred yards behind the black Suburban.

Austin turned to peer out the rear windshield at the wreck. As they sped away from the scene, Austin thought he saw Mack's head of white hair emerging from the crashed Suburban, hands in the air as he walked slowly toward the officers.

CHAPTER FORTY-THREE

"CAN YOU CATCH IT?" Austin asked.

"*Should* he catch it?" Anna interjected, before Brian could answer.

Brian glanced at them in the rearview mirror. "At times like this, I consider what my employer would want me to do. Since she's passed out back home, I don't think it's the right time to call her. Unless I have this wrong, her father is in that Suburban. The one she thought was dead her whole life."

"And it turns out," Anna added, "he's been running drugs through Pike Place Market for decades. Not to mention the fact that he ordered the family's beloved chef to murder her mother."

Brian pressed the gas, and the limo lurched forward.

Austin nodded down at Anna's phone, but she was already on it. Jackson picked up right away.

"Before you say anything," Anna said, hurriedly, "we had nothing to do with the crash."

"What crash?" Jackson barked.

"Nevermind that," Austin said. "John Johnson is now heading north on Alaskan way. A few blocks past the ferries."

"On it," Jackson said before ending the call.

Brian said, "What should I do?"

"Just stay with them," Austin said. "Don't do anything crazy. Jackson will send backup. Let's just keep them in our sights."

For three blocks Brian stayed about fifty yards back, maneuvering past the smattering of cars and running red lights when needed to keep up with the Suburban.

At a traffic light, the Suburban suddenly veered left, across the train tracks and toward the water.

"There's nothing down there," Anna said. "Where the hell could they be going?"

They crossed the tracks, then followed the Suburban along a narrow frontage road that ran parallel with the water.

"The Miller Docks," Anna said suddenly.

"What's that?"

"Private marina down here. It's... complicated. Just a few boats but with murky legal status."

"You think Johnson could have a slip here?"

"Seems like they'd be headed this way for a reason," Anna said.

"If they get to the boat..." Brian said.

He didn't need to finish the thought. Austin's mind raced. "How far ahead is the marina?"

Anna said, "Mile, maybe."

Austin swallowed hard. "If Chief Jackson asks, none of what is about to happen ever happened."

"I don't like the sound of that," Brian said. "I promised Karen, not a scratch."

"Don't worry," Austin said, pulling out his gun. "This works and it won't be *your* vehicle that gets scratched. Shift as far as you can to the left side of the road."

Austin rolled down the window as Brian veered slowly to the left. They were only doing about thirty miles an hour on the curvy, narrow road that hugged the shape of the bay, but the cold wind blew his hair back and stung his eyes. A heavy fog hung over the water and shrouded the road in gray mist. There were no streetlights, but he could make out the taillights of the

Suburban about forty yards ahead. "Now, speed up, get as close as you can."

Brian hit the gas.

"You sure you want to do this?" Anna asked.

Austin ignored the question. Knee pressed into the seat, he extended his arms and shoulders out the window, gun raised. "Step on it!" he shouted.

Brian slammed the gas, but they hit a pothole as they rounded a curve. Austin rocked up, his back striking the ceiling as he was almost thrown out the window. Anna grabbed his leg.

The Suburban had slowed as the curves in the road increased. This was his chance.

Steadying himself, Austin aimed at the left rear tire. He fired a single shot. It missed, striking the road. They took another curve, then another, the Suburban moving in and out of view as the fog grew more and less dense.

Finally, they emerged onto a long straightaway.

"That's the entry gate," Anna called.

Austin had already seen it. It was a tall chain link fence that appeared to have no guard. But it did have a heavy gate, most likely a key fob entry, like many small marinas used.

The Suburban had accelerated and was over seventy-five yards away. Austin aimed again and fired.

Almost instantly, the Suburban veered right as the left rear tire was punctured. It slowed, but didn't stop.

"Speed up," he shouted to Brian.

They were gaining on the Suburban now and Austin fired again, this time taking out the right rear tire. Metal scraped against concrete and the Suburban skidded out, jutting left as though the driver had overcorrected. It careened down the embankment toward the water, crashing into a ditch.

"Stop!" Austin shouted, pulling his upper half back into the limo.

"We're close," Anna said, "why—"

"Stop!"

Brian slammed on the brakes.

"You two stay here. They are armed. I'm the only one with a gun. Call Jackson again. Find out where the hell they are. Do not leave this limo."

He leapt out and bolted at a full sprint toward the wrecked Suburban. Smoke rose out of the ditch, mingling with the fog and blanketing the road.

Best case scenario, everyone had been knocked out. Alive but incapacitated. He didn't let himself imagine another scenario.

He stopped on the road above the ditch. Four feet below, the Suburban was smashed into a bank of dirt. The front windshield had blown out, but overall the thing had done pretty well in the crash.

He saw movement.

John Johnson had made it out of the back seat and was already thirty yards away, jogging toward a side gate at the marina.

Austin was ready to take off after him, but just as he stepped down the embankment, another figure emerged from the Suburban. The guard with the scarred cheeks and perpetual scowl.

Fortunately, the man's back was to Austin and his first move was to follow Johnson. Austin charged down the low hill, shoulder lowered, and connected with the man's lower back.

They toppled face first into the dirt, but the man swung an elbow, connecting with Austin's jaw, which released a loud *crack*. Then the man sprung up, more quickly than he should have been able, given the blow Austin had just delivered. The man reached for his gun, but it wasn't there. His scowl fell away for the first time, replaced with a confused frown.

"Must have fallen out in the crash," Austin said, looking up from the ground. "That's the problem with storing a firearm improperly. A real holster and I'd be dead right now. Store it in your waist like in the movies and, well..." Austin pulled out his gun and raised it slowly. "Hands on your head."

The man shot a look into the back seat, but obeyed.

Austin cast a quick glance into the driver's seat. The driver appeared to have passed out in the crash. Standing, gun still on the man, he popped the trunk. In the storage area, he found duct tape, which he used to bind the guard's wrists. He used the rest of the roll to secure him to the bumper. Next he found the man's .45, emptied the magazine, and shoved the weapon in the pocket of his jeans.

Without another word, he took off in the direction of the marina.

CHAPTER FORTY-FOUR

JOHNSON HAD ALREADY MADE it through a side gate and into the dark open area of the marina. He was heading for the water, where a single dock ran about a hundred yards into the bay, three or four small but fancy-looking boats on each side.

Reaching the gate, Austin skidded to a stop. Locked.

The chainlink fence surrounding the marina was at least ten feet high. He'd climbed higher, but that was when he was younger and in better shape.

Johnson disappeared into the shadows of a small building about a hundred yards from the dock.

Austin began climbing. To his surprise, he made easy progress, angling onto his back when he reached the top, his leather bomber jacket eating up the thin patch of barbed wire. Sliding down the other side, he landed hard, twisting his ankle and toppling to the ground.

As he stood, trying to keep all his weight on his left leg, he saw Johnson emerge around the other side of the building, heading for the dock.

Taking off as fast as he could, dragging his leg behind him, he gained on Johnson easily. Despite being in good shape for his age, Johnson still moved like a man in his late seventies. Johnson reached another gate. As he fumbled with his keys, Austin increased his speed.

Johnson turned when he heard footsteps and Austin's heavy breath, but he was too late. Austin connected with his ribcage shoulder first, smashing him into the gate.

With one deft motion, Austin turned him around, pressing his face into the fence and twisting both wrists behind him. Holding firm with one hand, he patted him down with the other. "I can't arrest you. But the people who can are on their way. It's over."

"I'm not armed. I told you I abhor violence."

"You don't seem to mind when others commit it on your behalf."

Johnson wriggled his arms, but it was useless.

Austin spun him around and Johnson went limp, sliding down the fence to sit on the ground.

Austin took a step back, eyes on Johnson's face, which was half shadowed and half lit by a single light that cut through the fog.

His first thought was to ask him about the man in the photograph. For fifty years, the world had believed John Johnson was dead, that he'd taken his own life. Not only was he alive and well, someone else was dead, someone who presumably had a family, had people missing him, wondering where he was. He should have asked about Simon, the farmhand Eleanor mentioned in her diary.

Instead, he heard himself asking. "What do you know about my wife?"

Johnson pulled his knees into his chest. His linen suit was wrinkled and dirty, but he still moved with the refinement and grace of a much younger man. He gave Austin a disconcerting look. Not a smile, but a knowing nod. "I don't know everything. But I know some things." He glanced back through the gate toward the dock. "You know what business I'm in, I presume."

"So does the SPD. Your game is over."

He nodded as though he already knew this. "Tell you what, Thomas Austin. I know people in New York, people you and Fiona spent your life trying to put behind bars. Let me go, let me walk through that gate to my boat, and I will deliver the ones who pulled the trigger. Within thirty days. You have my word."

Austin almost leapt forward and kicked him, but he stopped himself. The sound of Fiona's name coming from this man sickened him, angered him. But it was well beyond that. What bothered him most was that—despite everything—he was tempted.

"You're lying," Austin said. "Even if I'd consider that offer, which I wouldn't." He took another step back. "SPD will be here soon. I..." He trailed off, his head spinning.

"I don't know everything. You're too smart to believe me if I told you I know exactly what happened. But I think you know as well as I do that I could find out. But only if I'm free." Johnson scratched his chin. "One thing I can tell you is that factions of your beloved NYPD are deeply enmeshed with certain Southeast Asian purveyors of narcotics. That's how I heard about a DA who got taken out in the first place."

Austin shook his head, as though he could shake off any temptation. "Who was the dead man in the photograph?"

Johnson smiled.

"You were under investigation," Austin said. "You knew you were going away. So you killed someone who looked enough like you to pass—"

Johnson's laughter interrupted him. "You're a crummy detective, Thomas Austin."

Austin glared at him, his hardest New York glare, but the way Johnson looked up at him wiped it off his face.

"I killed Simon Lorie because he slept with my wife. It just so happened that he looked a little like me."

Austin stared down at him. As he did, he heard the faint sounds of sirens in the distance.

"Eleanor had secrets," Johnson said. "Have you ever considered the fact that your darling wife had secrets, too."

"Talk about your own screwed up life if you want. Don't talk about Fiona again."

"Ever consider the fact that maybe it was a lover who killed her? As a homicide detective, you know as well as anyone that most murders arise from domestic disputes. Maybe she'd been having an affair for years and finally broke it off, and that's what got her shot through her pretty little head."

Austin lunged for him, dropping to his knees and grabbing his lapel. "Shut up you sick bastard."

Johnson spat in his face.

Austin shoved a forearm into his throat and pressed him into the gate.

Through shallow half breaths, Johnson said, "I hear the sirens. When they get here, they're going to arrest you, too."

Austin heard movement behind him. Then a voice. "Let the old man go!" Grip still firm on Johnson's lapel, Austin turned.

A man stood behind him, half shadowed. Not one of Johnson's thugs. He was about Austin's size but younger, and he wore the gray uniform of a janitorial service, complete with a little patch on the left side of his chest.

"It's okay," Austin said. "I'm with the police."

The man glanced at Johnson, then back at Austin. Without another word, he pulled something from behind his back and swung violently at Austin's head. Austin ducked, but he was too late.

The butt end of a broom smashed his head and, for an instant, he went limp.

CHAPTER FORTY-FIVE

AUSTIN CAME to when he heard a gate slam. His vision was blurred and now his head hurt as much as his ankle. John Johnson was gone, but the man in the janitorial uniform stood over him. As Austin's vision adjusted, he saw that the man didn't look menacing. Instead, he looked almost surprised at what he'd done.

And yet, he held the thick broom handle like a baseball bat, as though he'd swing it again if necessary.

"Look Mr., I don't know who you are, but Mr. Min Hui is a member here and no one beats up one of our members on my watch."

Austin inched away, pressing his back against the fence. "His real name is John Johnson. He's a drug dealer. A murderer. He's going to escape."

"You were beating up an old man." He gripped the broom handle tighter.

"You hear those sirens?" Austin asked. "The police will be here in a few minutes."

"You said you were with them. Show me your badge."

"I'm a consultant."

"A... what?"

Austin put out both hands as he slid his back up the gate, standing shakily.

"Don't move any more," the man said. "Don't want to hit you again, but I will."

Austin had two choices. Try to fight this guy on a bad ankle, with his head ringing, or talk his way out of this. The guy was a janitor working the night shift and trying to be a good Samaritan. He'd seen Austin beating up an old guy who probably tipped this dude well. "Look, you know as well as I do that it's odd he's heading down the dock late at night, by himself. And you hear those sirens, right? Look in my eyes." He did. "I am a former NYPD detective. I'm armed, but I'm not pulling my weapon because I'm not here to shoot a guy who just thought he was protecting an old man." He hardened his look into the man's eyes. "Do you trust me?"

The man let the broom handle fall back slowly.

Austin pulled back his jacket, revealing his gun.

"You don't want me to pull this out, and I don't want to. Not on you. You're going to turn around, wait for the police, and tell them what happened. You're not going to get in any trouble for hitting me. You thought you were doing the right thing. Understand?"

He nodded again, eyes on Austin's gun.

"I am going to turn and climb over this fence now. You're not going to hit me again because you believe I'm telling the truth. You know how shady it is that an old man is heading for his boat late at night."

The man's face quivered slightly, but he didn't say anything.

Austin turned to climb over the fence. He heard movement and a metallic rattle. Turning quickly, ready to strike, Austin saw the man coming at him, but this time he held his keys.

A moment later, he'd let Austin through the gate.

Limping badly, pain coursing up from his ankle like hot daggers, Austin hobbled for the end of the dock, where faint red lights glowed in the foggy night. When he was fifty yards away, the lights began to move. Slowly, almost imperceptibly.

Johnson's boat.

Stuffing the pain down as far as he could, he picked up speed and reached the edge of the dock, launching himself onto the side of the boat, then rolling onto the deck.

It wasn't a huge boat, maybe thirty or forty feet, and Austin had never been a boat guy, so he didn't know what type it was. But he could tell a fancy boat from a cheap one. This one had gleaming dark wood railing contrasting with bright white side-boards and a glass-enclosed cabin, where Johnson stood, holding the steering wheel.

Austin pulled out his gun. With his free hand he opened the brass handle of the door to the cabin. "John Johnson. Turn off the boat."

Johnson turned, smiled. "I'm going to reach for the keys," he said, calmly.

Austin had the gun trained on his chest.

Johnson turned off the boat. Slowly, the sound of the engine died down.

The boat drifted. Silence engulfed them.

"You mind if I sit?" Johnson asked.

Austin nodded at the captain's chair.

Johnson sat. "Eleanor decided she was only into women after she got pregnant with John Junior. I was fine with that, at least I thought I was. I always had women on the side. I thought, so what if she does, too?"

"But then Simon Lorrie happened?"

"He worked on one of my farms. We did have legitimate farms and I'm proud of the fact that we supplied some of the finest fruits and vegetables to the people of Seattle at Pike Place."

"You also supplied them with heroin, opium, who knows what else?"

Johnson shrugged. "They had to get it somewhere. Simon

was from Idaho, maybe one of the Dakotas. All those states are the same to me. How would you have felt if Fiona was pregnant and decided she was into women, then you found out she was sleeping with an intern at the NYPD?"

"Don't say my wife's name again."

Johnson smiled.

"Did you kill him because he looked enough like you to pass off as you, or because he was having an affair with Eleanor?"

Johnson seemed to be considering this. "Both, I guess. Eleanor and I had a... *complicated* relationship. We were already planning my escape. I was just going to disappear. When I found out about Simon, I figured, why not slap her across the face and give myself extra cover? Stroke of genius. When a man disappears, people look for him. When he's dead..."

"And she sent you money every year through the charity?"

Johnson nodded. "Multiple charities. She had to. She was trying to be what her father wanted. A good girl. The benevolent rich lady, born into money and privilege but determined to help those less fortunate."

"She *did* help a lot of people who were less fortunate."

Johnson waved a hand dismissively. "All for show. In her heart, she was a cold bitch."

"And you found out about her memoir through Mack?"

He nodded. "He was the only other one who knew I was alive. Eleanor sent me money, but he kept me clued in about the family business. Only one I could really trust."

The sirens had grown louder and louder as they spoke and now Austin could see the flashing lights from the parking lot of the marina. Any moment he expected to hear boots jogging down the dock.

What he couldn't understand was why hearing about the memoir led Johnson to have Mack kill Eleanor. He still didn't believe that Eleanor was going to reveal all the family secrets. Doing so would have implicated her almost as much as him.

As though reading his thoughts, Johnson said, "The memoir

was going to be pitched as finally revealing the secrets of the past. Mack told me that one of the titles she was considering was *The Shadows of Pike Place*. She was going to write about how I had been involved in drugs, murder, how I'd helped grow Pike Place into Seattle's greatest attraction, but had profited from it, selling drugs in the shadows. But she was going to leave *herself* out of it. Wasn't going to admit that she knew about Simon. She planned to have that reporter cast her in the most positive light, to pin it all on me, and to make it look like she'd only recently found out about everything. Poor little rich girl taken advantage of by the scruffy low life." He shook his head. "Mack even told me that she fired the first memoir lady because she was too good of a reporter. The other guy, Brandon or whatever, he was willing to write any bullshit she fed him."

As he heard multiple sets of boots running down the dock, Austin almost smiled. Anna would be happy to hear that.

Johnson turned in the direction of the sound, his face growing angry, then afraid. He glanced around desperately. Austin watched him like a hawk. "Don't even think about running."

The footsteps grew louder.

"You know," Johnson said, "Whoever killed Fiona did us all a favor."

Austin stowed his weapon in the holster. The footsteps were right on top of them, along with shouts from the dock.

Austin stepped forward. He felt his foot and leg begin to move back. A swift kick to Johnson's exposed throat could end this man.

"Seattle Police. Anyone on this boat, hands up. We are boarding the vessel."

Through the cabin window he saw an officer reaching toward the boat with a long wooden pole. Slowly, he began pulling it back toward the dock. They'd only drifted about ten feet.

"Did us a favor," Johnson repeated. "The war on drugs is over. Your side lost. Fiona's side lost. Now they're making most of them legal after idiots like her spent years trying to put people like me behind bars for giving people what they wanted."

Austin let out a hot breath and knelt down, leaning in so his face was only inches from Johnson's. His voice was somewhere between rage and anguish. "Don't ever say her name again."

Johnson said nothing.

Austin stood and stepped away.

Boots landed on the ship's deck.

He couldn't allow himself to take vengeance on Johnson. But he'd be sure to testify at his trial. To make sure he ended up where he belonged. In prison until he was finally laid to rest in the grave that had been marked with his tombstone for the last fifty years.

CHAPTER FORTY-SIX

GREEN HILLS CEMETERY sat on a low hill just north of Seattle. It had been three days since John Johnson's arrest, long enough for Chief Jackson to obtain an order to dig up his grave. A grave they were quite certain contained the remains of a farmhand named Simon Lorie.

Austin stood next to Anna, watching the process from across the cemetery. A small dirt digger had been at it over half an hour, and appeared to be close to reaching the coffin.

Anna wasn't watching. She sat on the ground, typing furiously on a small tablet. As though sensing Austin's attention, she looked up, "Deadline. Promised my editor I'd have this in as soon as the photographs hit his desk."

"Photographs?"

Anna pointed to the other side of the cemetery, where a young woman in jeans and a black jacket snapped pictures of the exhumation. Anna smiled. "Sheriff Jackson gave me the exclusive. No other reporters allowed in the cemetery."

"How'd you get her to agree to that?'

Anna smiled. "Believe it or not, no blackmail was involved. She genuinely felt she owed me since I kinda cracked this case for her."

Austin raised an eyebrow as she tucked the tablet in her purse and stood.

"Okay," she admitted. "You may have helped a little."

"What did I tell you about running around like a drunken cowboy in my city?" It was Sheriff Jackson's voice. Austin turned and, thankfully, she was smiling.

She held out a hand to shake. "Seriously, good job, Austin."

"Thanks."

Suddenly her face grew stern. "Lucky break with that Suburban swerving off the road. You wouldn't happen to know anything about how the two rear tires got blown out, would you?"

Austin froze.

She looked from Austin to Anna, then back to Austin. "My theory is that they had bad luck with a couple nails left on the road." She was choosing her words carefully. "Tires were probably thin on tread to begin with."

"Sounds plausible," Anna said.

"Because I'm sure you know," Jackson continued, "that shooting out the tires of an SUV, while draped halfway out the window of a limousine would be well beyond reckless."

"Yes," Austin said carefully. "I am aware of that."

"Good," Jackson said. "Then the nails thing it is." She smiled warmly, shook his hand again, and headed over to the gravesite, where the digger was dropping another scoop of dirt into a pile between nearby headstones.

Austin spotted Jimmy, Lucy, and Ridley walking over from the parking lot and met them halfway across the cemetery. "Didn't expect to see you here."

"Didn't expect to be here," Ridley said, offering up his hand to shake. "Looks like you find your way into trouble on both sides of the Sound."

Austin smiled.

Jimmy patted him on the back. "Any chance you'll reconsider Ridley's offer? Join us as a consultant."

Austin shook his head. "Not unless you can promise me I'll have plenty of time to fish and come up with new recipes."

"No problem," Lucy said. "From here on out it'll be graffiti investigations and traffic violations."

"Lucy O-Liar," Jimmy said. "How can you not want to be in on the biggest cases in the county, in the state?"

Austin thought about this. Truth was, he *did* want to be in on them. No, that wasn't quite right. It was more like an addiction, something that may not be good for him, but he was drawn to anyway.

He'd moved across the country in hopes of outrunning it, but the cases seemed to find him. Still, he didn't know why, but he couldn't bring himself to sign on with Ridley and the Kitsap County Sheriff's department for anything more than a case-by-case basis.

Austin shrugged. "My kitchen renovation ends tomorrow. Spring season will be busy. But call me if you get any serial graffiti artists. Maybe I'll help you track them down."

CHAPTER FORTY-SEVEN

THEY STROLLED ACROSS THE CEMETERY, stopping about ten feet from Karen and Susan, who stood arm-in-arm, wearing matching designer outfits in jet black. John Junior was there as well, but he stood off to the side, away from the crowd.

Karen turned. "Oh, Anna, Austin. I didn't know you were here."

"We've been watching from the back," Anna said. "I know this must be hugely difficult for you."

Karen nodded toward a small gravestone. "Kyon. We buried him yesterday. No public service or anything. Junior wanted to keep it quiet."

"We didn't attend my father's funeral," Susan said. "At least, that's what mother told us. We're wearing black today for Kyon and because, even though our father is still alive, he's dead to us."

Karen said, "Chief Jackson told us everything."

Austin wanted to say something conciliatory, but nothing came to mind. These were mature women who, in the space of ten days, had seen their mother murdered by their chef, had their nephew take his own life while in police custody, and then found out their father was not only alive, but was one of the most-wanted drug dealers on the west coast. Sometimes silence was the only appropriate response.

Anna was less comfortable with the silence. She made a dramatic low bow. "You have redeemed the name of Karen forevermore."

Austin cringed. The gesture seemed wildly out of place.

But Karen smiled sadly. "Good to hear."

Anna said, "Getting us that diary, letting us use the limo. And Brian. Without all three, your father... I mean John, I mean... well, he would have gotten away."

"Thank you," Karen said.

"I will be sure to let the internet know that the name 'Karen' can no longer be used as a slur."

Karen smiled, but said nothing. She reached into her purse. "I was going to send this later today." She handed Anna an envelope. "The money. You earned it."

Anna took it, eyes down. "Thank you. I'm sorry this led where it did, I really am."

The digger revved its engine and Karen flinched like she'd been struck by a blow. "Chief Jackson told us about Simon Lorie. They confirmed what our father told you. He was a poor farmhand from Idaho. They even had pictures of him. Same age as our father. Looked enough like him."

Austin doubted Jackson had told them that Eleanor had been sleeping with him. He'd told Jackson everything, but he didn't think they needed to know that. At least not yet. Despite Eleanor's flaws, they'd suffered enough this week to have the memory of their mother tarnished even further.

"Apparently Simon Lorie disappeared without a trace," Susan said. "And no one bothered to look for him. There was a missing person report put in by another farmworker, but everyone just believed the dead guy was our father so no one suspected." She shook her head, squeezing her eyes tight as though she could block out the pain. "And mother identified him as such."

Karen reached out and squeezed Anna's arm, then walked

away in the direction of John Junior, followed by Susan, who now wept openly.

When they were gone, Austin turned to Anna. "I'm not sure that's how the internet works. I don't think you can tell people to stop making fun of the name 'Karen.'"

"Oh, like you're an expert."

"Never said I was an *expert* but..." He scratched his head. "I'm not sure they're going to listen."

"Well, I guess I can write an article about her and her name will be redeemed by virtue of the story I'll tell."

They walked along the edge of the graveyard. Austin could tell that, like him, Anna wanted to be there for the exhumation, but didn't want to get too close. The whole thing felt wrong, so deeply wrong, and yet, like a car crash, they couldn't look away.

"By the way," Austin said, "I wanted to tell you, I looked a little deeper into those paragraphs. The ones you thought might be non-fiction."

"Yeah, I was wondering." She looked away. "Honestly thought you might disappear from the Eleanor Johnson case to look into it."

"Is my obsession that obvious?"

"What reason could you have for not wanting to date a gorgeous, broke, brilliant single mom like myself, other than being obsessed with that case?"

"You're a little less broke than you were ten minutes ago."

Anna laughed. "That twenty-five grand is amazing, but it's already spent. College."

"Wait a second." There was something in the way she'd connected his unwillingness to go out with her to his obsession about Fiona's death. "Have you been talking to Pastor Johnson?"

She smiled. "Is it that obvious?"

"Last time I confide in that guy."

"Hey, he's a long-time source. And he didn't tell me anything I didn't already know, that *everyone* doesn't already know. You know how often it is that handsome men who aren't creepy as hell move into the county?"

"Do they keep statistics on that sort of thing?"

"Trust me," Anna said, "*I* do."

Austin didn't know why, but he heard himself saying, "Dinner at my place this weekend?"

Anna looked at him long and hard, a look somewhere between surprise and skepticism. "Okay," she said at last, "I guess I did promise you my famous meatballs."

CHAPTER FORTY-EIGHT

"YOU READY FOR AN ELEVATED IKEA MEAL?"

Austin stared at her blankly, watching from his kitchen table as she moved from the counter to the stove. It was their first date, and she'd brought a small cardboard box to carry the supplies needed for their dinner.

"Furniture store," she said. "They have a cafeteria with famous meatballs. Their signature thing. Like how Costco has cheap hot dogs."

Austin shrugged.

"In New York you probably ate a lot of Italian food. Our meatballs are a little different." Anna stirred as Austin sipped a beer, then kicked his feet up on the spare chair.

"How so?" he asked. "I mean, you're right that we ate a lot of Italian food. I think I might have had Swedish food once or twice, but..."

"You'd remember if you'd had *my* meatballs," Anna said. "Tonight it'll be like you're dining at an Ikea fit for a king. Meatballs with cream sauce, mashed potatoes, and homemade lingonberry sauce."

When she turned to see his reaction, Austin raised an eyebrow. "I didn't see you making any lingonberry sauce."

"I didn't say it was homemade by *me*. My cousin in Sweden sends it to me every year for Christmas. This is my last jar for the year."

"I'm honored you're sharing it with me," Austin said.

Anna had made Austin promise to let her cook for their first date. Austin wasn't entirely sure what made it different than all the other times they'd gotten together, but he definitely felt more pressure. He'd always found her attractive, that was never the issue. It was that the space inside him that could open to another romantic interest had closed so tight he'd forgotten it existed.

More than that, though, he was also distracted. He'd done the grief counseling offered by the NYPD, he'd read a few books on grieving and letting go of those we've lost, and yet, alone in a kitchen with a smart, beautiful woman who clearly liked him, all he could think about were eight words uttered by John Johnson. *Whoever killed her did us all a favor.*

Anna, though, was still talking about meatballs. "The core is similar—usually beef and pork—but we season our meatballs with allspice and nutmeg. And the cream sauce, as rich as any you've had, is obviously nothing like the marinara you'd get at a nice Italian place. Don't get me wrong, I *love* Italian food, but... Austin?"

"Yeah?" He looked up. He'd only been half listening. "I'm sorry."

"You seem distracted."

"I'm sorry. I *was* listening, too, but yeah. It smells amazing, and I can't wait to try it."

She set the wooden spoon on the edge of the pan and turned down the burner, then sat across from him. Her stare wasn't angry, but it also wasn't sweet. Something more like quizzical, as though she was trying to puzzle something out. "Okay, let's have it."

"Have what?"

"What are you obsessing on?"

"No... really..." Austin stammered. "Let's eat. I—"

"It's Fiona."

Austin nodded.

"The sauce needs to simmer for ten minutes. I'll talk it through with you if you promise to move on—at least temporarily—and eat dinner with me in ten minutes."

"Deal," Austin said. "It's John Johnson. Something he said."

He told Anna what Johnson had said, along with his research into Michael Lee. "Assuming Lee was Korean-American, and a Cambodian crime family in New York attempted to kill him..." he trailed off, hoping Anna would make some brilliant connection. "And then John Johnson, smuggling fentanyl into Seattle via Vietnam."

"I mean, I see the Southeast Asia connection," Anna said. "But where are you going with this?"

"He said that someone did them *all* a favor when they killed Fiona. Taking him at his word for a moment, this is where my mind goes: John Johnson had some connection to a Southeast Asian drug gang in New York City. Maybe they worked together from time to time, or maybe he even had his own crew there. Maybe he had an agreement not to beef over territory."

"As in, he took Seattle, another gang took New York?"

"Could be. Or something like that. Point is, what he said implies that Fiona was working on prosecuting a case or cases there that would have harmed not only the NY drug trade, but harmed John Johnson's business as well."

Anna stood and walked a lap around the kitchen, sipping from a small mason jar of white wine. Austin suddenly felt embarrassed. "I'm sorry I don't have any real wine glasses."

She glanced down at the jar. "No biggie. I should have known. You're a bachelor. Here's an idea." She sat down next to him, clearly excited. "What if she was working with the FBI on a case that spanned the whole country? Possible she was bringing what she knew about New York to the table in a case that also touched on Seattle, and therefore on Johnson."

"That's not a bad thought," Austin said. "Michael Lee, then, could have been a dealer who was going to flip, a witness who was going to testify, maybe even a former high level member of a gang Fiona was going to prosecute. One way or another he was involved in the case in a way that pissed off a lot of people, and they decided to take him out."

Anna moved back to the stove to check on her sauce. "And what better way to take a man out than to lure him to his death through an online dating app? Most men will do anything when a woman they find attractive is on the other end of the bar, or, in this case, a phone screen."

"Secrets," Austin said quietly.

"Huh?"

"It's just... I'm convinced something big was going on. Maybe an FBI thing, like you said, maybe something else. But why did I never hear about it? Why did nothing come up when the NYPD did their investigation?"

He stared at Anna, who had a concerned look on her face. She dropped her eyes.

"What?" Austin asked.

"I'm a reporter, you're a cop."

"Former detective, but okay."

"My view of the way police do things might be slightly different than yours."

"What are you getting at?"

"I'm no radical," Anna said. "You've seen how I worked with Ridley, Jimmy, and Lucy. Respect the hell out of them. But there are a good number of corrupt cops out there, prosecutors sometimes take bribes, and interactions between the FBI and local police departments are often fraught with politics, competing interests, and financial considerations. Real life isn't like *Law and Order*."

"I know all that," Austin said.

"My point is, if Fiona was involved in a big case that involved the feds, there could be a hundred reasons the FBI—or even the NYPD—would want to cover up what happened to her."

It was certainly plausible. He knew of a few cases in which informants had been killed and one where an undercover FBI agent had been murdered after infiltrating a drug gang. Their deaths had been covered up in order to keep the ongoing investigations alive. So it was possible, though it would have taken a hell of a coverup to bury what happened to an up-and-coming DA. Either way, there was no way they could do anything more than speculate.

He smiled, trying to sound upbeat. "Let's move on. Our ten minutes are up and I want to show your food the attention it deserves."

Anna began serving and Austin propped open the screen door that led to the little yard facing the beach. Run, who'd been occupied with a ball out front, perked up when she saw him. "Want some meatballs?" Austin asked.

She barked once, quietly, the way he'd trained her to answer direct questions.

He was pretty sure she didn't know what meatballs were, but he'd trained her to respond to a certain tone of voice. *Want to go to the beach? Want some treats?* Whenever he used that tone, she responded with a little bark and it always led to something she enjoyed.

The evening was cool but not cold, and Austin could feel spring in the air. He lit the candle on the little metal table he'd set out in the yard, then headed back in, Run at his heels.

"You might want your sweater," Austin said. "I set up the table out there, but it's a little chilly."

Anna put on her cardigan and carried plates to the table. Austin snuck Run a tiny bite of meatball she'd left in the pan, because he couldn't help himself. Then he joined her at the table.

"Dig in," she said.

It smelled of rich cream and savory meat, spices and cracked pepper. "Truly impressive."

"I'm glad." She chuckled softly. "It's the only thing I know how to make."

Austin laughed, then shot up from his chair. "I'll be right back. I have a surprise."

He jogged around the side of the building to his store, which was empty save for the teenager who worked the counter on weekday evenings. From the back of the cold case he grabbed a six pack of *Norrlands Guld*, a Swedish beer he'd added to his regular order for the occasion.

He stopped at the counter on his way out. "How's it going, Dezy?"

The young woman looked up from her phone. "Slow."

"You can close at eight instead of nine if you want."

"Thanks. I gotta go pick up my sister, so that's great."

As Austin turned to leave, he spotted the front page of the *New York Times*, one of four newspapers they carried and stocked by the front register. Out of habit, he scanned the headlines, stopping on one on the bottom right side of the page.

Leader of Purported Korean Drug Ring Arrested in the Bronx

He grabbed the paper and headed back to the table, where Anna was feeding Run a bite of meatball.

"I know I'm not supposed to feed her at the table," Anna said. "But life is short."

Austin slid the newspaper under his chair and set the beer on the table. "Sometimes I can't help myself either. She's just too cute." He popped a couple beers. "It's supposed to be the most popular beer in Sweden. I hear it goes great with meatballs."

Anna took a swig and smiled.

They ate quietly for a while, but it wasn't an awkward quiet. He was comfortable with her, and she was comfortable with him, too. He'd never been good at reading women, but he could tell.

"This is nice," she said after a long silence.

"It is," Austin said.

"But..."

Austin looked up. "What?"

"Look. You're a great guy. You know I'm interested. And I *think* you're interested."

Austin frowned. "There's a *but* coming."

"There is," she said, "and it's coming from *you*, Austin. Even if you don't know it." She leaned down and pulled the newspaper out from under his chair. "I read three newspapers cover to cover every day. And I'm a pretty good investigative reporter. Tell me if I'm wrong..."

Austin held up his hands to object, but he couldn't lie.

"You went to get the beer—very thoughtful, by the way—and saw the front page. The story on the Korean drug ring bust. Figured you'd stash it away for later. Maybe after I was gone you'd follow up with some pals in the NYPD? See if there's a connection to Michael Lee, to Fiona?"

Austin couldn't help but smile. "You got me."

Anna took another bite of food, chewed for a long time, then stood. "I can't get involved in a drawn out investigation of your wife's murder. I grieve for you, I really do. But I don't want to be a buddy who helps you solve crimes. I want more than that."

Austin opened his mouth, but nothing came out.

"I'm gonna go now." She pulled up the collar of her sweater. "I'm not storming out, and I'm not angry." The flickering candle lit her face from below, casting flecks of golden light across her pale skin. "I understand how important it is to you, but wherever you're going, I can't follow."

"I—"

"Don't object. You want to say something to make me feel better because you're a good guy, but don't." She knelt and gave Run a friendly pet, then strolled to the gate and turned. "You're about to sink into the past, Austin. I can tell. And when people do that, sometimes they never make it back to the present."

She walked away, the gate clanging shut behind her.

"Sorry," he said, but she was too far away to hear.

Run snuggled up around his ankles as he watched her SUV

kick up gravel and disappear from his parking lot. Austin opened the newspaper.

The sound of her car receded, then disappeared.

The night had gone eerily quiet, the only sound the faint crashing of waves on the beach. A cold wind blew out the candle.

Austin stared blankly at the newspaper, unable to focus, but unable to look away.

—The End—

Continue the Series in The Fallen of Foulweather Bluff, Book 3 of the Thomas Austin Crime Thrillers

A NOTE FROM THE AUTHOR

Thomas Austin and I have three things in common. First, we both live in a small beach town not far from Seattle. Second, we both like to cook. And third, we both spend more time than we should talking to our corgis.

If you enjoyed *The Shadows of Pike Place*, I encourage you to check out the whole series of Thomas Austin novels online. Each book can be read as a standalone, although relationships and situations develop from book to book, so they will be more enjoyable if read in order.

In the digital world, authors rely more than ever on mysterious algorithms to spread the word about our books. One thing I know for sure is that ratings and reviews help. So, if you'd take the time to offer a quick rating of this book, I'd be very grateful.

If you enjoy pictures of corgis, the beautiful Pacific Northwest beaches, or the famous Point No Point lighthouse, consider joining my VIP Readers Club. When you join, you'll receive no spam and you'll be the first to hear about free and discounted eBooks, author events, and new releases.

Thanks for reading!

D.D. Black

ALSO BY D.D. BLACK

The Thomas Austin Crime Thrillers

Standalone Crime Novels

ABOUT D.D. BLACK

D.D. Black is the author of the Thomas Austin Crime Thrillers and other Pacific Northwest crime novels that are on their way. When he's not writing, he can be found strolling the beaches of the Pacific Northwest, cooking dinner for his wife and son, or throwing a ball for his corgi over and over and over. Find out more at ddblackauthor.com, or on the sites below.

f facebook.com/ddblackauthor

instagram.com/ddblackauthor

tiktok.com/@d.d.black

amazon.com/D-D-Black/e/BoB6H2XTTP

BB bookbub.com/profile/d-d-black

Made in the USA
Columbia, SC
22 October 2023

24768732R00162